CW0741762

THE CAMBRIDGE CENTENNIAL EDITION OF

THE GREAT GATSBY

"I have always loved and admired *The Great Gatsby*, but this Cambridge edition gives us something quite unique and universal, offering more than a path into a literary masterpiece. This book is an extraordinary resource and a companion for life. A striking achievement."

Elif Shafak, author of *The Island of Missing Trees* and Booker Finalist for *10 Minutes 38 Seconds in this Strange World*

"*The Great Gatsby* is not only one of the most admired and beloved novels ever written: it is also one of the most studied, in both schools and universities. Teachers, students, and indeed all lovers of the novel have long needed a readily accessible edition that presents and explains its evolution and context. That is what the Cambridge Centennial *Gatsby* superbly provides. F. Scott Fitzgerald was an inveterate reviser of his work, and a highlight of the edition is its attention to the striking changes he made as his masterpiece went through the press."

Sir Jonathan Bate, author of *Bright Star, Green Light: The Beautiful Works and Damned Lives of John Keats and F. Scott Fitzgerald*

"This fascinating and comprehensive new edition of *The Great Gatsby*, which includes detailed analysis in its riveting notes and introduction, will delight fans and newcomers alike."

Jillian Cantor, *USA Today* bestselling author of *Beautiful Little Fools*

"A beautifully presented edition of one of the great novels. It was important for the Centennial Edition to do justice to a book that defined its era and remains profoundly relevant today: this stunning edition does exactly that, supporting the text with a superb introduction by Sarah Churchwell and a host of other rich and engaging resources."

Alex Preston, author of *Winchelsea*

"With a thoughtful introduction and a striking lineup of illustrations and behind-the-scenes information, this new Centennial Edition of *The Great Gatsby* from Cambridge does what all new editions should be doing – taking a fresh and ambitious look at this classic for a new generation of readers."

Michael Farris Smith, author of *Nick*

"One of the most exquisitely written books in modern literature has finally been given the edition it deserves."

Elizabeth Day, author and broadcaster

"F. Scott Fitzgerald's *The Great Gatsby* is a jewel-box of a novel, and Cambridge's Centennial Edition invites us to an intimate understanding of how such a wonder came about. At first glance, with its lyrical prose and deft character work, Gatsby looks effortless, but the Centennial Edition shows us it is anything but. We're offered a look backstage, where it is revealed that only iron-clad structure and ruthless attention to detail could give us the words that seem to float so lightly. This is the book I wish I had when I was writing *The Chosen and the Beautiful*."

Nghi Vo, Hugo Award-winning author of *The Chosen and the Beautiful* and *The Singing Hills Cycle*

13

for Jordan and me in the front seat. Tentatively he pushed about the unfamiliar gears; then ~~rigid with heat~~ we shot off toward the city through the oppressive afternoon.

When we reached West Egg Tom became visibly aware of it, turning his head from side to side ~~as though he had never seen it before~~ to look at the shops and houses,* as though he had never seen it before

"What kind of a town is this anyhow? I thought it was a cheap place."

"Most expensive town on Long Island," answered Jordan, "Full of moving picture people, playwriters, ~~and~~ singers and cartoonists and kept women. You'd love it."

~~[illegible]," said Tom~~

"No, I wouldn't" he said ~~quickly~~ vigorously, "~~I~~ ~~bet it smells bad~~. I wouldn't build a stable here."

I began to laugh.

"It doesn't seem quite as bad as that to me."

"You're different," he apologized, "But these theatrical people are like Jews. One Jew is all right but when you get a crowd of them —"

"Gatsby's different too," said Jordan maliciously, "He's an Oxford man."

"He is!" Tom was incredulous, "Like hell he is! He had on a pink suit."

"Nevertheless he's an Oxford man."

"Oxford, South Dakota," Tom ~~laughed~~ snorted contemptuously, "Oxford, New Mexico or something like that."

"Listen, Tom, if your such a snob why did you invite him to lunch?" demanded Jordan crossly,

"I didn't. Daisy invited him. He was a friend of hers before

Chapter VI, leaf 13, manuscript of *The Great Gatsby*.
Princeton University Library.

THE CAMBRIDGE CENTENNIAL EDITION OF

The GREAT GATSBY

F. SCOTT FITZGERALD

Edited by James L W West III
with an introduction by Sarah Churchwell

Shaftesbury Road, Cambridge CB2 8EA, United Kingdom

One Liberty Plaza, 20th Floor, New York, NY 10006, USA

477 Williamstown Road, Port Melbourne, VIC 3207, Australia

314–321, 3rd Floor, Plot 3, Splendor Forum, Jasola District Centre,
New Delhi – 110025, India

103 Penang Road, #05–06/07, Visioncrest Commercial, Singapore 238467

Cambridge University Press is part of Cambridge University Press &
Assessment, a department of the University of Cambridge.

We share the University's mission to contribute to society through the pursuit of
education, learning, and research at the highest international levels of excellence.

www.cambridge.org
Information on this title: www.cambridge.org/9781009414593

DOI: 10.1017/9781009414579

Quotations from the manuscript of *The Great Gatsby* in this volume have been taken
from *The Great Gatsby: An Edition of the Manuscript*, ed. James L. W. West III
and Don C. Skemer (Cambridge: Cambridge University Press, 2018). Misspellings
have been corrected; a few marks of punctuation have been added for readability.

Quotations from the unrevised text of the galley proofs have been taken
from *Trimalchio: An Early Version of The Great Gatsby*,
ed. James L. W. West III (Cambridge: Cambridge University Press, 2000).

The manuscript and galleys are in the F. Scott Fitzgerald Papers, Department
of Rare Books and Special Collections, Princeton University Library. Digital
reproductions of both documents are available on the website of the department.

First published 2025

Printed in the United Kingdom by CPI Group Ltd, Croydon CR0 4YY

A catalogue record for this publication is available from the British Library

*A Cataloging-in-Publication data record for this book is available from the
Library of Congress*

ISBN 978-1-009-41459-3 Hardback

CONTENTS

A plate section can be found between pages 204 - 205.

ILLUSTRATIONS

PLATES

CHRONOLOGY OF COMPOSITION AND PUBLICATION

JUNE 1922 Fitzgerald begins to consider ideas and themes for a new novel while correcting proofs for *Tales of the Jazz Age* (1922), his second collection of short fiction. He and his wife and daughter are living at White Bear Lake, a resort near his home town of St. Paul, Minnesota. Fitzgerald is at work on a play, *The Vegetable*, which he hopes to see produced on Broadway.

OCTOBER 1922 The Fitzgeralds move to the East and rent a house in Great Neck, a community on the North Shore of Long Island. Fitzgerald publishes "Winter Dreams," a short story with close connections to *The Great Gatsby*, in the December issue of *Metropolitan Magazine*.

APRIL 1923 Scribner's publishes *The Vegetable* in book form, this to encourage interest in a Broadway production. The veteran producer Sam H. Harris acquires stage rights; he signs Sam Forrest to direct the play.

SUMMER 1923 Fitzgerald produces some 18,000 words for his new novel but is dissatisfied with what he has written. Most of this material will be discarded. From this false start he salvages the short story "Absolution," which he will publish in the June 1924 issue of *The American Mercury*.

NOVEMBER 1923 *The Vegetable* opens on November 19 for a one-week trial run in Atlantic City. The play is a flop. Fitzgerald attempts repairs in subsequent rehearsals but without success. Harris decides not to mount a Broadway production. Fitzgerald is left in debt; he writes himself back to solvency by producing short stories for the magazine market.

MARCH–APRIL 1924 Fitzgerald reconceives his novel; he sets it in a fictional version of Long Island, with East Egg corresponding to Manhasset Neck and West Egg to Great Neck. He produces three chapters in manuscript.

MAY 1924 The Fitzgeralds sail for France in early May on the liner *Minnewaska*. They visit Paris, then travel to the Riviera. In June they settle in Villa Marie, Valescure, Saint-Raphaël. Fitzgerald returns to work on his novel.

SUMMER 1924 The first draft, handwritten, is completed late in the summer. Working with stenographers, Fitzgerald carries out revisions in a series of typescripts.

OCTOBER 1924 Fitzgerald finishes the novel; its title is "The Great Gatsby." After sending a complete typescript to Perkins via transatlantic mail on October 27, he and his wife and daughter depart from the Riviera and move to Rome, where they will live at the Hôtel des Princes, Piazza di Spagna, until February 1925.

NOVEMBER 1924 In letters dated November 18 and 20, Perkins sends praise, criticism, and suggestions to Fitzgerald. Perkins' chief concern is that Jay Gatsby, as a character, is "somewhat vague." Fitzgerald changes the title temporarily to "Trimalchio in West Egg."

DECEMBER 1924 Perkins has the novel typeset at the Scribner Press. Two sets of galley proofs are pulled and sent to Fitzgerald, who contemplates major revisions. He reverts to "The Great Gatsby" as his title.

JANUARY–FEBRUARY 1925 Fitzgerald revises and restructures the novel in galleys while living in Rome. He returns a master set of proofs to Perkins and keeps the working proofs for himself. He continues to consider other titles, including "Gold-Hatted Gatsby" and "Trimalchio."

MARCH 1925 Perkins supervises the correction of the text from Fitzgerald's master proofs. The revisions are so extensive that some portions must be entirely reset. Perkins sees the novel through to page proof; there is not time for Fitzgerald, who is still in Europe, to review these proofs. At almost the last moment, Fitzgerald suggests "Under the Red, White and Blue" as a title, but Perkins dissuades him from making the change.

APRIL 10, 1925 Publication of the first edition of *The Great Gatsby* in a print run of 20,870 copies.

INTRODUCTION

BY SARAH CHURCHWELL

On April 10, 1925, the day *The Great Gatsby* was published, F. Scott Fitzgerald wrote to Max Perkins, his editor, asking that great care be taken promoting his novel about modern carelessness. "Be sure and keep all such trite phrases as 'Surely the book of the Spring!' out of the advertising," he directed. "That one is my pet abomination."[1] Later that summer, he asked Perkins to "delete the man who says I 'deserve the huzza's of those who want to further a worthy American Literature.' Perhaps I deserve their huzzas but I'd rather they'd express their appreciation in some less boisterous way" (*LL* 124). A far more fastidious writer than his reputation suggests, Fitzgerald was withering about clichés, his letters peppered with objections to inherited phrases and ideas. Despite his best efforts, however, Fitzgerald's most acclaimed novel arrives a century after its publication encrusted with them: the American dream, the Roaring Twenties, Gatsby's

[1] F. Scott Fitzgerald, *A Life in Letters*, ed. Matthew J. Bruccoli, with Judith S. Baughman (New York: Scribner's, 1994): 105–6; hereafter, this title is cited in parentheses as '*LL*'.

green light, hot jazz and cold gin, feathered flappers dancing the Charleston, a book that's all one extravagant spree.

If Fitzgerald would have been delighted to know that *Gatsby* would one day be acclaimed as an American masterpiece, he would probably find our hackneyed ideas about it disappointing. And he would certainly be frustrated by the lack of credit he is routinely given for producing that masterpiece, as if it accidentally emerged from a callow and permanently tipsy brain. As Fitzgerald himself once exasperatedly observed, his writing did not spring fully formed "out of the mind of a temperamental child without taste or judgment."[2] *The Great Gatsby* would change how America understood itself: that is not done by accident.

"I want to write something *new*," Fitzgerald famously told Perkins when he started thinking about *Gatsby*, "something extraordinary and beautiful and simple and intricately patterned."[3] That was in 1922, the year in which he would set the novel. Most readers readily appreciate that *Gatsby* is extraordinary, beautiful, and simple, while many scholars have mapped *Gatsby*'s modernism to show how new it was. Its intricate patterns can be harder to discern, however—especially beneath a century's accumulated clichés. *Gatsby* has not been set in amber, which might at least have reflected its rich and lambent peculiarity, so much as shrink-wrapped in plastic and slapped with stock labels.

The Great Gatsby was Fitzgerald's third novel, written when he was just twenty-eight. It is also his shortest book,

[2] F. Scott Fitzgerald, *The Letters of F. Scott Fitzgerald*, ed. Andrew Turnbull (New York: Scribner's, 1963): 560; hereafter, this title is cited in parentheses as 'Turnbull'.

[3] F. Scott Fitzgerald, *Correspondence of F. Scott Fitzgerald*, ed. Matthew J. Bruccoli, Margaret M. Duggan, and Susan Walker (New York: Random House, 1980): 112.

which is crucial to its genius: the tightly compacted language accelerates its force. As he settled into hard work on the manuscript, Fitzgerald told Perkins that he intended to produce "a consciously artistic achievement," and so would not be ready to submit it until "it has the very best I'm capable of in it, or even as I feel sometimes, something better than I'm capable of" (*LL* 67, 65). That paradox shaped the novel he was writing, a story about aspiration as the measure of the human soul. If Robert Browning famously described heaven as the desire to reach beyond our grasp, Fitzgerald went further, implying that aspiration can remake us, that even our intrinsic capability can be surpassed—and that the measure of art is thus how far it transcends the limits of its creator. For Fitzgerald, that meant releasing his mysterious genius for language and taking it somewhere dazzling and profound.

When he finished *Gatsby*, Fitzgerald knew what he had accomplished, to the point of believing it was "about the best American novel ever written" (*LL* 80). A great many readers today concur with that assessment, but not about what makes this deceptive story of adulterous love—and dreams, disillusionment, and power—among the super-rich in Jazz-Age New York as extraordinary as Fitzgerald intended. There are many theories about what makes *Gatsby* so great, and the ability of this brief novel to keep producing different reasons is part of the answer.

In our culture's collective memory, greatly influenced by Hollywood, *The Great Gatsby* embodies the Roaring Twenties, and everyone wants to join the party. There are in fact only three party scenes in the novel, the first of which, in Myrtle Wilson's apartment, is frankly sordid. Of the other two, both thrown by Jay Gatsby, only one sparkles with glamour; the other is so disappointing to everyone who matters, especially

Gatsby himself, that he abruptly ends the festivities. Our familiar images of lavish bacchanals in palatial homes, of chorus girls and jazz orchestras and champagne glasses the size of finger bowls, infinitely defer the ending, as if the party went on forever. But *Gatsby*'s parties come crashing down after a mere six chapters, while its troubling hero ends shot dead in a swimming pool. "The poor son-of-a-bitch," says Owl Eyes at Jay Gatsby's funeral: nothing ends well in the novel everyone thinks made the Roaring Twenties sound like so much fun.

Before he leaves Long Island at story's end, Nick finds an obscene word scrawled on the porch of Gatsby's preposterous house—a word he proceeds to erase. Just as this may suggest Nick's tendency to idealize the story he tells, so our collective memory of *Gatsby* has tended to relieve itself of troubling details about the moral of the story. But Fitzgerald recognized that the story America tells itself is a fable, and that fables require a moral. In *Gatsby*, he returns the question of morals to the story of America, and in the process turns a fable into a modernist masterpiece.

Gatsby is not really about the Roaring Twenties, any more than it is really about a love affair. The Jazz Age is the novel's setting, not its subject (and Fitzgerald would have hooted with laughter at some of our most cherished ideas about the 1920s), while its converging storylines about marital infidelity enable Fitzgerald to ask deeper questions about fidelity in a fallen world. Jay Gatsby has remained faithful to Daisy Buchanan for five long years, through war, marriage, her child, and his career in organized crime, amassing the fortune he believes will win her back, while Daisy's husband Tom is chronically unfaithful to her. The plot is driven by a simple question: will Daisy keep faith with Gatsby? But the story enacts a larger struggle between good faith and bad faith, asking what it takes to keep faith with a dream or an ideal.

Fitzgerald's poetry has a way of distracting readers from noticing the novel's profound sense of unease, the haunting sense of failure upon which it ends. Gatsby's gift for hope does not survive its encounter with the "hard malice" of the powerful; he is sacrificed to Daisy's selfish unconcern. (When Nick Carraway calls George Wilson's murder of Gatsby and subsequent suicide a "holocaust" at the end of the novel, this sometimes confuses readers accustomed only to the word's postwar meanings. But in 1925, the genocide of European Jews had not yet taken place; for Fitzgerald and his readers, "holocaust" denoted only its original meaning of "sacrifice.")

Although dramatic adaptations persist in depicting Gatsby and Daisy as star-crossed lovers, that is only Gatsby's highly romantic perspective on their story: there is no evidence that Daisy shares his view. On the contrary, she is consistently hard-headed. After Daisy and Gatsby have sex for the first time, in 1917, it is "Gatsby who was breathless, who was, somehow, betrayed," when they meet again two days later. Daisy waits for Gatsby through the war, but then accepts Tom's proposal because she needs her life shaped immediately by "some force—of love, of money, of unquestionable practicality," equating the practical and mercenary with love. Gatsby's response to Daisy's engagement upsets her enough that she gets very drunk, but the next day she marries Tom "without so much as a shiver." Five years later, she has a brief affair with Gatsby, lasting about six weeks, during which time she attends one of his parties and is "offended" by the world he inhabits. When her reckless driving kills Myrtle a few weeks later, Daisy sacrifices Gatsby to save herself and we never see her again. Her repudiation is total.

Gatsby's world is an illusion he has created to impress Daisy—one that Fitzgerald conveys so successfully that a great many readers fall for it. But few, if any, of the people in the novel make that mistake for long. Even Owl Eyes, who has been drunk for a week, is surprised to discover that Gatsby's library is real, as he's so obviously putting on a show. Nick similarly sees in Gatsby "an elegant young rough-neck, a year or two over thirty, whose elaborate formality of speech just missed being absurd," a man who gives the "strong impression that he was picking his words with care."

Like his catchphrase "old sport" and his pink suit, Gatsby's habit of picking his words with care betrays him: in trying too hard, he gives the game away. But Gatsby's care is also weighed specifically against Daisy's carelessness, making her Gatsby's antithesis, as well as his antagonist. "It was all very careless and confused," Nick concludes, after tragedy has struck. "They were careless people, Tom and Daisy—they smashed up things and creatures and then retreated back into their money or their vast carelessness, or whatever it was that kept them together, and let other people clean up the mess they had made."

Gatsby's care—his fidelity and tenacity—is both redemptive, and a tragic flaw, as fatal as hubris. Out of all his superlative, inchoate aspirations, when "a universe of ineffable gaudiness" spun itself out in his mind, in the end he settled for wanting the rich girl, the big house, the fancy car. Gatsby is faithful, but to the wrong ideal, and the fact that he can't survive without his idealism is at the heart of the novel's tragic vision.

The Great Gatsby was far less commercially successful than Fitzgerald hoped, selling only modestly during his lifetime; he would not live to see its genius recognized. An exceptionally prescient book, *Gatsby* apprehended an emerging reality in America—but by definition the prophetic cannot be recognized until history has proven it right. After the Great Depression and the Second World War, the novel's elegiac sense that America kept betraying its own ideals seemed considerably more persuasive. By the 1950s, *The Great Gatsby* had been recognized as not merely a great American novel, but one of our greatest novels about America.

In 1925, deep in the midst of a booming Jazz-Age party, Americans were mostly deaf to cautionary tales about heedless waste. A century later, *Gatsby*'s warning that crass materialism was destroying America resonates deeply with our knowledge that a history of reckless consumption has pushed the world to the precipice of climate disaster. But *Gatsby*'s warning goes beyond our society's thrall to material goods per se, to our misplaced faith in material realism as an ideology—meaning that even our ideas about Fitzgerald's critique of materialism are diminished from the conceptual to the literal, in a way he would doubtless have found symptomatic.

From the autumn of 1922 to the spring of 1924, Scott and Zelda Fitzgerald lived in the small village of Great Neck, some 20 miles east of Manhattan on Long Island. Increasingly colonized by the newly rich of show-business New York, villages such as Great Neck were changing the tone of the "slender riotous island" where the raw energy of rising America clashed with the old monied elite in villages like Manhasset to the east. Fitzgerald soon came to see in 1920s Long Island a parable about modern America, and in early May 1924 the Fitzgeralds sailed for France, where he would write his novel about it. *Gatsby*'s villages of West Egg and East Egg indicate Fitzgerald's dual symbolic and satiric intentions: if these places are originary in some way, they are still in "a very rudimentary state of life" (*LL* 235), and faintly ludicrous.

Between Manhattan and West Egg, where Jay Gatsby and Nick Carraway live, spreads "a certain desolate area of land," where Myrtle and George Wilson dwell, which Fitzgerald calls the "valley of ashes," "a fantastic farm where ashes grow like wheat into ridges and hills and grotesque gardens; where ashes take the forms of houses and chimneys and rising smoke and, finally, with a transcendent effort, of men who move dimly and already crumbling through the powdery air." Reworking "ashes to ashes, dust to dust," Fitzgerald creates a modern travesty of the cycle of life, in which ashes remake themselves, through a transcendent effort, into men who are already crumbling back into ash and dust. The ash heaps suggest not merely a world that is burning and disintegrating, but one in which any kind of "transcendent effort" goes to die among the cinders—while also reminding us that even among the ashes of our dreams, transcendent efforts can be found.

The valley of ashes tipped Fitzgerald's hat to T. S. Eliot's "The Waste Land," published at the end of 1922—but it was also a realistic feature of New York at the time. The Flushing Ash Dumps, known locally as "Mount Corona," were mountainous piles of ash, up to 90 feet high in places, a malodorous stretch of swampland in which coal ash, cinders, garbage, and human waste had been dumped for decades between Long Island and Manhattan. Lone figures wandered the desolate heaps searching for treasure, or anything they could sell, a perfect image of a nation squandering its promise in search of a buck. A century later, the valley of ashes also symbolizes to an increasing number of readers the Anthropocene climate disaster that is the consequence of such wasteful destructiveness.

Most of the novel's memorable details function in the same way, as realistic features of New York in 1922, and as symbols that fuse social satire with the novel's metaphysical meanings. *Gatsby* is peppered with familiar symbols—the valley of ashes, the green light, the eyes of Dr. Eckleburg that are mistaken by George Wilson for the eyes of God. In fact, it's a novel that understands how signs and emblems can expand our capacity for thought. Gatsby's green light has become one of the most famous images in literature, standing for Gatsby's envy of the Buchanans' world and his hope that he can attain it. It suggests his, and his nation's, aspirationalism, their faith in renewal, in the fresh green hope of starting over—and it suggests their mutual drive for the color of American money.

It has been said that *Gatsby* is secretly a novel of ideas, but Fitzgerald wasn't trying to keep it a secret. He might well have retorted, with some asperity, that any novel worth reading has ideas. One of the more stubborn clichés about Scott Fitzgerald is that he could write, but he couldn't think. (That slander comes primarily from his erstwhile friend and eternal rival Ernest Hemingway, who could write, but couldn't relent.) Good writers have to be able to think, it's something of a predicate. They must generalize and abstract, drawing wider conclusions from discrete, telling details.

Gatsby is a deeply thoughtful novel, in every sense: it is a book about the meanings of America, yes—and about visionary dreams and Platonic ideals and minds that can romp like the mind of God. It famously culminates in an image of mankind being "compelled into an aesthetic contemplation he neither understood nor desired," that celebrated phrase invoking different modes of imaginative thought and subjective experience—and our deep resistance to them.

Most of *Gatsby*'s characters are defined in relation to systems of thought in subtle ways, and symbolized by what they read. Gatsby's visionary mind endows him with the potential for greatness, and he acquires an entire, vast library of books—but their pages remain uncut, suggesting both the scope of his ambition and his failure to realize it. Tom Buchanan can only "nibble at the edge of stale ideas," and is introduced to us parroting "impassioned gibberish" he's read about scientific racism, surprising Nick with the discovery that Tom is even capable of being depressed by a book. When Tom precipitates tragedy, it is primarily because "there is no confusion like the confusion of a simple mind." Myrtle Wilson reads gossip magazines and *Simon Called Peter*, a scandalous story of an adulterous affair that Fitzgerald considered a "really immoral" book (Turnbull 476). Jordan Baker is a "clean, hard, limited person, who dealt in universal skepticism" and reads the *Saturday Evening Post*, the voice of 1920s middle America. Only Daisy proves an exception, as Fitzgerald's plot requires that her interiority remain in suspense until he is ready to reveal the tragic consequences of her shallowness.

Nick, meanwhile, was "rather literary in college," making him the best-read and most informed of the lot. Contrary to Hollywood's determination to depict Nick Carraway as a callow youth dazzled by Jay Gatsby's glamour, Fitzgerald makes clear that Tom and Gatsby are only a couple of years older than Nick, who turns thirty during the story. Nick and Gatsby are also both veterans. (How Tom evaded wartime service is a question the novel leaves open.) Nick is an Ivy League graduate; he is contemptuous of Tom's ignorance and lightly mocks Gatsby's absurdities. Tom is aristocratic and Nick middle-class, while Gatsby is working-class trying to pass as an aristocrat: Nick's attitudes consistently map onto this social hierarchy. Nick has developed philosophies of life, including that it is "much more successfully looked at from a single window"—an image that likely alludes to the philosopher Immanuel Kant, said to have developed his ideas about the difference between material realism and transcendental idealism while looking out the same window every day and contemplating the view of the local church.

There is a reason for Kant's sudden appearance by name in the middle of *Gatsby*, in other words, when Nick wryly muses that he was regarding Gatsby's mansion "like Kant at his church steeple." This is not a bit of random name-dropping in an "intricately patterned" masterpiece. Fitzgerald was interested in neo-Platonic philosophy and its ideas about the relationship between aesthetics, metaphysics, and morals, to the extent of carrying histories of philosophy with him through his unsettled life. When Nick informs us that Jay Gatsby "sprang from his Platonic conception of himself," we should recognize that we are in a novel of ideas: Gatsby's pursuit of the Platonic ideal defines him. Nick responds so strongly to Gatsby's romantic idealism not because he is naïve, but because he sees the limits of Jordan's "hardy skepticism" and seeks something greater than his own judgmental cynicism.

When Gatsby and Daisy are reunited at last, after his five years of unswerving devotion, Nick imagines that, for Gatsby, "the colossal significance" of the green light had suddenly "vanished forever." It had seemed to symbolize their distance and the magnitude of his desire, but "now it was again a green light on a dock. His count of enchanted objects had diminished by one." That is the difference between what Kant called transcendental idealism and empirical realism—as the metaphysical collapses back into the limits of the merely physical.

Where Gatsby seeks the extravagant, Nick endlessly registers limits. He opens the story with the limits of his tolerance and ends it on the limits of human sympathy. He calls Tom a man of "limited excellence" physically, Jordan "clean, hard, limited," and himself that "most limited of all specialists, the 'well-rounded man.'" Even the ocean, that familiar symbol of the limitless, hits "the blue cool limit of the sky." But Nick's sensitivity to limits is also a symptom of his own desire to be transported beyond the disappointing actual—to the point that he may project all of Gatsby's greatness onto him.

The irony in Fitzgerald's title shapes the novel: Gatsby's greatness is suspect, to say the least. Calling him "The Great Gatsby" suggests a vaudeville showman, a conjuror, or illusionist; Gatsby falls for cheap American tricks, tries to pull one off himself, and is destroyed in the attempt. A gangster implicated in every racket in a corrupt city, including financial swindles and bootlegging (often associated at the time with narcotics as well), Gatsby is a vulgarized, brutal Quixote: he is romantically tilting at windmills, but he will also take what he wants at any cost. In this, at least, he mirrors the Buchanans: all three are equally ruthless (equally American) in their pursuit of what they want.

Gatsby also bears a disquieting resemblance to Myrtle Wilson: both are chronic outsiders given to violent affectation, social climbers trying to reinvent themselves. Gatsby constantly teeters on the brink of Myrtle's sheer vulgarity: the "Marie Antoinette music-rooms" in Gatsby's mansion are just a more expensive version of the toile de Jouy furniture that features "scenes of ladies swinging in the gardens of Versailles" in Myrtle's apartment. Gatsby and Myrtle both find in one Buchanan the symbol of all they desire—wealth, power, glamour—and both are destroyed by the other Buchanan, whom they foolishly think they can replace.

The Buchanans' mutual cold power ("anybody would have said that they were conspiring together") triumphs, as Gatsby's belief in the ideal shatters against their selfish cynicism. Gatsby's "responsiveness," his "heightened sensitivity to the promises of life," makes him an artist and a mystic, dreaming of the sacramental, seeking "a satisfactory hint of the unreality of reality." Gatsby's problem is not that he fails to find an object worthy of his passionate adoration, but that the world cannot offer one. When he limits his "unutterable visions" to Daisy Buchanan's "perishable breath, his mind would never romp again like the mind of God." *Gatsby* asks what it means to make a transcendent effort: to transcend one's origins, to transcend our own limits, the limits of other people, and the limits of the world.

On the opening flyleaf of a book on the history of philosophy in Fitzgerald's personal library, he once jotted a note: "Our souls: the name we use for how much training we can take: how much organic volition we have for forcing our minds to a realization of our organic capacities."[4] In writing *Gatsby*, Fitzgerald was putting this proposition to the test: could he, through sheer mental will, force his own mind to realize its organic capacities? Could he pull out of his soul more than he was capable of, define an artistic ideal and create something transcendent?

Jay Gatsby tries through force of will to turn himself into his own Platonic ideal—and fails, even comically at times. But Nick comes to feel that merely making a transcendent effort,

[4] Herbert Ernest Cushman, *A Beginner's History of Philosophy*, 2 vols. (Boston: Houghton Mifflin, 1910), annotated by F. Scott Fitzgerald; Department of Rare Books and Special Collections, Princeton University Library. The note Fitzgerald jotted down is on the opening flyleaf of the first volume, while *Gatsby* recognizably alludes to ideas and language in the second volume (see pp. xxxix–xl below).

the attempt to nurture any kind of ideal in a degraded world, is redemptive. He opens the novel by objecting to the fact that the revelations of the young men he knows, "or at least the terms in which they express them, are usually plagiaristic," which is to say, hackneyed and banal. "Reserving judgments is a matter of infinite hope," Nick adds, because it allows for the possibility that someone, someday, might offer a genuine revelation. And that's why Gatsby matters: because he surprises Nick out of his cynical judgmentalism.

Clichés are limited thoughts expressed in plagiaristic terms. *The Great Gatsby* constantly pushes beyond them, stylistically and thematically, reserving judgment in infinite hope. Jay Gatsby is himself a cliché, a faux aristocrat invented by seventeen-year-old James Gatz out of bad magazine fiction—who upends our stock ideas by turning out to have the soul of an artist, which is why we need to reserve judgment. The novel's romance with possibility is predicated on faith that people can transcend their limits. The route to transcendence is through language, its potential to convey the ineffable, the inexpressible, the mystical—everything that goes beyond the physical world and our limited consciousness of it, toward something "commensurate to [our] capacity for wonder."

Its first readers did not see in *The Great Gatsby* a classic treatise on "the American dream," not least because the phrase "American dream" would not be popularized as an idiom until the 1930s; it would take another twenty years or so for the expression to become indelibly associated with *The Great Gatsby*. Nor did its first readers consider *Gatsby* a profound reflection on the future of America, or an elegy for a lost national promise. But they did recognize its black satire of a wasteful, decadent, hollowed age.

Gatsby's original audience had good reasons to see in it only a hyperlocal novel about a small segment of New York society at a very specific moment in time. They lacked the distance necessary for perspective, recognizing all too clearly an assemblage of familiar realistic details. "'The Great Gatsby' is not necessarily a novel of wide appeal," wrote one critic, in typical terms. "I don't even know whether it is fully intelligible to anyone who has not had glimpses of the kind of life it depicts."[5] *Gatsby* could only leave readers to "bewail the waste of so much talent upon such trivial subjects,"[6] agreed another. The "lugubrious gambols of a little clique on Long Island" were "so sordid and depressing that if the cleverness is there it is obscured by the details of his story."[7] Its particularity was so conspicuous that it seemed impossible for any more universal meanings to emerge beyond their immediate milieu. It was a beautifully written book about instantly recognizable people whose very realism made them illegible.

But we should pause before congratulating ourselves too readily on our greater discernment, for if our distance from the reality behind the novel makes it easier for us to apprehend its artistry and symbolism, it has equally led to widespread misreadings of its realistic details. Nick tells us that he kept a timetable from the summer of Gatsby's parties dated "July 5th, 1922." One day after the traditional birth of the nation,

[5] *Collier's*, August 8, 1925.

[6] McAlister Coleman, "The Gin Age: The Great Gatsby, by Scott Fitzgerald." *New Leader*, 2.25 (June 20, 1925): 11; Zelda Fitzgerald, Scrapbook, ca. 1905–1926. Manuscripts Division, Department of Rare Books and Special Collections, Princeton University Library, vol. IV, p. 009.

[7] *Kansas City Star*, May 9, 1925.

it suggests America's great hopes have already receded behind it. But it also locates the story precisely, on Long Island in the summer of 1922. As the novel opens, Nick tells us that the events he is narrating ended "last autumn," so he is writing from the perspective of 1923 about events that stretch back to 1917.

Many of our favorite ideas about the world of *Gatsby* derive from well after its publication in 1925, however. We have inherited banal revelations expressed in plagiaristic terms: they arose partly from carelessness, but also from seeing what we hoped to see, rather than what was there—exactly the fatal mistake that Jay Gatsby makes.

For example, there is not a single flapper dancing the Charleston, a word that never appears in *The Great Gatsby*, because it didn't become a dance craze until the summer of 1926. Fitzgerald likely had never seen it danced when he wrote *Gatsby* and may well have never heard of it. The young woman at Gatsby's party who dances out alone onto the canvas platform is mistaken for Gilda Gray's understudy at the Follies—which means she is probably doing the shimmy, the dance that made Gilda Gray a star.

And her dress of "trembling opal" would not have been short, spaghetti-strapped, spangled or pleated. In the summer of 1922, hems were variable but high fashion dictated a length from mid-calf to the ankle. The party in Myrtle's apartment takes place "a few days before the Fourth of July," after which Nick ends up reading the *New York Tribune* in the small hours of the morning as he waits for a train home. If he was reading the July 2, 1922 edition, he may have seen the *Tribune*'s fashion section advising elegant women to adopt the "Charm of Studied Simplicity" for their Fourth of July outfits, featuring long column dresses in crepe or chiffon with hemlines at the ankle (Image 1).

8 IV NEW YORK TRIBUNE, SUNDAY, JULY 2, 1922

The Charm of Studied Simplicity

BY SARA MARSHALL COOK

Novelty Woolens

THE styles brought out at this time of the year in a very large measure predate the fashions of the coming autumn. Women have proved that their tastes in dress are simple, for out of the multitude of ideas constantly launched, and many of them pushed to the utmost, those embodying simplicity invariably take a firm hold. The greatest successes known in the history of dressmaking have been made in recent years by designers who worked along these lines. Those who have eschewed complication and held to an almost stern simplicity have been the ones whose models have had the greatest vitality and endurance.

No stronger current has run through the stream of fashions during the last few years than the Vionnet genre or type of dress. It never can be said of Vionnet's models that they definitely date themselves, as do most fashions that rage for a time. They are beautiful, artistic and becoming, and no one can deny that they are enduring. Women who have become accustomed to this type of dress continue from season to season to have a similar thing, and often in ordering a model have the same style copied two or three times, the only difference being in the color.

Tan the Shade and Crepella the Fabric

THE strong point in Vionnet's line is that the dresses are so simple in effect that they look almost as if the wearer had made the dress herself. However, the studied simplicity is the result of a very original and frequently complicated manner of handling fabrics. She is [illegible]

[illegible] light weight wool material of crepe weave, known as Crepella, which is now being used for hand-made dresses of the sort that have been so popular in crepe de Chine, voile and handkerchief linen. These show drawn work and Venetian ladder embroidery.

Two typical models of wool Crepella are sketched on this page. They are in a soft tan shade. This shade will be quite as popular as the material—Crepella.

A Material Suitable For Summer and Fall

IT SEEMS a contrariety that dressmakers should manifest so strong an interest in woolen materials at a season of the year when the mercury stands at its highest, but this novelty woolen, which is a Rodier creation, is lighter in weight than many crepe de Chines and is particularly suitable for dresses being made up at this time. It makes delightful frocks for the mountains or sea shore, and models made from this fine wool crepe need not be packed away for another season when one comes back to town, but will be found very serviceable throughout the autumn and winter.

They no doubt are an outcome of two fashions which developed into veritable crazes — that is, for the frocks made from materials of crepy weave and the hand-made lingerie dress carrying work of the type shown on the later models of crepella.

It is in keeping with the continued vogue for clothes of simple outline without applied ornamentation that the hand-made lingerie frock should become so much the fashion of the moment, for it may be said to be at the height of its season just now not only in this country, where quantities of models have been imported, but in Paris as well.

Paris dressmakers are making much of frocks of these types. It is interesting to note that such [illegible]

Hand-Drawn Work a Universal Trimming

Summer Evening Dresses That Bespeak Simplicity

The Veil Returns

Long Chiffon Models In Masque Effect

The Deft Art of Draping a Veil

1 Fashionable women's clothing from the period. These garments might have been worn by Daisy and Jordan. *New York Tribune*, July 2, 1922. Image provided by Library of Congress, Washington, DC.

When Nick enters the Buchanans' salon as the novel begins, he is arrested by the sight of Daisy and Jordan in the center of a crimson room stirred by the breeze from an open window: "They were both in white, and their dresses were rippling and fluttering as if they had just been blown back in after a short flight around the house." Long dresses of chiffon would ripple and flutter in a breeze; short, boxy skirts, which came into vogue at the end of the decade, would not.

Hollywood routinely helps itself to any details from the 1920s that let it gesture toward the Jazz Age. Baz Luhrmann's 2013 film adaptation of *Gatsby*, for example, features Prada dresses in silhouettes that were not worn until around 1928. This may sound like pedantic quibbling—what's six years in Hollywood time? But, socially and culturally, the 1920s ended in a very different place from where they began: the styles of 1922 were far closer to those of 1919 than to those of 1929. The same is true of the 1960s: if a story set in 1962 featured the hair, music, and clothes of 1969, it would rightly be ridiculed, but that is effectively what most film adaptations of *Gatsby* do in their depictions of a generic "Roaring Twenties."

Luhrmann's Broadway is also thronged with familiar yellow taxicabs—but New York taxis were not uniformly yellow in the early 1920s. There were yellow taxis, but also red taxis, blue taxis, brown taxis, black taxis, cream-colored taxis, checkered taxis, and by the summer of 1923, there were lavender taxis, like the one Myrtle Wilson selects after letting four others pass her by. The lavender taxis were known for being expensive, and thus could seem pretentious, an impression heightened by the violence of their color scheme: "cerise and lavender taxis with red and green checkers and an ivory chauffeur."[8] A night out in Prohibition New York, it was said, "begins in a bierstube [beer hall] and ends in a purple taxi."[9] Meanwhile,

[8] *Boston Globe*, July 23, 1923.
[9] *Rock Island Argus* (IL), Nov. 19, 1924.

car manufacturers were promising "to please the women" with new "color schemes." "Smart cars are painted in brighter tints," women were advised in 1922, and neutral tones "have lost caste."[10] Myrtle Wilson, with her violent affectations and her social climbing, wants terribly to be smart. Naturally she would choose a lavender taxi.

Filmmakers have every right to create their own artwork from source material, but these deadening clichés distort our view of *Gatsby* in important ways. They keep us from registering how rich and strange and alien its world is: the New York of *Gatsby* lures us in while we're reading, even if we aren't conscious of it, because it is a surreal and surprising city, without a trite yellow cab in sight—but a lavender taxi with gray upholstery is waiting for those who care to notice.

At the same time, Fitzgerald's New York was far more conservative than Hollywood imagines. Many old formalities were just starting to break down: Nick remarks, for example, that he and Myrtle Wilson are already using first names, thanks to the whiskey they've drunk, a sign of growing informality in the cultural changes to come. Gatsby's "graceful, conservative fox-trot" surprises Nick, while Daisy and Tom are both marked out as especially conservative in a society most people today would probably find already suffocatingly straitlaced.

Tom is frankly reactionary, as revealed by his enthusiasm for the white supremacist tract he urges Nick to read, "'The Rise of the Colored Empires' by this man Goddard": "The idea is if we don't look out the white race will be—will be utterly submerged," he adds. "It's all scientific stuff; it's been proved. … It's up to us, who are the dominant race, to watch out

[10] *New York Times*, January 8, 1922.

or these other races will have control of things." Tom's white supremacism symbolizes his malignant power (and his stupidity), but it is also entirely realistic, representing the typical attitudes of a rich conservative American at that time. Known as "Nordicism" in the United States in the early 1920s, and functionally synonymous with the ideas of "Aryanism" being developed at the same time in Germany, scientific racism held that people of Northern European heritage (hence "Nordic") were biologically superior to people from everywhere else.

Fitzgerald is specifically referring to Lothrop Stoddard, author of the wildly popular 1920 white replacement screed *The Rising Tide of Color against White World-Supremacy*, which warned that America,

> originally settled almost exclusively by Nordics, was toward the close of the nineteenth century invaded by hordes of immigrant Alpines and Mediterraneans, not to mention Asiatic elements like Levantines and Jews. As a result, the Nordic native [i.e., native-born] American has been crowded out with amazing rapidity by these swarming, prolific aliens, and after two short generations he has in many of our urban areas become almost extinct.[11]

Altering the book's author and title, but keeping them easily identifiable, Fitzgerald is either lightly fictionalizing (perhaps deliberately conflating Lothrop Stoddard with two other men named Goddard who were also well-known eugenicist lecturers)—or he is suggesting that Tom is too obtuse to get the details right about the wretched book he so admires.

Buchanan's white supremacism defines his malevolence, and is certainly an object of Fitzgerald's satirical contempt

[11] Lothrop Stoddard, *The Rising Tide of Color against White World-Supremacy* (New York: Scribner's, 1920): 165.

(calling it "gibberish" clearly reveals Nick's judgment, but we can also look beyond *Gatsby* to an essay Fitzgerald wrote in 1923 that explicitly declared: "No one has a greater contempt than I have for the recent hysteria about the Nordic theory"[12]). Opening with Buchanan's diatribe against the "rising tide of color" is precisely equivalent to a contemporary novelist today introducing a rich white New York banker by having him share a garbled version of a Fox News episode he just watched about invading immigrants: it is a metonymic detail, portraiture through association.

But *The Great Gatsby* does not entirely transcend the material racism that defined the American 1920s. When Nick sees African Americans (whom he calls "two bucks and a girl") being driven in a limousine by a white chauffeur across the Queensboro Bridge, it becomes an image of the world turned upside down, in which the supposedly natural order of things, in the form of racist hierarchies, has been inverted. Nick similarly finds Wolfshiem, Gatsby's Jewish business partner, comically sinister, with his personified nose and his human molar cufflinks and his "business gonnegtion." Readers today find this depiction of Wolfshiem far from funny, but we also know that the extermination of six million Jewish people was less than twenty years away: Hitler would publish *Mein Kampf* three months after Gatsby appeared, in July 1925. But even without the benefit of history, Fitzgerald was perfectly capable of extending imaginative sympathy beyond poor white men like Gatsby, and any novel that finds tragedy in failures of moral imagination can fairly be judged by its own standards.

Daisy may not share Tom's violently racist politics, but she is no less socially or culturally conservative than her husband.

[12] *New York Evening Post*, May 26, 1923.

She does not fortuitously wander into Gatsby's parties the way Jordan does—and the way Gatsby hoped she would, which is why he resorts to involving her cousin Nick in arranging a tryst—because she is safely ensconced in aristocratic East Egg. When she ventures to West Egg, Daisy is "offended" and "appalled" by what she encounters:

> The rest offended her ... She was appalled by West Egg, this unprecedented "place" that Broadway had begotten upon a Long Island fishing village—appalled by its raw vigor that chafed under the old euphemisms ... She saw something awful in the very simplicity she failed to understand.

Daisy's friend Jordan Baker is more at home in West Egg. Named for two models of the cars marketed to women, Jordan is by implication sleek, modern, and fast—with all that word implied in the 1920s. (In Fitzgerald's earlier *This Side of Paradise*, a young woman with a sexual reputation is known as "a Speed.") Nick suggests that Jordan is fast in the sexual sense when he tells us that she habitually used subterfuge "to keep that cool, insolent smile turned to the world and yet satisfy the demands of her hard, jaunty body"—and when there is a long, suggestive gap between the moment Nick kisses her in a carriage in Central Park at sunset, and his arrival home afterwards at two o'clock in the morning. The world of *Gatsby* sits on the cusp of the world we know—but it's still cloaked in "the old euphemisms," which can mislead readers who are no longer accustomed to deciphering them. *The Great Gatsby* is a novel of implications: to understand it well, we must learn to read between the lines, as Jay Gatsby fails to do.

All these carefully chosen details also keep suggesting a world beyond the merely mimetic—what John Updike once called the ability of language to be "worked into a supernatural, supermimetic bliss."[13] The reason everyone who reads *Gatsby* wants to join the fun, in other words, has far less to do with our often ludicrous ideas of what a Jazz-Age party looked like than with the vital strangeness of Fitzgerald's writing. The lavender taxi is hyper-realistic, but it is also surrealistic, capturing the phantasmagorical qualities of *Gatsby*'s New York.

Fitzgerald's fidelity to physical reality and at the same time to its metaphysical surreality is what makes the experience of reading *Gatsby* so uncanny: it keeps transporting us to the edge of reality, without ever quite leaving it behind. And that's what the novel is about: our dreams of transcending reality. Fifth Avenue is so "warm and soft, almost pastoral" that Nick "wouldn't have been surprised to see a great flock of white sheep turn the corner." It is a New York in which Nick believes anything can happen, including Gatsby himself.

A nightingale sings in the Buchanans' garden in the opening chapter, but nightingales don't inhabit America. Daisy quips that it must have come over on an ocean liner, but it seems more likely that the nightingale flew in from the pages of John Keats, Fitzgerald's favorite poet; his "Ode to a Nightingale" would give Fitzgerald the title for his next novel, *Tender Is the Night*. The nightingale suggests that beauty in *Gatsby* matters more than realism. The mystical properties of language—its ability to be supernatural and supermimetic—mean that suddenly anything *is* possible. A flock of sheep might cross Fifth Avenue; a nightingale can sail to America on an ocean liner.

Our capacity to transform the world sits at *Gatsby*'s heart and runs through its capillaries, phrase by phrase, as

[13] John Updike, "The Doctor's Son," *The New Yorker* (November 6, 1978): 213.

Fitzgerald shows that he can indeed make anything happen with language. *Gatsby* is a tour de force of literary synesthesia, the interchange of sensory perceptions. Critics frequently note the use of synesthesia in *Gatsby* ("yellow cocktail music" being the plagiaristic example), but few if any mention why it matters. Synesthesia changes our perception: it increases the world's potential.

An opening description sends us whizzing cinematically across the grounds of the Buchanan estate, where lawns jump, and gardens burn:

> The lawn started at the beach and ran toward the front door for a quarter of a mile, jumping over sun-dials and brick walks and burning gardens—finally when it reached the house drifting up the side in bright vines as though from the momentum of its run. The front was broken by a line of French windows, glowing now with reflected gold.

The yellow cocktail music floats past triumphant hat-boxes and humming lights out into the Sound, which is a body of water and ambient noise, music and conversation and the growing "echolalia of the garden." One woman appears at the side of her flirtatious husband "like an angry diamond," another is a "scarcely human orchid." Odors in *Gatsby* can be sparkling or frothy or pale gold. Clamor becomes time at "roaring noon." This is language as alchemy: "The moon had risen higher, and floating in the Sound was a triangle of silver scales, trembling a little to the stiff, tinny drip of the banjoes on the lawn," as water, music, metal, and light melt and reform.

The verbal exuberance of *Gatsby* belies its exacting prose and carefully controlled perspective. The gilded, art deco opera of Fitzgerald's language is extremely risky, always in danger of becoming as kitschy as Gatsby's pink suit. In one or two places, he may tip over the line. But, for the most part, Fitzgerald's prose is a kind of experiment in restrained extravagance. The novel's style is nearly paradoxical in its ability to be simultaneously excessive and withholding, romantic and judgmental. Its effect depends entirely upon the contrast between the modern jazz of its setting and the formal romanticism of Fitzgerald's style: all of its energy comes from the high tension between the two. That resistant pull is how Fitzgerald achieves the novel's tautness, its finely tuned elegiac satire.

For all its historical specificity, Fitzgerald ruthlessly stripped *Gatsby* of any Jazz-Age slang that might have dated it—there are no bee's knees or cat's pajamas to be found. He was using Keats to write jazz, not the other way around; the controlled, conservative style followed logically. The formality of Nick's narration is not fortuitous: it reflects his moral fastidiousness, his declaration at the novel's start that, after the carelessness of New York, he wants the world to be standing at "moral attention" forever. *Gatsby* recognizes the joys of intemperance but it comes down on the side of moral vigilance as a response to the dangers of carelessness.

Many of our most recycled, plagiaristic observations about *Gatsby* miss the point, failing to read between the lines or grasp the full implications of Fitzgerald's choices. For example, it is often noted that Jimmy Gatz's old copy of *Hopalong Cassidy* suggests his dime-novel dreams, but less often that it explains why Nick declares that *Gatsby* is "a story of the West," but not a Western, because the forces of good do not triumph over evil: it is a tragedy in which the dreams of the West have already died.

Similarly, it is often noted that Benjamin Franklin's schedule for self-improvement provides Gatsby with a manual for upward social mobility, that he is a representative American who buys into the nation's founding dreams, and thus follows the original American self-help book. But Jimmy Gatz's plan focuses only on physical activity and hard work, omitting the spiritual dimension that Franklin's schedule emphasized. Franklin said he asked himself every morning, "What good shall I do this day?"; and every evening, "What good have I done today?" In other words, Franklin centered morality as well as industry, and Fitzgerald expected his audience to recognize what was missing. *The Great Gatsby* renders a society that no longer reflects on spiritual self-improvement—and has confused material enterprise with moral achievement. Gatsby, like the country he embodies, forgets that he should be trying not just to be great, but to do good.

If we accept that there are no incidental details in the intricate pattern of *Gatsby*, then we are tasked with interpreting a system of thought. Ben Franklin and Hopalong Cassidy are easy enough to read. Kant takes more work, but once we credit Fitzgerald's philosophical interests, a philosopher's presence becomes equally legible. The same applies to the novel's closing reference to El Greco, a beautiful sentence that is often quoted and almost never interpreted. In fact, El Greco serves as an emblem of the novel's aesthetics and its efforts to capture something commensurate to the capacity of the human soul in art.

Looking back on the story at the end of the novel, Nick says: "I see it as a night scene by El Greco: a hundred houses, at once conventional and grotesque, crouching under a sullen, overhanging sky and a lustreless moon." The meaning of his sentence goes beyond West Egg, specifically, to the story he has just finished telling: in other words, he sees *Gatsby* itself as a night scene by El Greco.

The night scene in question was El Greco's *View of Toledo*, on display from the early 1920s at New York's Metropolitan Museum, and with which Fitzgerald was long familiar through American literary and periodical culture (Image 2). Widely held to have captured the mystery of the human soul in art, El Greco was acclaimed in the early decades of the twentieth century as the "modern old master," and celebrated by writers Fitzgerald admired, including H. L. Mencken, while W. Somerset Maugham devoted pages of his 1915 novel *Of Human Bondage* to an exalted paean to the *View of Toledo* specifically. By the early 1920s, El Greco had become a familiar cultural shorthand for artistic greatness, just as Picasso might be invoked today.

Many writers Fitzgerald was reading offered tributes to El Greco's unease and intensity, the strange, dark beauty of his canvases, his distorted perspective and grotesque shapes, his ability to suggest the inexpressible and ineffable, the material world turned surreal and nightmarish. One of the most important of these writers for Fitzgerald was Maugham, whose impact on *Gatsby* has been all but entirely overlooked in favor of influences such as Keats and Joseph Conrad. Maugham's *The Moon and Sixpence* (1919) opens with El Greco as the image of the great artist who, "sensual and tragic, proffers the mystery of his soul like a standing sacrifice."[14] In his earlier *Of Human Bondage,* Maugham argued that the greatest artists painted both "man and the intention of his soul; Rembrandt and El Greco; it's only

[14] W. Somerset Maugham, *The Moon and Sixpence* (New York: P. F. Collier and Son, 1919): 8.

2 El Greco, *View of Toledo*, ca. 1600. Nick's dreams in Chapter IX are haunted by "a night scene by El Greco." Metropolitan Museum of Art, New York City. (A color version of this image appears in the plate section.)

the second-raters who've only painted man." If an artist can capture both a "man and the intention of his soul," Maugham added, then "you become literary."[15] Becoming

[15] W. Somerset Maugham, *Of Human Bondage* (London: William Heinemann, 1915): 240.

literary is precisely what Fitzgerald wanted to show the world he had done in the pages of *The Great Gatsby.*

In his Toledo paintings, Maugham declared, El Greco reconciled the conflict between local, physical realism and a universalizing, spiritual idealism:

> Here was something better than the realism which he had adored; but certainly it was not [a] bloodless idealism […] It accepted life in all its vivacity, ugliness and beauty, squalor and heroism; it was realism still; but it was realism carried to some higher pitch, in which facts were transformed by the more vivid light in which they were seen.

El Greco shows how a hyperlocal realism might be transformed by a higher pitch and more vivid light into a universal work of art. The *View of Toledo* suggests much of Fitzgerald's style in *Gatsby*—its vivid light, luminous colors, and distorted shapes. Fitzgerald even matches his novel's color palette to El Greco's blue grounds and grey skies: in Gatsby's "blue gardens men and girls came and went like moths." At dawn, "ghostly birds began to sing among the blue leaves." After "a blue quickening by the window," it is "blue enough outside to snap off the light" as "small gray clouds took on fantastic shapes." West Egg becomes, like Toledo, a grotesque, nightmare city: not the glamorous bright lights of careless flappers, but a place of gathered gloom, perhaps even on the edge of apocalypse.

It is not clear when Fitzgerald jotted his note on the first flyleaf of his two-volume history of philosophy, in which he defines our souls as the name we give to the limits of our "volition […] for forcing our minds to a realization of our organic capacities." But its second volume offers an extended discussion of idealist philosophy, including a section that outlines the relation between mysticism and aesthetics. It describes the mystic as someone who finds the natural world too "definite"—too limited—and too "transitory" to satisfy their sense of reality. For the mystic:

> There is only one reality, and that is within the soul; all else is an illusion [...] Mysticism is frequently allied with aesthetics; the love of God is apparently the same as the love for a work of art [...] [or as] the artistic ecstasy over a thing of beauty. Both result in the absorption of the soul in its object, and in the presence of either all else seems illusory.[16]

El Greco painted the mystical in the modern world, and so did Fitzgerald: El Greco's mystical city gives Fitzgerald his ideal emblem for the world of *Gatsby*. When Daisy abandons Gatsby and he must give up his colossal vision, Nick imagines Gatsby stripped bare, shivering as he confronted "what a grotesque thing a rose is and how raw the sunlight was upon the scarcely created grass. A new world, material without being real, where poor ghosts, breathing dreams like air, drifted fortuitously about." It is then that Gatsby must die—because he is a mystic to whom modern America is material, but not real. The real world lacks the wonder and grandeur of his visionary ideals and so he cannot survive it.

After Gatsby is sacrificed to Tom and Daisy's carelessness, Nick wanders out to the shore and offers his famous valedictory to Gatsby and to the promise of America, imagining the first Europeans landing there to settle:

> for a transitory enchanted moment man must have held his breath in the presence of this continent, compelled into an aesthetic contemplation he neither understood nor desired, face to face for the last time in history with something commensurate to his capacity for wonder.

[16] Cushman, vol. II, 319.

Many people misremember this famous scene, but in a way that is telling, substituting Puritan pilgrims in Massachusetts for the Dutch settlers of New York whom Nick actually imagines. The shift from spiritualism to mercantilism is the whole point: America has lost faith with its spiritual ideal and built a new world that is merely material, without being real, because it has lost its capacity for idealism and wonder.

Nick views his experience of West Egg as a night scene by El Greco: a nightmare version of a city on a hill, both idealized and distorted, grotesque, and fantastic. The America that Nick contemplates is no longer the shining city of Puritan utopia, or the neo-Platonic ideal of Kantian aesthetics, but a society of vast, vulgar, and meretricious beauty. Its soul is coming to judgment in a darkening city of spiritual unease, the early mystical dream of America already abandoned in the dark fields of the republic under gathering clouds. If the novel's great sin is carelessness, Fitzgerald's elegy for Gatsby becomes his requiem for the utopian dreams of the nation that succumbed to it.

THE GREAT GATSBY

THE GREAT GATSBY

BY

F. SCOTT FITZGERALD

Then wear the gold hat, if that will move her;
If you can bounce high, bounce for her too,
Till she cry "Lover, gold-hatted, high-bouncing lover,
I must have you!"

—Thomas Parke D'Invilliers.

ONCE AGAIN

TO

ZELDA

CHAPTER I

In my younger and more vulnerable years my father gave me some advice that I've been turning over in my mind ever since.

"Whenever you feel like criticizing anyone," he told me, "just remember that all the people in this world haven't had the advantages that you've had."

He didn't say any more, but we've always been unusually communicative in a reserved way, and I understood that he meant a great deal more than that. In consequence, I'm inclined to reserve all judgments, a habit that has opened up many curious natures to me and also made me the victim of not a few veteran bores. The abnormal mind is quick to detect and attach itself to this quality when it appears in a normal person, and so it came about that in college I was unjustly accused of being a politician, because I was privy to the secret griefs of wild, unknown men. Most of the confidences were unsought—frequently I have feigned sleep, preoccupation, or a hostile levity when I realized by some unmistakable sign that an intimate revelation was quivering on the horizon; for the intimate revelations of young men, or at least the terms in which they express them, are usually plagiaristic and marred by obvious suppressions. Reserving judgments is a matter of infinite hope. I am still a little afraid of missing something if I forget that, as my father snobbishly suggested, and I snobbishly repeat, a sense of the fundamental decencies is parcelled out unequally at birth.

And, after boasting this way of my tolerance, I come to the admission that it has a limit. Conduct may be founded on the hard rock or the wet marshes, but after a certain point I don't care what it's founded on. When I came back from the East last autumn I felt that I wanted the world to be in uniform and at a sort of moral attention forever; I wanted no more riotous excursions with privileged glimpses into the human heart. Only Gatsby, the man who gives his name to this book, was exempt from my reaction—Gatsby, who represented everything for which I have an unaffected scorn. If personality is an unbroken series of successful gestures, then there was something gorgeous about him, some heightened sensitivity to the promises of life, as if he were related to one of those intricate machines that register earthquakes ten thousand miles away. This responsiveness had nothing to do with that flabby impressionability which is dignified under the name of the "creative temperament"—it was an extraordinary gift for hope, a romantic readiness such as I have never found in any other person and which it is not likely I shall ever find again. No—Gatsby turned out all right at the end; it is what preyed on Gatsby, what foul dust floated in the wake of his dreams that temporarily closed out my interest in the abortive sorrows and short-winded elations of men.

My family have been prominent, well-to-do people in this Middle Western city for three generations. The Carraways are something of a clan, and we have a tradition that we're descended from the Dukes of Buccleuch, but the actual founder of my line was my grandfather's brother, who came here in fifty-one, sent a substitute to the Civil War, and started the wholesale hardware business that my father carries on today.

I never saw this great-uncle, but I'm supposed to look like him—with special reference to the rather hard-boiled painting that hangs in father's office. I graduated from New Haven in 1915, just a quarter of a century after my father, and a little later I participated in that delayed Teutonic migration known as the Great War. I enjoyed the counter-raid so thoroughly that I came back restless. Instead of being the warm center of the world, the Middle West now seemed like the ragged edge of the universe—so I decided to go East and learn the bond business. Everybody I knew was in the bond business, so I supposed it could support one more single man. All my aunts and uncles talked it over as if they were choosing a prep school for me, and finally said, "Why—ye-es," with very grave, hesitant faces. Father agreed to finance me for a year, and after various delays I came East, permanently, I thought, in the spring of twenty-two.

The practical thing was to find rooms in the city, but it was a warm season, and I had just left a country of wide lawns and friendly trees, so when a young man at the office suggested that we take a house together in a commuting town, it sounded like a great idea. He found the house, a weatherbeaten cardboard bungalow at eighty a month, but at the last minute the firm ordered him to Washington, and I went out to the country alone. I had a dog—at least I had him for a few days until he ran away—and an old Dodge and a Finnish woman, who made my bed and cooked breakfast and muttered Finnish wisdom to herself over the electric stove.

It was lonely for a day or so until one morning some man, more recently arrived than I, stopped me on the road.

"How do you get to West Egg Village?" he asked helplessly.

I told him. And as I walked on I was lonely no longer. I was a guide, a pathfinder, an original settler. He had casually conferred on me the freedom of the neighborhood.

And so with the sunshine and the great bursts of leaves growing on the trees, just as things grow in fast movies, I had that familiar conviction that life was beginning over again with the summer.

There was so much to read, for one thing, and so much fine health to be pulled down out of the young breath-giving air. I bought a dozen volumes on banking and credit and investment securities, and they stood on my shelf in red and gold like new money from the mint, promising to unfold the shining secrets that only Midas and Morgan and Maecenas knew. And I had the high intention of reading many other books besides. I was rather literary in college—one year I wrote a series of very solemn and obvious editorials for the Yale News—and now I was going to bring back all such things into my life and become again that most limited of all specialists, the "well-rounded man." This isn't just an epigram—life is much more successfully looked at from a single window, after all.

It was a matter of chance that I should have rented a house in one of the strangest communities in North America. It was on that slender riotous island which extends itself due east of New York—and where there are, among other natural curiosities, two unusual formations of land. Twenty miles from the city a pair of enormous eggs, identical in contour and separated only by a courtesy bay, jut out into the most domesticated body of salt water in the Western hemisphere, the great wet barnyard of Long Island Sound. They are not perfect ovals—like the egg in the Columbus story, they are both crushed flat at the contact end—but their physical resemblance must be a source of perpetual confusion to the gulls that fly overhead. To the wingless a more arresting phenomenon is their dissimilarity in every particular except shape and size.

I lived at West Egg, the—well, the less fashionable of the two, though this is a most superficial tag to express the bizarre and not a little sinister contrast between them. My house was at the very tip of the egg, only fifty yards from the Sound, and squeezed between two huge places that rented for twelve or fifteen thousand a season. The one on my right was a colossal affair by any standard—it was a factual imitation of some Hôtel de Ville in Normandy, with a tower on one side, spanking new under a thin beard of raw ivy, and a marble swimming pool, and more than forty acres of lawn and garden. It was Gatsby's mansion. Or, rather, as I didn't know Mr. Gatsby, it was a mansion inhabited by a gentleman of that name. My own house was an eyesore, but it was a small eyesore, and it had been overlooked, so I had a view of the water, a partial view of my neighbor's lawn, and the consoling proximity of millionaires—all for eighty dollars a month.

Across the courtesy bay the white palaces of fashionable East Egg glittered along the water, and the history of the summer really begins on the evening I drove over there to have dinner with the Tom Buchanans. Daisy was my second cousin once removed, and I'd known Tom in college. And just after the war I spent two days with them in Chicago.

Her husband, among various physical accomplishments, had been one of the most powerful ends that ever played football at New Haven—a national figure in a way, one of those men who reach such an acute limited excellence at twenty-one that everything afterward savors of anti-climax. His family were enormously wealthy—even in college his freedom with money was a matter for reproach—but now he'd left Chicago and come East in a fashion that rather took your breath away: for instance, he'd brought down a string of polo ponies from Lake Forest. It was hard to realize that a man in my own generation was wealthy enough to do that.

Why they came East I don't know. They had spent a year in France for no particular reason, and then drifted here and there unrestfully wherever people played polo and were rich together. This was a permanent move, said Daisy over the telephone, but I didn't believe it—I had no sight into Daisy's heart, but I felt that Tom would drift on forever seeking, a little wistfully, for the dramatic turbulence of some irrecoverable football game.

And so it happened that on a warm windy evening I drove over to East Egg to see two old friends whom I scarcely knew at all. Their house was even more elaborate than expected, a cheerful red-and-white Georgian Colonial mansion, overlooking the bay. The lawn started at the beach and ran toward the front door for a quarter of a mile, jumping over sun-dials and brick walks and burning gardens—finally when it reached the house drifting up the side in bright vines as though from the momentum of its run. The front was broken by a line of

French windows, glowing now with reflected gold and wide open to the warm windy afternoon, and Tom Buchanan in riding clothes was standing with his legs apart on the front porch.

He had changed since his New Haven years. Now he was a sturdy straw-haired man of thirty with a rather hard mouth and a supercilious manner. Two shining arrogant eyes had established dominance over his face and gave him the appearance of always leaning aggressively forward. Not even the effeminate swank of his riding clothes could hide the enormous power of that body—he seemed to fill those glistening boots until he strained the top lacing, and you could see a great pack of muscle shifting when his shoulder moved under his thin coat. It was a body capable of enormous leverage—a cruel body.

His speaking voice, a gruff husky tenor, added to the impression of fractiousness he conveyed. There was a touch of paternal contempt in it, even toward people he liked—and there were men at New Haven who had hated his guts.

"Now, don't think my opinion on these matters is final," he seemed to say, "just because I'm stronger and more of a man than you are." We were in the same senior society, and while we were never intimate I always had the impression that he approved of me and wanted me to like him with some harsh, defiant wistfulness of his own.

We talked for a few minutes on the sunny porch.

"I've got a nice place here," he said, his eyes flashing about restlessly.

Turning me around by one arm, he moved a broad flat hand along the front vista, including in its sweep a sunken Italian garden, a half acre of deep, pungent roses, and a snub-nosed motor-boat that bumped the tide offshore.

"It belonged to Demaine, the oil man." He turned me around again, politely and abruptly. "We'll go inside."

We walked through a high hallway into a bright rosy-colored space, fragilely bound into the house by French windows at either end. The windows were ajar and gleaming white against the fresh grass outside that seemed to grow a little way into the house. A breeze blew through the room, blew curtains in at one end and out the other like pale flags, twisting them up toward the frosted wedding-cake of the ceiling, and then rippled over the wine-colored rug, making a shadow on it as wind does on the sea.

The only completely stationary object in the room was an enormous couch on which two young women were buoyed up as though upon an anchored balloon. They were both in white, and their dresses were rippling and fluttering as if they had just been blown back in after a short flight around the house. I must have stood for a few moments listening to the whip and snap of the curtains and the groan of a picture on the wall. Then there was a boom as Tom Buchanan shut the rear windows and the caught wind died out about the room, and the curtains and the rugs and the two young women ballooned slowly to the floor.

The younger of the two was a stranger to me. She was extended full length at her end of the divan, completely motionless, and with her chin raised a little, as if she were balancing something on it which was quite likely to fall. If she saw me out of the corner of her eyes she gave no hint of it—indeed, I was almost surprised into murmuring an apology for having disturbed her by coming in.

The other girl, Daisy, made an attempt to rise—she leaned slightly forward with a conscientious expression—then she laughed, an absurd, charming little laugh, and I laughed too and came forward into the room.

"I'm p-paralyzed with happiness."

She laughed again, as if she said something very witty, and held my hand for a moment, looking up into my face, promising that there was no one in the world she so much wanted to see. That was a way she had. She hinted in a murmur that the surname of the balancing girl was Baker. (I've heard it said that Daisy's murmur was only to make people lean toward her; an irrelevant criticism that made it no less charming.)

At any rate, Miss Baker's lips fluttered, she nodded at me almost imperceptibly, and then quickly tipped her head back again—the object she was balancing had obviously tottered a little and given her something of a fright. Again a sort of apology arose to my lips. Almost any exhibition of complete self-sufficiency draws a stunned tribute from me.

I looked back at my cousin, who began to ask me questions in her low, thrilling voice. It was the kind of voice that the ear follows up and down, as if each speech is an arrangement of notes that will never be played again. Her face was sad and lovely with bright things in it, bright eyes and a bright passionate mouth, but there was an excitement in her voice that men who had cared for her found difficult to forget: a singing compulsion, a whispered "Listen," a promise that she had done gay, exciting things just a while since and that there were gay, exciting things hovering in the next hour.

I told her how I had stopped off in Chicago for a day on my way East, and how a dozen people had sent their love through me.

"Do they miss me?" she cried ecstatically.

"The whole town is desolate. All the cars have the left rear wheel painted black as a mourning wreath, and there's a persistent wail all night along the North Shore."

"How gorgeous! Let's go back, Tom. Tomorrow!" Then she added irrelevantly: "You ought to see the baby."

"I'd like to."

"She's asleep. She's three years old. Haven't you ever seen her?"

"Never."

"Well, you ought to see her. She's——"

Tom Buchanan, who had been hovering restlessly about the room, stopped and rested his hand on my shoulder.

"What you doing, Nick?"

"I'm a bond man."

"Who with?"

I told him.

"Never heard of them," he remarked decisively.

This annoyed me.

"You will," I answered shortly. "You will if you stay in the East."

"Oh, I'll stay in the East, don't you worry," he said, glancing at Daisy and then back at me, as if he were alert for something more. "I'd be a God Damn fool to live anywhere else."

At this point Miss Baker said: "Absolutely!" with such suddenness that I started—it was the first word she had uttered since I came into the room. Evidently it surprised her as much as it did me, for she yawned and with a series of rapid, deft movements stood up into the room.

"I'm stiff," she complained. "I've been lying on that sofa for as long as I can remember."

"Don't look at me," Daisy retorted. "I've been trying to get you to New York all afternoon."

"No, thanks," said Miss Baker to the four cocktails just in from the pantry. "I'm absolutely in training."

Her host looked at her incredulously.

"You are!" He took down his drink as if it were a drop in the bottom of a glass. "How you ever get anything done is beyond me."

I looked at Miss Baker, wondering what it was she "got done." I enjoyed looking at her. She was a slender, small-breasted girl, with an erect carriage, which she accentuated by throwing her body backward at the shoulders like a young cadet. Her gray sun-strained eyes looked back at me with polite reciprocal curiosity out of a wan, charming, discontented face. It occurred to me now that I had seen her, or a picture of her, somewhere before.

"You live in West Egg," she remarked contemptuously. "I know somebody there."

"I don't know a single——"

"You must know Gatsby."

"Gatsby?" demanded Daisy. "What Gatsby?"

Before I could reply that he was my neighbor dinner was announced; wedging his tense arm imperatively under mine, Tom Buchanan compelled me from the room as though he were moving a checker to another square.

Slenderly, languidly, their hands set lightly on their hips, the two young women preceded us out onto a rosy-colored porch, open toward the sunset, where four candles flickered on the table in the diminished wind.

"Why *candles?*" objected Daisy, frowning. She snapped them out with her fingers. "In two weeks it'll be the longest day in the year." She looked at us all radiantly. "Do you always watch for the longest day of the year and then miss it? I always watch for the longest day in the year and then miss it."

"We ought to plan something," yawned Miss Baker, sitting down at the table as if she were getting into bed.

"All right," said Daisy. "What'll we plan?" She turned to me helplessly: "What do people plan?"

Before I could answer her eyes fastened with an awed expression on her little finger.

"Look!" she complained. "I hurt it."

We all looked—the knuckle was black and blue.

"You did it, Tom," she said accusingly. "I know you didn't mean to, but you *did* do it. That's what I get for marrying a brute of a man, a great, big, hulking physical specimen of a——"

"I hate that word hulking," objected Tom crossly, "even in kidding."

"Hulking," insisted Daisy.

Sometimes she and Miss Baker talked at once, unobtrusively and with a bantering inconsequence that was never quite chatter, that was as cool as their white dresses and their impersonal eyes in the absence of all desire. They were here, and they accepted Tom and me, making only a polite pleasant effort to entertain or to be entertained. They knew that presently dinner would be over and a little later the evening too would be over and casually put away. It was sharply different from the West, where an evening was hurried from phase to phase toward its close, in a continually disappointed anticipation or else in sheer nervous dread of the moment itself.

"You make me feel uncivilized, Daisy," I confessed on my second glass of corky but rather impressive claret. "Can't you talk about crops or something?"

I meant nothing in particular by this remark, but it was taken up in an unexpected way.

"Civilization's going to pieces," broke out Tom violently. "I've gotten to be a terrible pessimist about things. Have you read 'The Rise of the Colored Empires' by this man Goddard?"

"Why, no," I answered, rather surprised by his tone.

"Well, it's a fine book, and everybody ought to read it. The idea is if we don't look out the white race will be—will be utterly submerged. It's all scientific stuff; it's been proved."

"Tom's getting very profound," said Daisy, with an expression of unthoughtful sadness. "He reads deep books with long words in them. What was that word we——"

"Well, these books are all scientific," insisted Tom, glancing at her impatiently. "This fellow has worked out the whole thing. It's up to us, who are the dominant race, to watch out or these other races will have control of things."

"We've got to beat them down," whispered Daisy, winking ferociously toward the fervent sun.

"You ought to live in California—" began Miss Baker, but Tom interrupted her by shifting heavily in his chair.

"This idea is that we're Nordics. I am, and you are, and you are, and—" After an infinitesimal hesitation he included Daisy with a slight nod, and she winked at me again. "—And we've produced all the things that go to make civilization—oh, science and art, and all that. Do you see?"

There was something pathetic in his concentration, as if his complacency, more acute than of old, was not enough to him any more. When, almost immediately, the telephone rang inside and the butler left the porch Daisy seized upon the momentary interruption and leaned toward me.

"I'll tell you a family secret," she whispered enthusiastically. "It's about the butler's nose. Do you want to hear about the butler's nose?"

"That's why I came over tonight."

"Well, he wasn't always a butler; he used to be the silver polisher for some people in New York that had a silver service for two hundred people. He had to polish it from morning till night, until finally it began to affect his nose——"

"Things went from bad to worse," suggested Miss Baker.

"Yes. Things went from bad to worse, until finally he had to give up his position."

For a moment the last sunshine fell with romantic affection upon her glowing face; her voice compelled me forward breathlessly as I listened—then the glow faded, each light deserting her with lingering regret, like children leaving a pleasant street at dusk.

The butler came back and murmured something close to Tom's ear, whereupon Tom frowned, pushed back his chair, and without a word went inside. As if his absence quickened something within her, Daisy leaned forward again, her voice glowing and singing.

"I love to see you at my table, Nick. You remind me of a—of a rose, an absolute rose. Doesn't he?" She turned to Miss Baker for confirmation: "An absolute rose?"

This was untrue. I am not even faintly like a rose. She was only extemporizing, but a stirring warmth flowed from her, as if her heart was trying to come out to you concealed in one of those breathless, thrilling words. Then suddenly she threw her napkin on the table and excused herself and went into the house.

Miss Baker and I exchanged a short glance consciously devoid of meaning. I was about to speak when she sat up alertly and said "Sh!" in a warning voice. A subdued impassioned murmur was audible in the room beyond, and Miss Baker leaned forward unashamed, trying to hear. The murmur trembled on the verge of coherence, sank down, mounted excitedly, and then ceased altogether.

"This Mr. Gatsby you spoke of is my neighbor—" I said.

"Don't talk. I want to hear what happens."

"Is something happening?" I inquired innocently.

"You mean to say you don't know?" said Miss Baker, honestly surprised. "I thought everybody knew."

"I don't."

"Why—" she said hesitantly, "Tom's got some woman in New York."

"Got some woman?" I repeated blankly.

Miss Baker nodded.

"She might have the decency not to telephone him at dinner-time. Don't you think?"

Almost before I had grasped her meaning there was the flutter of a dress and the crunch of leather boots, and Tom and Daisy were back at the table.

"It couldn't be helped!" cried Daisy with tense gayety.

She sat down, glanced searchingly at Miss Baker and then at me, and continued: "I looked outdoors for a minute, and it's very romantic outdoors. There's a bird on the lawn that I think must be a nightingale come over on the Cunard or White Star Line. He's singing away—" Her voice sang: "It's romantic, isn't it, Tom?"

"Very romantic," he said, and then miserably to me: "If it's light enough after dinner, I want to take you down to the stables."

The telephone rang inside, startlingly, and as Daisy shook her head decisively at Tom the subject of the stables, in fact all subjects, vanished into air. Among the broken fragments of the last five minutes at table I remember the candles being lit again, pointlessly, and I was conscious of wanting to look squarely at everyone and yet to avoid all eyes. I couldn't guess what Daisy and Tom were thinking, but I doubt if even Miss Baker, who seemed to have mastered a certain hardy skepticism, was able utterly to put this fifth guest's shrill metallic urgency out of mind. To a certain temperament the situation might have seemed intriguing—my own instinct was to telephone immediately for the police.

The horses, needless to say, were not mentioned again. Tom and Miss Baker, with several feet of twilight between them, strolled back into the library, as if to a vigil beside a perfectly tangible body, while, trying to look pleasantly interested and a little deaf, I followed Daisy around a chain of connecting verandas to the porch in front. In its deep gloom we sat down side by side on a wicker settee.

Daisy took her face in her hands as if feeling its lovely shape, and her eyes moved gradually out into the velvet dusk. I saw that turbulent emotions possessed her, so I asked what I thought would be some sedative questions about her little girl.

"We don't know each other very well, Nick," she said suddenly. "Even if we are cousins. You didn't come to my wedding."

"I wasn't back from the war."

"That's true." She hesitated. "Well, I've had a very bad time, Nick, and I'm pretty cynical about everything."

Evidently she had reason to be. I waited but she didn't say any more, and after a moment I returned rather feebly to the subject of her daughter.

"I suppose she talks, and—eats, and everything."

"Oh, yes." She looked at me absently. "Listen, Nick; let me tell you what I said when she was born. Would you like to hear?"

"Very much."

"It'll show you how I've gotten to feel about—things. Well, she was less than an hour old and Tom was God knows where. I woke up out of the ether with an utterly abandoned feeling, and asked the nurse right away if it was a boy or a girl. She told me it was a girl, and so I turned my head away and wept. 'All right,' I said, 'I'm glad it's a girl. And I hope she'll be a fool—that's the best thing a girl can be in this world, a beautiful little fool.'

"You see I think everything's terrible anyhow," she went on in a convinced way. "Everybody thinks so—the most advanced people. And I *know*. I've been everywhere and seen everything and done everything." Her eyes flashed around her in a defiant way, rather like Tom's, and she laughed with thrilling scorn. "Sophisticated—God, I'm sophisticated!"

The instant her voice broke off, ceasing to compel my attention, my belief, I felt the basic insincerity of what she had said. It made me uneasy, as though the whole evening had been a trick of some sort to exact a contributary emotion from me. I waited, and sure enough, in a moment she looked at me with an absolute smirk on her lovely face, as if she had asserted her membership in a rather distinguished secret society to which she and Tom belonged.

Inside, the crimson room bloomed with light. Tom and Miss Baker sat at either end of the long couch and she read aloud to him from the Saturday Evening Post—the words, murmurous and uninflected, running together in a soothing tune. The lamp-light, bright on his boots and dull on the autumn-leaf yellow of her hair, glinted along the paper as she turned a page with a flutter of slender muscles in her arms.

When we came in she held us silent for a moment with a lifted hand.

"To be continued," she said, tossing the magazine on the table, "in our very next issue."

Her body asserted itself with a restless movement of her knee, and she stood up.

"Ten o'clock," she remarked, apparently finding the time on the ceiling. "Time for this good girl to go to bed."

"Jordan's going to play in the tournament tomorrow," explained Daisy, "over at Westchester."

"Oh—you're *Jor*dan Baker."

I knew now why her face was familiar—its pleasing contemptuous expression had looked out at me from many rotogravure pictures of the sporting life at Asheville and Hot Springs and Palm Beach. I had heard some story of her too, a critical, unpleasant story, but what it was I had forgotten long ago.

"Good night," she said softly. "Wake me at eight, won't you."

"If you'll get up."

"I will. Good night, Mr. Carraway. See you anon."

"Of course you will," confirmed Daisy. "In fact I think I'll arrange a marriage. Come over often, Nick, and I'll sort of—oh—fling you together. You know—lock you up accidentally in linen closets and push you out to sea in a boat, and all that sort of thing——"

"Good night," called Miss Baker from the stairs. "I haven't heard a word."

"She's a nice girl," said Tom after a moment. "They oughtn't to let her run around the country this way."

"Who oughtn't to?" inquired Daisy coldly.

"Her family."

"Her family is one aunt about a thousand years old. Besides, Nick's going to look after her, aren't you, Nick? She's going to spend lots of weekends out here this summer. I think the home influence will be very good for her."

Daisy and Tom looked at each other for a moment in silence.

"Is she from New York?" I asked quickly.

"From Louisville. Our white girlhood was passed together there. Our beautiful white——"

"Did you give Nick a little heart-to-heart talk on the veranda?" demanded Tom suddenly.

"Did I?" She looked at me. "I can't seem to remember, but I think we talked about the Nordic race. Yes, I'm sure we did. It sort of crept up on us and first thing you know——"

"Don't believe everything you hear, Nick," he advised me.

I said lightly that I had heard nothing at all, and a few minutes later I got up to go home. They came to the door with me and stood side by side in a cheerful square of light. As I started my motor Daisy peremptorily called: "Wait!

"I forgot to ask you something, and it's important. We heard you were engaged to a girl out West."

"That's right," corroborated Tom kindly. "We heard that you were engaged."

"It's a libel. I'm too poor."

"But we heard it," insisted Daisy, surprising me by opening up again in a flower-like way. "We heard it from three people, so it must be true."

Of course I knew what they were referring to, but I wasn't even vaguely engaged. The fact that gossip had published the banns was one of the reasons I had come East. You can't stop going with an old friend on account of rumors, and on the other hand I had no intention of being rumored into marriage.

Their interest rather touched me and made them less remotely rich—nevertheless, I was confused and a little disgusted as I drove away. It seemed to me that the thing for Daisy to do was to rush out of the house, child in arms—but apparently there were no such intentions in her head. As for Tom, the fact that he "had some woman in New York" was really less surprising than that he had been depressed by a book. Something was making him nibble at the edge of stale ideas as if his sturdy physical egotism no longer nourished his peremptory heart.

Already it was deep summer on roadhouse roofs and in front of wayside garages, where new red gas-pumps sat out in pools of light, and when I reached my estate at West Egg I ran the car under its shed and sat for a while on an abandoned grass roller in the yard. The wind had blown off, leaving a loud, bright night, with wings beating in the trees and a persistent organ sound as the full bellows of the earth blew the frogs full of life. The silhouette of a moving cat wavered across the moonlight, and turning my head to watch it, I saw that I was not alone—fifty feet away a figure had emerged from the shadow of my neighbor's mansion and was standing with his hands in his pockets regarding the silver pepper of the stars. Something in his leisurely movements and the secure position of his feet upon the lawn suggested that it was Mr. Gatsby himself, come out to determine what share was his of our local heavens.

I decided to call to him. Miss Baker had mentioned him at dinner, and that would do for an introduction. But I didn't call to him, for he gave a sudden intimation that he was content to be alone—he stretched out his arms toward the dark water in a curious way, and, far as I was from him, I could have sworn he was trembling. Involuntarily I glanced seaward—and distinguished nothing except a single green light, minute and far away, that might have been at the end of a dock. When I looked once more for Gatsby he had vanished, and I was alone again in the unquiet darkness.

CHAPTER II

ABOUT half way between West Egg and New York the motor-road hastily joins the railroad and runs beside it for a quarter of a mile, so as to shrink away from a certain desolate area of land. This is a valley of ashes—a fantastic farm where ashes grow like wheat into ridges and hills and grotesque gardens; where ashes take the forms of houses and chimneys and rising smoke and, finally, with a transcendent effort, of men who move dimly and already crumbling through the powdery air. Occasionally a line of gray cars crawls along an invisible track, gives out a ghastly creak, and comes to rest, and immediately the ash-gray men swarm up with leaden spades and stir up an impenetrable cloud, which screens their obscure operations from your sight.

But above the gray land and the spasms of bleak dust which drift endlessly over it, you perceive, after a moment, the eyes of Doctor T. J. Eckleburg. The eyes of Doctor T. J. Eckleburg are blue and gigantic—their retinas are one yard high. They look out of no face, but, instead, from a pair of enormous yellow spectacles which pass over a non-existent nose. Evidently some wild wag of an oculist set them there to fatten his practice in the borough of Queens, and then sank down himself into eternal blindness, or forgot them and moved away. But his eyes, dimmed a little by many paintless days under sun and rain, brood on over the solemn dumping ground.

The valley of ashes is bounded on one side by a small foul river, and, when the drawbridge is up to let barges through, the passengers on waiting trains can stare at the dismal scene for as long as half an hour. There is always a halt there of at least a minute, and it was because of this that I first met Tom Buchanan's mistress.

The fact that he had one was insisted upon wherever he was known. His acquaintances resented the fact that he turned up in popular restaurants with her and, leaving her at a table, sauntered about, chatting with whomsoever he knew. Though I was curious to see her, I had no desire to meet her—but I did. I went up to New York with Tom on the train one afternoon, and when we stopped by the ashheaps he jumped to his feet and, taking hold of my elbow, literally forced me from the car.

"We're getting off," he insisted. "I want you to meet my girl."

I think he'd tanked up a good deal at luncheon, and his determination to have my company bordered on violence.

The supercilious assumption was that on Sunday afternoon I had nothing better to do.

I followed him over a low whitewashed railroad fence, and we walked back a hundred yards along the road under Doctor Eckleburg's persistent stare. The only building in sight was a small block of yellow brick sitting on the edge of the waste land, a sort of compact Main Street ministering to it, and contiguous to absolutely nothing. One of the three shops it contained was for rent and another was an all-night restaurant, approached by a trail of ashes; the third was a garage—*Repairs*. GEORGE B. WILSON. *Cars bought and sold.*—and I followed Tom inside.

The interior was unprosperous and bare; the only car visible was the dust-covered wreck of a Ford which crouched in a dim corner. It had occurred to me that this shadow of a garage must be a blind, and that sumptuous and romantic apartments were concealed overhead, when the proprietor himself appeared in the door of an office, wiping his hands on a piece of waste. He was a blond, spiritless man, anæmic, and faintly handsome. When he saw us a damp gleam of hope sprang into his light blue eyes.

"Hello, Wilson, old man," said Tom, slapping him jovially on the shoulder. "How's business?"

"I can't complain," answered Wilson unconvincingly. "When are you going to sell me that car?"

"Next week; I've got my man working on it now."

"Works pretty slow, don't he?"

"No, he doesn't," said Tom coldly. "And if you feel that way about it, maybe I'd better sell it somewhere else after all."

"I don't mean that," explained Wilson quickly. "I just meant——"

His voice faded off and Tom glanced impatiently around the garage. Then I heard footsteps on a stairs, and in a moment the thickish figure of a woman blocked out the light from the office door. She was in the middle thirties, and faintly stout, but she carried her surplus flesh sensuously as some women can. Her face, above a spotted dress of dark blue crêpe-de-chine, contained no facet or gleam of beauty, but there was an immediately perceptible vitality about her as if the nerves of her body were continually smouldering. She smiled slowly and, walking through her husband as if he were a ghost, shook hands with Tom, looking him flush in the eye. Then she wet her lips, and without turning around spoke to her husband in a soft, coarse voice:

"Get some chairs, why don't you, so somebody can sit down."

"Oh, sure," agreed Wilson hurriedly, and went toward the little office, mingling immediately with the cement color of the walls. A white ashen dust veiled his dark suit and his pale hair as it veiled everything in the vicinity—except his wife, who moved close to Tom.

"I want to see you," said Tom intently. "Get on the next train."

"All right."

"I'll meet you by the newsstand on the lower level."

She nodded and moved away from him just as George Wilson emerged with two chairs from his office door.

We waited for her down the road and out of sight. It was a few days before the Fourth of July, and a gray, scrawny Italian child was setting torpedoes in a row along the railroad track.

"Terrible place, isn't it," said Tom, exchanging a frown with Doctor Eckleburg.

"Awful."

"It does her good to get away."

"Doesn't her husband object?"

"Wilson? He thinks she goes to see her sister in New York. He's so dumb he doesn't know he's alive."

So Tom Buchanan and his girl and I went up together to New York—or not quite together, for Mrs. Wilson sat discreetly in another car. Tom deferred that much to the sensibilities of those East Eggers who might be on the train.

She had changed her dress to a brown figured muslin, which stretched tight over her rather wide hips as Tom helped her to the platform in New York. At the newsstand she bought a copy of Town Tattle and a moving-picture magazine, and in the station drug-store some cold cream and a small flask of perfume. Upstairs in the solemn echoing drive she let four taxi cabs drive away before she selected a new one, lavender-colored with gray upholstery, and in this we slid out from the mass of the station into the glowing sunshine. But immediately she turned sharply from the window and, leaning forward, tapped on the front glass.

"I want to get one of those dogs," she said earnestly. "I want to get one for the apartment. They're nice to have—a dog."

We backed up to a gray old man who bore an absurd resemblance to John D. Rockefeller. In a basket swung from his neck cowered a dozen very recent puppies of an indeterminate breed.

"What kind are they?" asked Mrs. Wilson eagerly, as he came to the taxi window.

"All kinds. What kind do you want, lady?"

"I'd like to get one of those police dogs; I don't suppose you got that kind?"

The man peered doubtfully into the basket, plunged in his hand and drew one up, wriggling, by the back of the neck.

"That's no police dog," said Tom.

"No, it's not exactly a pol*ice* dog," said the man with disappointment in his voice. "It's more of an Airedale." He passed his hand over the brown wash-rag of a back. "Look at that coat. Some coat. That's a dog that'll never bother you with catching cold."

"I think it's cute," said Mrs. Wilson enthusiastically. "How much is it?"

"That dog?" He looked at it admiringly. "That dog will cost you ten dollars."

The Airedale—undoubtedly there was an Airedale concerned in it somewhere, though its feet were startlingly white—changed hands and settled down into Mrs. Wilson's lap, where she fondled the weatherproof coat with rapture.

"Is it a boy or a girl?" she asked delicately.

"That dog? That dog's a boy."

"It's a bitch," said Tom decisively. "Here's your money. Go and buy ten more dogs with it."

We drove over to Fifth Avenue, so warm and soft, almost pastoral, on the summer Sunday afternoon that I wouldn't have been surprised to see a great flock of white sheep turn the corner.

"Hold on," I said. "I have to leave you here."

"No, you don't," interposed Tom quickly. "Myrtle'll be hurt if you don't come up to the apartment. Won't you, Myrtle?"

"Come on," she urged. "I'll telephone my sister Catherine. She's said to be very beautiful by people who ought to know."

"Well, I'd like to, but——"

We went on, cutting back again over the Park toward the West Hundreds. At 158th Street the cab stopped at one slice in a long white cake of apartment-houses. Throwing a regal homecoming glance around the neighborhood, Mrs. Wilson gathered up her dog and her other purchases, and went haughtily in.

"I'm going to have the McKees come up," she announced as we rose in the elevator. "And, of course, I got to call up my sister, too."

The apartment was on the top floor—a small living-room, a small dining-room, a small bedroom, and a bath. The living-room was crowded to the doors with a set of tapestried furniture entirely too large for it, so that to move about was to stumble continually over scenes of ladies swinging in the gardens of Versailles. The only picture was an over-enlarged photograph, apparently a hen sitting on a blurred rock. Looked at from a distance, however, the hen resolved itself into a bonnet, and the countenance of a stout old lady beamed down into the room. Several old copies of Town Tattle lay on the table together with a copy of "Simon Called Peter," and some of the small scandal magazines of Broadway. Mrs. Wilson was first concerned with the dog. A reluctant elevator-boy went for a box full of straw and some milk, to which he added on his own initiative a tin of large, hard dog-biscuits—one of which decomposed apathetically in the saucer of milk all afternoon. Meanwhile Tom brought out a bottle of whiskey from a locked bureau door.

I have been drunk just twice in my life, and the second time was that afternoon; so everything that happened has a dim, hazy cast over it, although until after eight o'clock the apartment was full of cheerful sun. Sitting on Tom's lap Mrs. Wilson called up several people on the telephone; then there were no cigarettes, and I went out to buy some at the drug-store on the corner. When I came back they had disappeared, so I sat down discreetly in the living-room and read a chapter of "Simon Called Peter"—either it was terrible stuff or the whiskey distorted things, because it didn't make any sense to me.

Just as Tom and Myrtle (after the first drink Mrs. Wilson and I called each other by our first names) reappeared, company commenced to arrive at the apartment-door.

The sister, Catherine, was a slender, worldly girl of about thirty, with a solid, sticky bob of red hair, and a complexion powdered milky white. Her eyebrows had been plucked and then drawn on again at a more rakish angle, but the efforts of nature toward the restoration of the old alignment gave a blurred air to her face. When she moved about there was an incessant clicking as innumerable pottery bracelets jingled up and down upon her arms. She came in with such a proprietary haste and looked around so possessively at the furniture that I wondered if she lived here. But when I asked her she laughed immoderately, repeated my question aloud, and told me she lived with a girl friend at a hotel.

Mr. McKee was a pale, feminine man from the flat below. He had just shaved, for there was a white spot of lather on his cheekbone, and he was most respectful in his greeting to everyone in the room. He informed me that he was in the "artistic game," and I gathered later that he was a photographer and had made the dim enlargement of Mrs. Wilson's mother which hovered like an ectoplasm on the wall. His wife was shrill, languid, handsome, and horrible. She told me with pride that her husband had photographed her a hundred and twenty-seven times since they had been married.

Mrs. Wilson had changed her costume sometime before, and was now attired in an elaborate afternoon dress of cream-colored chiffon, which gave out a continual rustle as she swept about the room. With the influence of the dress her personality had also undergone a change. The intense vitality that had been so remarkable in the garage was converted into impressive hauteur. Her laughter, her gestures, her assertions became more violently affected moment by moment, and as she expanded the room grew smaller around her, until she seemed to be revolving on a noisy, creaking pivot through the smoky air.

"My dear," she told her sister in a high, mincing shout, "most of these fellas will cheat you every time. All they think of is money. I had a woman up here last week to look at my feet, and when she gave me the bill you'd of thought she had my appendicitus out."

"What was the name of the woman?" asked Mrs. McKee.

"Mrs. Eberhardt. She goes around looking at people's feet in their own homes."

"I like your dress," remarked Mrs. McKee. "I think it's adorable."

Mrs. Wilson rejected the compliment by raising her eyebrow in disdain.

"It's just a crazy old thing," she said. "I just slip it on sometimes when I don't care what I look like."

"But it looks wonderful on you, if you know what I mean," pursued Mrs. McKee. "If Chester could only get you in that pose I think he could make something of it."

We all looked in silence at Mrs. Wilson, who removed a strand of hair from over her eyes and looked back at us with a brilliant smile. Mr. McKee regarded her intently with his head on one side, and then moved his hand back and forth slowly in front of his face.

"I should change the light," he said after a moment. "I'd like to bring out the modelling of the features. And I'd try to get hold of all the back hair."

"I wouldn't think of changing the light," cried Mrs. McKee. "I think it's——"

Her husband said "*Sh!*" and we all looked at the subject again, whereupon Tom Buchanan yawned audibly and got to his feet.

"You McKees have something to drink," he said. "Get some more ice and mineral water, Myrtle, before everybody goes to sleep."

"I told that boy about the ice." Myrtle raised her eyebrows in despair at the shiftlessness of the lower orders. "These people! You have to keep after them all the time."

She looked at me and laughed pointlessly. Then she flounced over to the dog, kissed it with ecstasy, and swept into the kitchen, implying that a dozen chefs awaited her orders there.

"I've done some nice things out on Long Island," asserted Mr. McKee.

Tom looked at him blankly.

"Two of them we have framed downstairs."

"Two what?" demanded Tom.

"Two studies. One of them I call 'Montauk Point—The Gulls,' and the other I call 'Montauk Point—The Sea.'"

The sister Catherine sat down beside me on the couch.

"Do you live down on Long Island, too," she inquired.

"I live at West Egg."

"Really? I was down there at a party about a month ago. At a man named Gatsby's. Do you know him?"

"I live next door to him."

"Well, they say he's a nephew or a cousin of Kaiser Wilhelm's. That's where all his money comes from."

"Really?"

She nodded.

"I'm scared of him. I'd hate to have him get anything on me."

This absorbing information about my neighbor was interrupted by Mrs. McKee's pointing suddenly at Catherine:

"Chester, I think you could do something with *her,*" she broke out, but Mr. McKee only nodded in a bored way, and turned his attention to Tom.

"I'd like to do more work on Long Island, if I could get the entry. All I ask is that they should give me a start."

"Ask Myrtle," said Tom, breaking into a short shout of laughter as Mrs. Wilson entered with a tray. "She'll give you a letter of introduction, won't you, Myrtle?"

"Do what?" she asked, startled.

"You'll give McKee a letter of introduction to your husband, so he can do some studies of him." His lips moved silently for a moment as he invented. "'George B. Wilson at the Gasoline Pump,' or something like that."

Catherine leaned close to me and whispered in my ear:

"Neither of them can stand the person they're married to."

"Can't they?"

"Can't *stand* them." She looked at Myrtle and then at Tom. "What I say is, why go on living with them if they can't stand them? If I was them I'd get a divorce and get married to each other right away."

"Doesn't she like Wilson either?"

The answer to this was unexpected. It came from Myrtle, who had overheard the question, and it was violent and obscene.

"You see?" cried Catherine triumphantly. She lowered her voice again. "It's really his wife that's keeping them apart. She's a Catholic, and they don't believe in divorce."

Daisy was not a Catholic, and I was a little shocked at the elaborateness of the lie.

"When they do get married," continued Catherine, "they're going West to live for a while until it blows over."

"It'd be more discreet to go to Europe."

"Oh, do you like Europe?" she exclaimed surprisingly. "I just got back from Monte Carlo."

"Really."

"Just last year. I went over there with another girl."

"Stay long?"

"No, we just went to Monte Carlo and back. We went by way of Marseilles. We had over twelve hundred dollars when we started, but we got gypped out of it all in two days in the private rooms. We had an awful time getting back, I can tell you. God, how I hated that town!"

The late afternoon sky bloomed in the window for a moment like the blue honey of the Mediterranean—then the shrill voice of Mrs. McKee called me back into the room.

"I almost made a mistake, too," she declared vigorously. "I almost married a little kyke who'd been after me for years. I knew he was below me. Everybody kept saying to me: 'Lucille, that man's way below you!' But if I hadn't met Chester, he'd of got me sure."

"Yes, but listen," said Myrtle Wilson, nodding her head up and down. "At least you didn't marry him."

"I know I didn't."

"Well, I married him," said Myrtle, ambiguously. "And that's the difference between your case and mine."

"Why did you, Myrtle?" demanded Catherine. "Nobody forced you to."

Myrtle considered.

"I married him because I thought he was a gentleman," she said finally. "I thought he knew something about breeding, but he wasn't fit to lick my shoe."

"You were crazy about him for a while," said Catherine.

"Crazy about him!" cried Myrtle incredulously. "Who said I was crazy about him? I never was any more crazy about him than I was about that man there."

She pointed suddenly at me, and everyone looked at me accusingly. I tried to show by my expression that I had played no part in her past.

"The only *crazy* I was was when I married him. I knew right away I made a mistake. He borrowed somebody's best suit to get married in, and never even told me about it, and the man came after it one day when he was out." She looked to see who was listening. "'Oh, is that your suit?' I said. 'This is the first I ever heard about it.' But I gave it to him and then I lay down and cried to beat the band all afternoon."

"She really ought to get away from him," resumed Catherine to me. "They've been living over that garage for eleven years. And Tom's the first sweetie she ever had."

The bottle of whiskey—a second one—was now in constant demand by all present, excepting Catherine, who "felt just as good on nothing at all." Tom rang for the janitor and sent him for some celebrated sandwiches which were a complete supper in themselves. I wanted to get out and walk eastward toward the Park through the soft twilight, but each time I tried to go I became entangled in some wild, strident argument which pulled me back, as if with ropes, into my chair. Yet high over the city our line of yellow windows must have contributed their share of human secrecy to the casual watcher in the darkening streets, and I was him too, looking up and wondering. I was within and without, simultaneously enchanted and repelled by the inexhaustible variety of life.

Myrtle pulled her chair close to mine, and suddenly her warm breath poured over me the story of her first meeting with Tom.

"It was on the two little seats facing each other that are always the last ones left on the train. I was going up to New York to see my sister and spend the night. He had on a dress suit and patent leather shoes, and I couldn't keep my eyes off him, but every time he looked at me I had to pretend to be looking at the advertisement over his head. When we came into the station he was next to me, and his white shirt front pressed against my arm, and so I told him I'd have to call a policeman, but he knew I lied. I was so excited that when I got into a taxi with him I didn't hardly know I wasn't getting into a subway train. All I kept thinking about, over and over, was 'You can't live forever, you can't live forever.'"

She turned to Mrs. McKee and the room rang full of her artificial laughter.

"My dear," she cried, "I'm going to give you this dress as soon as I'm through with it. I've got to get another one tomorrow. I'm going to make a list of all the things I've got to get. A massage and a wave, and a collar for the dog, and one of those cute little ash trays where you touch a spring, and a wreath with a black silk bow for mother's grave that'll last all summer. I got to write down a list so I won't forget all the things I got to do."

It was nine o'clock—almost immediately afterward I looked at my watch and found it was ten. Mr. McKee was asleep on a chair with his fists clenched in his lap, like a photograph of a man of action. Taking out my handkerchief I wiped from his cheek the spot of dried lather that had worried me all the afternoon.

The little dog was sitting on the table looking with blind eyes through the smoke, and from time to time groaning faintly. People disappeared, reappeared, made plans to go somewhere, and then lost each other, searched for each other, found each other a few feet away. Some time toward midnight Tom Buchanan and Mrs. Wilson stood face to face discussing, in impassioned voices, whether Mrs. Wilson had any right to mention Daisy's name.

"Daisy! Daisy! Daisy!" shouted Mrs. Wilson. "I'll say it whenever I want to! Daisy! Dai——"

Making a short deft movement, Tom Buchanan broke her nose with his open hand.

Then there were bloody towels upon the bathroom floor, and women's voices scolding, and high over the confusion a long broken wail of pain. Mr. McKee awoke from his doze and started in a daze toward the door. When he had gone half way he turned around and stared at the scene—his wife and Catherine scolding and consoling as they stumbled here and there among the crowded furniture with articles of aid, and the despairing figure on the couch, bleeding fluently, and trying to spread a copy of Town Tattle over the tapestry scenes of Versailles. Then Mr. McKee turned and continued on out the door. Taking my hat from the chandelier, I followed.

"Come to lunch some day," he suggested, as we groaned down in the elevator.

"Where?"

"Anywhere."

"Keep your hands off the lever," snapped the elevator boy.

"I beg your pardon," said Mr. McKee with dignity. "I didn't know I was touching it."

"All right," I agreed, "I'll be glad to."

... I was standing beside his bed and he was sitting up between the sheets, clad in his underwear, with a great portfolio in his hands.

"Beauty and the Beast ... Loneliness ... Old Grocery Horse ... Brook'n Bridge ..."

Then I was lying half asleep in the cold lower level of the Pennsylvania Station, staring at the morning Tribune, and waiting for the four o'clock train.

CHAPTER III

THERE was music from my neighbor's house through the summer nights. In his blue gardens men and girls came and went like moths among the whisperings and the champagne and the stars. At high tide in the afternoon I watched his guests diving from the tower of his raft, or taking the sun on the hot sand of his beach while his two motor-boats slit the waters of the Sound, drawing aquaplanes over cataracts of foam. On weekends his Rolls-Royce became an omnibus, bearing parties to and from the city between nine in the morning and long past midnight, while his station wagon scampered like a brisk yellow bug to meet all trains. And on Mondays eight servants, including an extra gardener, toiled all day with mops and scrubbing-brushes and hammers and garden shears, repairing the ravages of the night before.

Every Friday five crates of oranges and lemons arrived from a fruiterer in New York—every Monday these same oranges and lemons left his back door in a pyramid of pulpless halves. There was a machine in the kitchen which could extract the juice of two hundred oranges in half an hour if a little button was pressed two hundred times by a butler's thumb.

At least once a fortnight a corps of caterers came down with several hundred feet of canvas and enough colored lights to make a Christmas tree of Gatsby's enormous garden. On buffet tables, garnished with glistening hors-d'œuvre, spiced baked hams crowded against salads of harlequin designs and pastry pigs and turkeys bewitched to a dark gold. In the main hall a bar with a real brass rail was set up, and stocked with gins and liquors and with cordials so long forgotten that most of his female guests were too young to know one from another.

By seven o'clock the orchestra has arrived, no thin five-piece affair, but a whole pitful of oboes and trombones and saxophones and viols and cornets and piccolos, and low and high drums. The last swimmers have come in from the beach now and are dressing upstairs; the cars from New York are parked five deep in the drive, and already the halls and salons and verandas are gaudy with primary colors, and hair shorn in strange new ways, and shawls beyond the dreams of Castile. The bar is in full swing, and floating rounds of cocktails permeate the garden outside, until the air is alive with chatter and laughter, and casual innuendo and introductions forgotten on the spot, and enthusiastic meetings between women who never knew each other's names.

The lights grow brighter as the earth lurches away from the sun, and now the orchestra is playing yellow cocktail music, and the opera of voices pitches a key higher. Laughter is easier minute by minute, spilled with prodigality, tipped out at a cheerful word. The groups change more swiftly, swell with new arrivals, dissolve and form in the same breath; already there are wanderers, confident girls who weave here and there among the stouter and more stable, become for a sharp, joyous moment the center of a group, and then, excited with triumph, glide on through the sea-change of faces and voices and color under the constantly changing light.

Suddenly one of these gypsies, in trembling opal, seizes a cocktail out of the air, dumps it down for courage and, moving her hands like Frisco, dances out alone on the canvas platform. A momentary hush; the orchestra leader varies his rhythm obligingly for her, and there is a burst of chatter as the erroneous news goes around that she is Gilda Gray's understudy from the Follies. The party has begun.

I believe that on the first night I went to Gatsby's house I was one of the few guests who had actually been invited. People were not invited—they went there. They got into automobiles which bore them out to Long Island, and somehow they ended up at Gatsby's door. Once there they were introduced by somebody who knew Gatsby, and after that they conducted themselves according to the rules of behavior associated with amusement parks. Sometimes they came and went without having met Gatsby at all, came for the party with a simplicity of heart that was its own ticket of admission.

I had been actually invited. A chauffeur in a uniform of robin's-egg blue crossed my lawn early that Saturday morning with a surprisingly formal note from his employer: the honor would be entirely Gatsby's, it said, if I would attend his "little party" that night. He had seen me several times, and had intended to call on me long before, but a peculiar combination of circumstances had prevented it—signed Jay Gatsby, in a majestic hand.

Dressed up in white flannels I went over to his lawn a little after seven, and wandered around rather ill at ease among swirls and eddies of people I didn't know—though here and there was a face I had noticed on the commuting train. I was immediately struck by the number of young Englishmen dotted about; all well-dressed, all looking a little hungry, and all talking in low, earnest voices to solid and prosperous Americans. I was sure that they were selling something: bonds or insurance or automobiles. They were at least agonizingly aware of the easy money in the vicinity and convinced that it was theirs for a few words in the right key.

As soon as I arrived I made an attempt to find my host, but the two or three people of whom I asked his whereabouts stared at me in such an amazed way, and denied so vehemently any knowledge of his movements, that I slunk off in the direction of the cocktail table—the only place in the garden where a single man could linger without looking purposeless and alone.

I was on my way to get roaring drunk from sheer embarrassment when Jordan Baker came out of the house and stood at the head of the marble steps, leaning a little backward and looking with contemptuous interest down into the garden.

Welcome or not, I found it necessary to attach myself to someone before I should begin to address cordial remarks to the passers-by.

"Hello!" I roared, advancing toward her. My voice seemed unnaturally loud across the garden.

"I thought you might be here," she responded absently as I came up. "I remembered you lived next door to——"

She held my hand impersonally, as a promise that she'd take care of me in a minute, and gave ear to two girls in twin yellow dresses, who stopped at the foot of the steps.

"Hello!" they cried together. "Sorry you didn't win."

That was for the golf tournament. She had lost in the finals the week before.

"You don't know who we are," said one of the girls in yellow, "but we met you here about a month ago."

"You've dyed your hair since then," remarked Jordan, and I started, but the girls had moved casually on and her remark was addressed to the premature moon, produced like the supper, no doubt, out of a caterer's basket. With Jordan's slender golden arm resting in mine, we descended the steps and sauntered about the garden. A tray of cocktails floated at us through the twilight, and we sat down at a table with the two girls in yellow and three men, each one introduced to us as Mr. Mumble.

"Do you come to these parties often?" inquired Jordan of the girl beside her.

"The last one was the one I met you at," answered the girl, in an alert confident voice. She turned to her companion: "Wasn't it for you, Lucille?"

It was for Lucille, too.

"I like to come," Lucille said. "I never care what I do, so I always have a good time. When I was here last I tore my gown on a chair, and he asked me my name and address—inside of a week I got a package from Croirier's with a new evening gown in it."

"Did you keep it?" asked Jordan.

"Sure I did. I was going to wear it tonight, but it was too big in the bust and had to be altered. It was gas blue with lavender beads. Two hundred and sixty-five dollars."

"There's something funny about a fellow that'll do a thing like that," said the other girl eagerly. "He doesn't want any trouble with *any*body."

"Who doesn't?" I inquired.

"Gatsby. Somebody told me——"

The two girls and Jordan leaned together confidentially.

"Somebody told me they thought he killed a man once."

A thrill passed over all of us. The three Mr. Mumbles bent forward and listened eagerly.

"I don't think it's so much *that,*" argued Lucille skeptically; "it's more that he was a German spy during the war."

One of the men nodded in confirmation.

"I heard that from a man who knew all about him, grew up with him in Germany," he assured us positively.

"Oh, no," said the first girl, "it couldn't be that, because he was in the American army during the war." As our credulity switched back to her she leaned forward with enthusiasm. "You look at him sometime when he thinks nobody's looking at him. I'll bet he killed a man."

She narrowed her eyes and shivered. Lucille shivered. We all turned and looked around for Gatsby. It was testimony to the romantic speculation he inspired that there were whispers about him from those who had found little that it was necessary to whisper about in this world.

The first supper—there would be another one after midnight—was now being served, and Jordan invited me to join her own party, who were spread around a table on the other side of the garden. There were three married couples and Jordan's escort, a persistent undergraduate given to violent innuendo, and obviously under the impression that sooner or later Jordan was going to yield him up her person to a greater or lesser degree. Instead of rambling this party had preserved a dignified homogeneity, and assumed to itself the function of representing the staid nobility of the country-side—East Egg condescending to West Egg, and carefully on guard against its spectroscopic gayety.

"Let's get out," whispered Jordan, after a somehow wasteful and inappropriate half hour; "this is much too polite for me."

We got up, and she explained that we were going to find the host: I had never met him, she said, and it was making me uneasy. The undergraduate nodded in a cynical, melancholy way.

The bar, where we glanced first, was crowded, but Gatsby was not there. She couldn't find him from the top of the steps, and he wasn't on the veranda. On a chance we tried an important-looking door, and walked into a high Gothic library, panelled with carved English oak, and probably transported complete from some ruin overseas.

A stout, middle-aged man, with enormous owl-eyed spectacles, was sitting somewhat drunk on the edge of a great table, staring with unsteady concentration at the shelves of books. As we entered he wheeled excitedly around and examined Jordan from head to foot.

"What do you think?" he demanded impetuously.

"About what?"

He waved his hand toward the bookshelves.

"About that. As a matter of fact you needn't bother to ascertain. I ascertained. They're real."

"The books?"

He nodded.

"Absolutely real—have pages and everything. I thought they'd be a nice durable cardboard. Matter of fact, they're absolutely real. Pages and— Here! Lemme show you."

Taking our skepticism for granted, he rushed to the bookcases and returned with Volume One of the "Stoddard Lectures."

"See!" he cried triumphantly. "It's a bona-fide piece of printed matter. It fooled me. This fella's a regular Belasco. It's a triumph. What thoroughness! What realism! Knew when to stop, too—didn't cut the pages. But what do you want? What do you expect?"

He snatched the book from me and replaced it hastily on its shelf, muttering that if one brick was removed the whole library was liable to collapse.

"Who brought you?" he demanded. "Or did you just come? I was brought. Most people were brought."

Jordan looked at him alertly, cheerfully, without answering.

"I was brought by a woman named Roosevelt," he continued. "Mrs. Claud Roosevelt. Do you know her? I met her somewhere last night. I've been drunk for about a week now, and I thought it might sober me up to sit in a library."

"Has it?"

"A little bit, I think. I can't tell yet. I've only been here an hour. Did I tell you about the books? They're real. They're——"

"You told us."

We shook hands with him gravely and went back outdoors.

There was dancing now on the canvas in the garden; old men pushing young girls backward in eternal graceless circles, superior couples holding each other tortuously, fashionably, and keeping in the corners—and a great number of single girls dancing individualistically or relieving the orchestra for a moment of the burden of the banjo or the traps. By midnight the hilarity had increased. A celebrated tenor had sung in Italian, and a notorious contralto had sung in jazz, and between the numbers people were doing "stunts" all over the garden, while happy, vacuous bursts of laughter rose toward the summer sky.

A pair of stage twins, who turned out to be the girls in yellow, did a baby act in costume, and champagne was served in glasses bigger than finger-bowls. The moon had risen higher, and floating in the Sound was a triangle of silver scales, trembling a little to the stiff, tinny drip of the banjoes on the lawn.

I was still with Jordan Baker. We were sitting at a table with a man of about my age and a rowdy little girl, who gave way upon the slightest provocation to uncontrollable laughter. I was enjoying myself now. I had taken two finger-bowls of champagne, and the scene had changed before my eyes into something significant, elemental, and profound.

At a lull in the entertainment the man looked at me and smiled.

"Your face is familiar," he said, politely. "Weren't you in the Third Division during the war?"

"Why, yes. I was in the Ninth Machine-Gun Battalion."

"I was in the Seventh Infantry until June nineteen-eighteen. I knew I'd seen you somewhere before."

We talked for a moment about some wet, gray little villages in France. Evidently he lived in this vicinity, for he told me that he had just bought a hydroplane, and was going to try it out in the morning.

"Want to go with me, old sport? Just near the shore along the Sound."

"What time?"

"Any time that suits you best."

It was on the tip of my tongue to ask his name when Jordan looked around and smiled.

"Having a gay time now?" she inquired.

"Much better." I turned again to my new acquaintance. "This is an unusual party for me. I haven't even seen the host. I live over there—" I waved my hand at the invisible hedge in the distance, "and this man Gatsby sent over his chauffeur with an invitation."

For a moment he looked at me as if he failed to understand.

"I'm Gatsby," he said suddenly.

"What!" I exclaimed. "Oh, I beg your pardon."

"I thought you knew, old sport. I'm afraid I'm not a very good host."

He smiled understandingly—much more than understandingly. It was one of those rare smiles with a quality of eternal reassurance in it, that you may come across four or five times in life. It faced—or seemed to face—the whole external world for an instant, and then concentrated on *you* with an irresistible prejudice in your favor. It understood you just so far as you wanted to be understood, believed in you as you would like to believe in yourself, and assured you that it had precisely the impression of you that, at your best, you hoped to convey. Precisely at that point it vanished—and I was looking at an elegant young rough-neck, a year or two over thirty, whose elaborate formality of speech just missed being absurd. Sometime before he introduced himself I'd got a strong impression that he was picking his words with care.

Almost at the moment when Mr. Gatsby identified himself a butler hurried toward him with the information that Chicago was calling him on the wire. He excused himself with a small bow that included each of us in turn.

"If you want anything just ask for it, old sport," he urged me. "Excuse me. I will rejoin you later."

When he was gone I turned immediately to Jordan—constrained to assure her of my surprise. I had expected that Mr. Gatsby would be a florid and corpulent person in his middle years.

"Who is he?" I demanded. "Do you know?"

"He's just a man named Gatsby."

"Where is he from, I mean? And what does he do?"

"Now *you*'re started on the subject," she answered with a wan smile. "Well, he told me once he was an Oxford man."

A dim background started to take shape behind him, but at her next remark it faded away.

"However, I don't believe it."

"Why not?"

"I don't know," she insisted. "I just don't think he went there."

Something in her tone reminded me of the other girl's "I think he killed a man," and had the effect of stimulating my curiosity. I would have accepted without question the information that Gatsby sprang from the swamps of Louisiana or from the Lower East Side of New York. That was comprehensible. But young men didn't—at least in my provincial inexperience I believed they didn't—drift coolly out of nowhere and buy a palace on Long Island Sound.

"Anyhow, he gives large parties," said Jordan, changing the subject with an urban distaste for the concrete. "And I like large parties. They're so intimate. At small parties there isn't any privacy."

There was the boom of a bass drum, and the voice of the orchestra leader rang out suddenly above the echolalia of the garden.

"Ladies and gentlemen," he cried. "At the request of Mr. Gatsby we are going to play for you Mr. Vladimir Tostoff's latest work, which attracted so much attention at Carnegie Hall last May. If you read the papers you know there was a big sensation." He smiled with jovial condescension, and added: "Some sensation!" Whereupon everybody laughed.

"The piece is known," he concluded lustily, "as 'Vladimir Tostoff's Jazz History of the World.'"

The nature of Mr. Tostoff's composition eluded me, because just as it began my eyes fell on Gatsby, standing alone on the marble steps and looking from one group to another with approving eyes. His tanned skin was drawn attractively tight on his face and his short hair looked as though it were trimmed every day. I could see nothing sinister about him. I wondered if the fact that he was not drinking helped to set him off from his guests, for it seemed to me that he grew more correct as the fraternal hilarity increased. When the "Jazz History of the World" was over, girls were putting their heads on men's shoulders in a puppyish, convivial way, girls were swooning backward playfully into men's arms, even into groups, knowing that someone would arrest their falls—but no one swooned backward on Gatsby, and no French bob touched Gatsby's shoulder, and no singing quartets were formed with Gatsby's head for one link.

"I beg your pardon."

Gatsby's butler was suddenly standing beside us.

"Miss Baker?" he inquired. "I beg your pardon, but Mr. Gatsby would like to speak to you alone."

"With me?" she exclaimed in surprise.

"Yes, madame."

She got up slowly, raising her eyebrows at me in astonishment, and followed the butler toward the house. I noticed that she wore her evening-dress, all her dresses, like sports clothes—there was a jauntiness about her movements as if she had first learned to walk upon golf courses on clean, crisp mornings.

I was alone and it was almost two. For some time confused and intriguing sounds had issued from a long, many-windowed room which overhung the terrace. Eluding Jordan's undergraduate, who was now engaged in an obstetrical conversation with two chorus girls, and who implored me to join him, I went inside.

The large room was full of people. One of the girls in yellow was playing the piano, and beside her stood a tall, red-haired young lady from a famous chorus, engaged in song. She had drunk a quantity of champagne, and during the course of her song she had decided, ineptly, that everything was very, very sad—she was not only singing, she was weeping too. Whenever there was a pause in the song she filled it with gasping, broken sobs, and then took up the lyric again in a quavering soprano. The tears coursed down her cheeks—not freely, however, for when they came into contact with her heavily beaded eyelashes they assumed an inky color, and pursued the rest of their way in slow black rivulets. A humorous suggestion was made that she sing the notes on her face, whereupon she threw up her hands, sank into a chair, and went off into a deep vinous sleep.

"She had a fight with a man who says he's her husband," explained a girl at my elbow.

I looked around. Most of the remaining women were now having fights with men said to be their husbands. Even Jordan's party, the quartet from East Egg, were rent asunder by dissension. One of the men was talking with curious intensity to a young actress, and his wife, after attempting to laugh at the situation in a dignified and indifferent way, broke down entirely and resorted to flank attacks—at intervals she appeared suddenly at his side like an angry diamond, and hissed: "You promised!" into his ear.

The reluctance to go home was not confined to wayward men. The hall was at present occupied by two deplorably sober men and their highly indignant wives. The wives were sympathizing with each other in slightly raised voices.

"Whenever he sees I'm having a good time he wants to go home."

"Never heard anything so selfish in my life."

"We're always the first ones to leave."

"So are we."

"Well, we're almost the last tonight," said one of the men sheepishly. "The orchestra left half an hour ago."

In spite of the wives' agreement that such malevolence was beyond credibility, the dispute ended in a short struggle, and both wives were lifted, kicking, into the night.

As I waited for my hat in the hall the door of the library opened and Jordan Baker and Gatsby came out together. He was saying some last word to her, but the eagerness in his manner tightened abruptly into formality as several people approached him to say good-by.

Jordan's party were calling impatiently to her from the porch, but she lingered for a moment to shake hands.

"I've just heard the most amazing thing," she whispered. "How long were we in there?"

"Why, about an hour."

"It was ... simply amazing," she repeated abstractedly. "But I swore I wouldn't tell it and here I am tantalizing you." She yawned gracefully in my face. "Please come and see me.... Phone book.... Under the name of Mrs. Sigourney Howard.... My aunt...." She was hurrying off as she talked—her brown hand waved a jaunty salute as she melted into her party at the door.

Rather ashamed that on my first appearance I had stayed so late, I joined the last of Gatsby's guests, who were clustered around him. I wanted to explain that I'd hunted for him early in the evening and to apologize for not having known him in the garden.

"Don't mention it," he enjoined me eagerly. "Don't give it another thought, old sport." The familiar expression held no more familiarity than the hand which reassuringly brushed my shoulder. “And don’t forget we’re going up in the hydroplane tomorrow morning, at nine o’clock.”

Then the butler, behind his shoulder:

“Philadelphia wants you on the phone, sir.”

“All right, in a minute. Tell them I’ll be right there.... Good night.”

“Good night.”

“Good night.” He smiled—and suddenly there seemed to be a pleasant significance in having been among the last to go, as if he had desired it all the time. “Good night, old sport.... Good night.”

But as I walked down the steps I saw that the evening was not quite over. Fifty feet from the door a dozen headlights illuminated a bizarre and tumultuous scene. In the ditch beside the road, right side up, but violently shorn of one wheel, rested a new coupé which had left Gatsby’s drive not two minutes before. The sharp jut of a wall accounted for the detachment of the wheel, which was now getting considerable attention from half a dozen curious chauffeurs. However, as they had left their cars blocking the road, a harsh, discordant din from those in the rear had been audible for some time, and added to the already violent confusion of the scene.

A man in a long duster had dismounted from the wreck and now stood in the middle of the road, looking from the car to the tire and from the tire to the observers in a pleasant, puzzled way.

“See!” he explained. “It went in the ditch.”

The fact was infinitely astonishing to him, and I recognized first the unusual quality of wonder, and then the man—it was the late patron of Gatsby’s library.

“How’d it happen?”

He shrugged his shoulders.

"I know nothing whatever about mechanics," he said decisively.

"But how did it happen? Did you run into the wall?"

"Don't ask me," said Owl Eyes, washing his hands of the whole matter. "I know very little about driving—next to nothing. It happened, and that's all I know."

"Well, if you're a poor driver you oughtn't to try driving at night."

"But I wasn't even trying," he explained indignantly. "I wasn't even trying!"

An awed hush fell upon the bystanders.

"Do you want to commit suicide?"

"You're lucky it was just a wheel! A bad driver and not even *try*ing!"

"You don't understand," explained the criminal. "I wasn't driving. There's another man in the car."

The shock that followed this declaration found voice in a sustained "Ah-h-h!" as the door of the coupé swung slowly open. The crowd—it was now a crowd—stepped back involuntarily, and when the door had opened wide there was a ghostly pause. Then, very gradually, part by part, a pale, dangling individual stepped out of the wreck, pawing tentatively at the ground with a large uncertain dancing shoe.

Blinded by the glare of the headlights and confused by the incessant groaning of the horns, the apparition stood swaying for a moment before he perceived the man in the duster.

"Wha's matter?" he inquired calmly. "Did we run outa gas?"

"Look!"

Half a dozen fingers pointed at the amputated wheel—he stared at it for a moment, and then looked upward as though he suspected that it had dropped from the sky.

"It came off," someone explained.

He nodded.

"At first I din' notice we'd stopped."

A pause. Then, taking a long breath and straightening his shoulders, he remarked in a determined voice:

"Wonder'ff tell me where there's a gas'line station?"

At least a dozen men, some of them little better off than he was, explained to him that wheel and car were no longer joined by any physical bond.

"Back out," he suggested after a moment. "Put her in reverse."

"But the *wheel's* off!"

He hesitated.

"No harm in trying," he said.

The caterwauling horns had reached a crescendo and I turned away and cut across the lawn toward home. I glanced back once. A wafer of a moon was shining over Gatsby's house, making the night fine as before, and surviving the laughter and the sound of his still glowing garden. A sudden emptiness seemed to flow now from the windows and the great doors, endowing with complete isolation the figure of the host, who stood on the porch, his hand up in a formal gesture of farewell.

Reading over what I have written so far, I see I have given the impression that the events of three nights several weeks apart were all that absorbed me. On the contrary, they were merely casual events in a crowded summer, and, until much later, they absorbed me infinitely less than my personal affairs.

Most of the time I worked. In the early morning the sun threw my shadow westward as I hurried down the white chasms of lower New York to the Probity Trust. I knew the other clerks and young bond-salesmen by their first names, and lunched with them in dark, crowded restaurants on little pig sausages and mashed potatoes and coffee. I even had a short affair with a girl who lived in Jersey City and worked in the accounting department, but her brother began throwing mean looks in my direction, so when she went on her vacation in July I let it blow quietly away.

I took dinner usually at the Yale Club—for some reason it was the gloomiest event of my day—and then I went upstairs to the library and studied investments and securities for a conscientious hour. There were generally a few rioters around, but they never came into the library, so it was a good place to work. After that, if the night was mellow, I strolled down Madison Avenue past the old Murray Hill Hotel, and over Thirty-third Street to the Pennsylvania Station.

I began to like New York, the racy, adventurous feel of it at night, and the satisfaction that the constant flicker of men and women and machines gives to the restless eye. I liked to walk up Fifth Avenue and pick out romantic women from the crowd and imagine that in a few minutes I was going to enter into their lives, and no one would ever know or disapprove. Sometimes, in my mind, I followed them to their apartments on the corners of hidden streets, and they turned and smiled back at me before they faded through a door into warm darkness. At the enchanted metropolitan twilight I felt a haunting loneliness sometimes, and felt it in others—poor young clerks who loitered in front of windows waiting until it was time for a solitary restaurant dinner—young clerks in the dusk, wasting the most poignant moments of night and life.

Again at eight o'clock, when the dark lanes of the Forties were five deep with throbbing taxi cabs, bound for the theatre district, I felt a sinking in my heart. Forms leaned together in the taxis as they waited, and voices sang, and there was laughter from unheard jokes, and lighted cigarettes outlined unintelligible gestures inside. Imagining that I, too, was hurrying toward gayety and sharing their intimate excitement, I wished them well.

For a while I lost sight of Jordan Baker, and then in midsummer I found her again. At first I was flattered to go places with her, because she was a golf champion, and everyone knew her name. Then it was something more. I wasn't actually in love, but I felt a sort of tender curiosity. The bored haughty face that she turned to the world concealed something—most affectations conceal something eventually, even though they don't in the beginning—and one day I found what it was. When we were on a house-party together up in Warwick, she left a borrowed car out in the rain with the top down, and then lied about it—and suddenly I remembered the story about her that had eluded me that night at Daisy's. At her first big golf tournament there was a row that nearly reached the newspapers—a suggestion that she had moved her ball from a bad lie in the semi-final round. The thing approached the proportions of a scandal—then died away. A caddy retracted his statement, and the only other witness admitted that he might have been mistaken. The incident and the name had remained together in my mind.

Jordan Baker instinctively avoided clever, shrewd men, and now I saw that this was because she felt safer on a plane where any divergence from a code would be thought impossible. She was incurably dishonest. She wasn't able to endure being at a disadvantage and, given this unwillingness, I suppose she had begun dealing in subterfuges when she was very young in order to keep that cool, insolent smile turned to the world and yet satisfy the demands of her hard, jaunty body.

It made no difference to me. Dishonesty in a woman is a thing you never blame deeply—I was casually sorry, and then I forgot. It was on that same house-party that we had a curious conversation about driving a car. It started because she passed so close to some workmen that our fender flicked a button on one man's coat.

"You're a rotten driver," I protested. "Either you ought to be more careful, or you oughtn't to drive at all."

"I am careful."

"No, you're not."

"Well, other people are," she said lightly.

"What's that got to do with it?"

"They'll keep out of my way," she insisted. "It takes two to make an accident."

"Suppose you met somebody just as careless as yourself."

"I hope I never will," she answered. "I hate careless people. That's why I like you."

Her gray, sun-strained eyes stared straight ahead, but she had deliberately shifted our relations, and for a moment I thought I loved her. But I am slow-thinking and full of interior rules that act as brakes on my desires, and I knew that first I had to get myself definitely out of that tangle back home. I'd been writing letters once a week and signing them: "Love, Nick," and all I could think of was how, when that certain girl played tennis, a faint mustache of perspiration appeared on her upper lip. Nevertheless there was a vague understanding that had to be tactfully broken off before I was free.

Everyone suspects himself of at least one of the cardinal virtues, and this is mine: I am one of the few honest people that I have ever known.

CHAPTER IV

On Sunday morning while church bells rang in the villages alongshore, the world and its mistress returned to Gatsby's house and twinkled hilariously on his lawn.

"He's a bootlegger," said the young ladies, moving somewhere between his cocktails and his flowers. "One time he killed a man who had found out that he was nephew to Von Hindenburg and second cousin to the devil. Reach me a rose, honey, and pour me a last drop into that there crystal glass."

Once I wrote down on the empty spaces of a time-table the names of those who came to Gatsby's house that summer. It is an old time-table now, disintegrating at its folds, and headed "This schedule in effect July 5th, 1922." But I can still read the gray names, and they will give you a better impression than my generalities of those who accepted Gatsby's hospitality and paid him the subtle tribute of knowing nothing whatever about him.

From East Egg, then, came the Chester Beckers and the Leeches, and a man named Bunsen, whom I knew at Yale, and Doctor Webster Civet, who was drowned last summer up in Maine. And the Hornbeams and the Willie Voltaires, and a whole clan named Blackbuck, who always gathered in a corner and flipped up their noses like goats at whosoever came near. And the Ismays and the Chrysties (or rather Hubert Auerbach and Mr. Chrystie's wife), and Edgar Beaver, whose hair, they say, turned cotton-white one winter afternoon for no good reason at all.

Clarence Endive was from East Egg, as I remember. He came only once, in white knickerbockers, and had a fight with a bum named Etty in the garden. From farther out on the Island came the Cheadles and the O. R. P. Schraeders, and the Stonewall Jackson Abrams of Georgia, and the Fishguards and the Ripley Snells. Snell was there three days before he went to the penitentiary, so drunk out on the gravel drive that Mrs. Ulysses Swett's automobile ran over his right hand. The Dancies came, too, and S. B. Whitebait, who was well over sixty, and Maurice A. Flink, and the Hammerheads, and Beluga the tobacco importer, and Beluga's girls.

From West Egg came the Poles and the Mulreadys and Cecil Roebuck and Cecil Schoen and Gulick the state senator and Newton Orchid, who controlled Films Par Excellence, and Eckhaust and Clyde Cohen and Don S. Schwartze (the son) and Arthur McCarty, all connected with the movies in one way or another. And the Catlips and the Bembergs and G. Earl Muldoon, brother to that Muldoon who afterward strangled his wife. Da Fontano the promoter came there, and Ed Legros and James B. ("Rot-Gut") Ferret and the De Jongs and Ernest Lilly—they came to gamble, and when Ferret wandered into the garden it meant he was cleaned out and Associated Traction would have to fluctuate profitably next day.

A man named Klipspringer was there so often and so long that he became known as "the boarder"—I doubt if he had any other home. Of theatrical people there were Gus Waize and Horace O'Donavan and Lester Myer and George Duckweed and Francis Bull. Also from New York were the Chromes and the Backhyssons and the Dennickers and Russel Betty and the Corrigans and the Kellehers and the Dewars and the Scullys and S. W. Belcher and the Smirkes and the young Quinns, divorced now, and Henry L. Palmetto, who killed himself by jumping in front of a subway train in Times Square.

Benny McClenahan arrived always with four girls. They were never quite the same ones in physical person, but they were so identical one with another that it inevitably seemed they had been there before. I have forgotten their names—Jaqueline, I think, or else Consuela, or Gloria or Judy or June, and their last names were either the melodious names of flowers and months or the sterner ones of the great American capitalists whose cousins, if pressed, they would confess themselves to be.

In addition to all these I can remember that Faustina O'Brien came there at least once and the Baedeker girls and young Brewer, who had his nose shot off in the war, and Mr. Albrucksburger and Miss Haag, his fiancée, and Ardita Fitz-Peters and Mr. P. Jewett, once head of the American Legion, and Miss Claudia Hip, with a man reputed to be her chauffeur, and a prince of something, whom we called Duke, and whose name, if I ever knew it, I have forgotten.

All these people came to Gatsby's house in the summer.

At nine o'clock, one morning late in July, Gatsby's gorgeous car lurched up the rocky drive to my door and gave out a burst of melody from its three-noted horn. It was the first time he had called on me, though I had gone to two of his parties, mounted in his hydroplane, and, at his urgent invitation, made frequent use of his beach.

"Good morning, old sport. You're having lunch with me today and I thought we'd ride up together."

He was balancing himself on the dashboard of his car with that resourcefulness of movement that is so peculiarly American—that comes, I suppose, with the absence of lifting work or rigid sitting in youth and, even more, with the formless grace of our nervous, sporadic games. This quality was continually breaking through his punctilious manner in the shape of restlessness. He was never quite still; there was always a tapping foot somewhere or the impatient opening and closing of a hand.

He saw me looking with admiration at his car.

"It's pretty, isn't it, old sport?" He jumped off to give me a better view. "Haven't you ever seen it before?"

I'd seen it. Everybody had seen it. It was a rich cream color, bright with nickel, swollen here and there in its monstrous length with triumphant hat-boxes and supper-boxes and tool-boxes, and terraced with a labyrinth of wind-shields that mirrored a dozen suns. Sitting down behind many layers of glass in a sort of green leather conservatory, we started to town.

I had talked with him perhaps half a dozen times in the past month and found, to my disappointment, that he had little to say. So my first impression, that he was a person of some undefined consequence, had gradually faded and he had become simply the proprietor of an elaborate roadhouse next door.

And then came that disconcerting ride. We hadn't reached West Egg Village before Gatsby began leaving his elegant sentences unfinished and slapping himself indecisively on the knee of his caramel-colored suit.

"Look here, old sport," he broke out surprisingly. "What's your opinion of me, anyhow?"

A little overwhelmed, I began the generalized evasions which that question deserves.

"Well, I'm going to tell you something about my life," he interrupted. "I don't want you to get a wrong idea of me from all these stories you hear."

So he was aware of the bizarre accusations that flavored conversation in his halls.

"I'll tell you God's truth." His right hand suddenly ordered divine retribution to stand by. "I am the son of some wealthy people in the Middle West—all dead now. I was brought up in America but educated at Oxford, because all my ancestors have been educated there for many years. It is a family tradition."

He looked at me sideways—and I knew why Jordan Baker had believed he was lying. He hurried the phrase "educated at Oxford," or swallowed it, or choked on it, as though it had bothered him before. And with this doubt, his whole statement fell to pieces, and I wondered if there wasn't something a little sinister about him, after all.

"What part of the Middle West?" I inquired casually.

"San Francisco."

"I see."

"My family all died and I came into a good deal of money."

His voice was solemn, as if the memory of that sudden extinction of a clan still haunted him. For a moment I suspected that he was pulling my leg, but a glance at him convinced me otherwise.

"After that I lived like a young rajah in all the capitals of Europe—Paris, Venice, Rome—collecting jewels, chiefly rubies, hunting big game, painting a little, things for myself only, and trying to forget something very sad that had happened to me long ago."

With an effort I managed to restrain my incredulous laughter. The very phrases were worn so threadbare that they evoked no image except that of a turbaned "character" leaking sawdust at every pore as he pursued a tiger through the Bois de Boulogne.

"Then came the war, old sport. It was a great relief, and I tried very hard to die, but I seemed to bear an enchanted life. I accepted a commission as first lieutenant when it began. In the Argonne Forest I took two machine-gun detachments so far forward that there was a half mile gap on either side of us where the infantry couldn't advance. We stayed there two days and two nights, a hundred and thirty men with sixteen Lewis guns, and when the infantry came up at last they found the insignia of three German divisions among the piles of dead. I was promoted to be a major, and every Allied government gave me a decoration—even Montenegro, little Montenegro down on the Adriatic Sea!"

Little Montenegro! He lifted up the words and nodded at them—with his smile. The smile comprehended Montenegro's troubled history and sympathized with the brave struggles of the Montenegrin people. It appreciated fully the chain of national circumstances which had elicited this tribute from Montenegro's warm little heart. My incredulity was submerged in fascination now; it was like skimming hastily through a dozen magazines.

He reached in his pocket, and a piece of metal, slung on a ribbon, fell into my palm.

"That's the one from Montenegro."

To my astonishment, the thing had an authentic look. "Orderi di Danilo," ran the circular legend, "Montenegro, Nicolas Rex."

"Turn it."

"Major Jay Gatsby," I read. "For Valour Extraordinary."

"Here's another thing I always carry. A souvenir of Oxford days. It was taken in Trinity Quad—the man on my left is now the Earl of Doncaster."

It was a photograph of half a dozen young men in blazers loafing in an archway through which were visible a host of spires. There was Gatsby, looking a little, not much, younger—with a cricket bat in his hand.

Then it was all true. I saw the skins of tigers flaming in his palace on the Grand Canal; I saw him opening a chest of rubies to ease, with their crimson-lighted depths, the gnawings of his broken heart.

"I'm going to make a big request of you today," he said, pocketing his souvenirs with satisfaction, "so I thought you ought to know something about me. I didn't want you to think I was just some nobody. You see, I usually find myself among strangers because I drift here and there trying to forget the sad thing that happened to me." He hesitated. "You'll hear about it this afternoon."

"At lunch?"

"No, this afternoon. I happened to find out that you're taking Miss Baker to tea."

"Do you mean you're in love with Miss Baker?"

"No, old sport, I'm not. But Miss Baker has kindly consented to speak to you about this matter."

I hadn't the faintest idea what "this matter" was, but I was more annoyed than interested. I hadn't asked Jordan to tea in order to discuss Mr. Jay Gatsby. I was sure the request would be something utterly fantastic, and for a moment I was sorry I'd ever set foot upon his overpopulated lawn.

He wouldn't say another word. His correctness grew on him as we neared the city. We passed Port Roosevelt, where there was a glimpse of red-belted ocean-going ships, and sped along a cobbled slum lined with the dark, undeserted saloons of the faded-gilt nineteen-hundreds. Then the valley of ashes opened out on both sides of us, and I had a glimpse of Mrs. Wilson straining at the garage pump with panting vitality as we went by.

With fenders spread like wings we scattered light through half Astoria—only half, for as we twisted among the pillars of the elevated I heard the familiar "jug-jug-*spat!*" of a motorcycle, and a frantic policeman rode alongside.

"All right, old sport," called Gatsby. We slowed down. Taking a white card from his wallet, he waved it before the man's eyes.

"Right you are," agreed the policeman, tipping his cap. "Know you next time, Mr. Gatsby. Excuse *me!*"

"What was that?" I inquired. "The picture of Oxford?"

"I was able to do the commissioner a favor once, and he sends me a Christmas card every year."

Over the great bridge, with the sunlight through the girders making a constant flicker upon the moving cars, with the city rising up across the river in white heaps and sugar lumps all built with a wish out of non-olfactory money. The city seen from the Queensboro Bridge is always the city seen for the first time, in its first wild promise of all the mystery and the beauty in the world.

A dead man passed us in a hearse heaped with blooms, followed by two carriages with drawn blinds, and by more cheerful carriages for friends. The friends looked out at us with the tragic eyes and short upper lips of southeastern Europe, and I was glad that the sight of Gatsby's splendid car was included in their somber holiday. As we crossed Blackwell's Island a limousine passed us, driven by a white chauffeur, in which sat three modish negroes, two bucks and a girl. I laughed aloud as the yolks of their eyeballs rolled toward us in haughty rivalry.

"Anything can happen now that we've slid over this bridge," I thought; "anything at all...."

Even Gatsby could happen, without any particular wonder.

Roaring noon. In a well-fanned Forty-second Street cellar I met Gatsby for lunch. Blinking away the brightness of the street outside, my eyes picked him out obscurely in the anteroom, talking to another man.

"Mr. Carraway, this is my friend Mr. Wolfshiem."

A small, flat-nosed Jew raised his large head and regarded me with two fine growths of hair which luxuriated in either nostril. After a moment I discovered his tiny eyes in the half darkness.

"—So I took one look at him," said Mr. Wolfshiem, shaking my hand earnestly, "and what do you think I did?"

"What?" I inquired politely.

But evidently he was not addressing me, for he dropped my hand and covered Gatsby with his expressive nose.

"I handed the money to Katspaugh and I sid: 'All right, Katspaugh, don't pay him a penny till he shuts his mouth.' He shut it then and there."

Gatsby took an arm of each of us and moved forward into the restaurant, whereupon Mr. Wolfshiem swallowed a new sentence he was starting and lapsed into a somnambulatory abstraction.

"Highballs?" asked the head waiter.

"This is a nice restaurant here," said Mr. Wolfshiem, looking at the Presbyterian nymphs on the ceiling. "But I like across the street better!"

"Yes, highballs," agreed Gatsby, and then to Mr. Wolfshiem: "It's too hot over there."

"Hot and small—yes," said Mr. Wolfshiem, "but full of memories."

"What place is that?" I asked Gatsby.

"The old Metropole."

"The old Metropole," brooded Mr. Wolfshiem gloomily. "Filled with faces dead and gone. Filled with friends gone now forever. I can't forget so long as I live the night they shot Rosy Rosenthal there. It was six of us at the table, and Rosy had eat and drunk a lot all evening. When it was almost morning the waiter came up to him with a funny look and says somebody wants to speak to him outside. 'All right,' says Rosy, and begins to get up, and I pulled him down in his chair.

"'Let the bastards come in here if they want you, Rosy, but don't you, so help me, move outside this room.'

"It was four o'clock in the morning then, and if we'd of raised the blinds we'd of seen daylight."

"Did he go?" I asked innocently.

"Sure he went." Mr. Wolfshiem's nose flashed at me indignantly. "He turned around in the door and says: 'Don't let that waiter take away my coffee!' Then he went out on the sidewalk, and they shot him three times in his full belly and drove away."

"Four of them were electrocuted," I said, remembering.

"Five, with Becker." His nostrils turned to me in an interested way. "I understand you're looking for a business gonnegtion."

The juxtaposition of these two remarks was startling. Gatsby answered for me:

"Oh, no," he exclaimed, "this isn't the man."

"No?" Mr. Wolfshiem seemed disappointed.

"This is just a friend. I told you we'd talk about that some other time."

"I beg your pardon," said Mr. Wolfshiem. "I had a wrong man."

A succulent hash arrived, and Mr. Wolfshiem, forgetting the more sentimental atmosphere of the old Metropole, began to eat with ferocious delicacy. His eyes, meanwhile, roved very slowly all around the room—he completed the arc by turning to inspect the people directly behind. I think that, except for my presence, he would have taken one short glance beneath our own table.

"Look here, old sport," said Gatsby, leaning toward me, "I'm afraid I made you a little angry this morning in the car."

There was the smile again, but this time I held out against it.

"I don't like mysteries," I answered, "and I don't understand why you won't come out frankly and tell me what you want. Why has it all got to come through Miss Baker?"

"Oh, it's nothing underhand," he assured me. "Miss Baker's a great sportswoman, you know, and she'd never do anything that wasn't all right."

Suddenly he looked at his watch, jumped up, and hurried from the room, leaving me with Mr. Wolfshiem at the table.

"He has to telephone," said Mr. Wolfshiem, following him with his eyes. "Fine fellow, isn't he? Handsome to look at and a perfect gentleman."

"Yes."

"He's an Oggsford man."

"Oh!"

"He went to Oggsford College in England. You know Oggsford College?"

"I've heard of it."

"It's one of the most famous colleges in the world."

"Have you known Gatsby for a long time?" I inquired.

"Several years," he answered in a gratified way. "I made the pleasure of his acquaintance just after the war. But I knew I had discovered a man of fine breeding after I talked with him an hour. I said to myself: 'There's the kind of man you'd like to take home and introduce to your mother and sister.'" He paused. "I see you're looking at my cuff buttons."

I hadn't been looking at them, but I did now. They were composed of oddly familiar pieces of ivory.

"Finest specimens of human molars," he informed me.

"Well!" I inspected them. "That's a very interesting idea."

"Yeah." He flipped his sleeves up under his coat. "Yeah, Gatsby's very careful about women. He would never so much as look at a friend's wife."

When the subject of this instinctive trust returned to the table and sat down Mr. Wolfshiem drank his coffee with a jerk and got to his feet.

"I have enjoyed my lunch," he said, "and I'm going to run off from you two young men before I outstay my welcome."

"Don't hurry, Meyer," said Gatsby, without enthusiasm. Mr. Wolfshiem raised his hand in a sort of benediction.

"You're very polite, but I belong to another generation," he announced solemnly. "You sit here and discuss your sports and your young ladies and your—" He supplied an imaginary noun with another wave of his hand. "As for me, I am fifty years old, and I won't impose myself on you any longer."

As he shook hands and turned away his tragic nose was trembling. I wondered if I had said anything to offend him.

"He becomes very sentimental sometimes," explained Gatsby. "This is one of his sentimental days. He's quite a character around New York—a denizen of Broadway."

"Who is he, anyhow, an actor?"

"No."

"A dentist?"

"Meyer Wolfshiem? No, he's a gambler." Gatsby hesitated, then added coolly: "He's the man who fixed the World's Series back in 1919."

"Fixed the World's Series?" I repeated.

The idea staggered me. I remembered, of course, that the World's Series had been fixed in 1919, but if I had thought of it at all I would have thought of it as a thing that merely *happened,* the end of some inevitable chain. It never occurred to me that one man could start to play with the faith of fifty million people—with the single-mindedness of a burglar blowing a safe.

"How did he happen to do that?" I asked after a minute.

"He just saw the opportunity."

"Why isn't he in jail?"

"They can't get him, old sport. He's a smart man."

I insisted on paying the check. As the waiter brought my change I caught sight of Tom Buchanan across the crowded room.

"Come along with me for a minute," I said; "I've got to say hello to someone."

When he saw us Tom jumped up and took half a dozen steps in our direction.

"Where've you been?" he demanded eagerly. "Daisy's furious because you haven't called up."

"This is Mr. Gatsby, Mr. Buchanan."

They shook hands briefly, and a strained, unfamiliar look of embarrassment came over Gatsby's face.

"How've you been, anyhow?" demanded Tom of me. "How'd you happen to come up this far to eat?"

"I've been having lunch with Mr. Gatsby."

I turned toward Mr. Gatsby, but he was no longer there.

One October day in nineteen-seventeen——

(said Jordan Baker that afternoon, sitting up very straight on a straight chair in the tea-garden at the Plaza Hotel)

—I was walking along from one place to another, half on the sidewalks and half on the lawns. I was happier on the lawns because I had on shoes from England with rubber nobs on the soles that bit into the soft ground. I had on a new plaid skirt also that blew a little in the wind, and whenever this happened the red, white, and blue banners in front of all the houses stretched out stiff and said *tut-tut-tut-tut,* in a disapproving way.

The largest of the banners and the largest of the lawns belonged to Daisy Fay's house. She was just eighteen, two years older than me, and by far the most popular of all the young girls in Louisville. She dressed in white, and had a little white roadster, and all day long the telephone rang in her house and excited young officers from Camp Taylor demanded the privilege of monopolizing her that night. "Anyways, for an hour!"

When I came opposite her house that morning her white roadster was beside the curb, and she was sitting in it with a lieutenant I had never seen before. They were so engrossed in each other that she didn't see me until I was five feet away.

"Hello, Jordan," she called unexpectedly. "Please come here."

I was flattered that she wanted to speak to me, because of all the older girls I admired her most. She asked me if I was going to the Red Cross and make bandages. I was. Well, then, would I tell them that she couldn't come that day? The officer looked at Daisy while she was speaking, in a way that every young girl wants to be looked at sometime, and because it seemed romantic to me I have remembered the incident ever since. His name was Jay Gatsby, and I didn't lay eyes on him again for over four years—even after I'd met him on Long Island I didn't realize it was the same man.

That was nineteen-seventeen. By the next year I had a few beaux myself, and I began to play in tournaments, so I didn't see Daisy very often. She went with a slightly older crowd—when she went with anyone at all. Wild rumors were circulating about her—how her mother had found her packing her bag one winter night to go to New York and say good-by to a soldier who was going overseas. She was effectually prevented, but she wasn't on speaking terms with her family for several weeks. After that she didn't play around with the soldiers any more, but only with a few flat-footed, short-sighted young men in town, who couldn't get into the army at all.

By the next autumn she was gay again, gay as ever. She had a début after the armistice, and in February she was presumably engaged to a man from New Orleans. In June she married Tom Buchanan of Chicago, with more pomp and circumstance than Louisville ever knew before. He came down with a hundred people in four private cars, and hired a whole floor of the Seelbach Hotel, and the day before the wedding he gave her a string of pearls valued at three hundred and fifty thousand dollars.

I was a bridesmaid. I came into her room half an hour before the bridal dinner, and found her lying on her bed as lovely as the June night in her flowered dress—and as drunk as a monkey. She had a bottle of Sauterne in one hand and a letter in the other.

" 'Gratulate me," she muttered. "Never had a drink before, but oh how I do enjoy it."

"What's the matter, Daisy?"

I was scared, I can tell you; I'd never seen a girl like that before.

"Here, deares'." She groped around in a wastebasket she had with her on the bed and pulled out the string of pearls. "Take 'em downstairs and give 'em back to whoever they belong to. Tell 'em all Daisy's change' her mine. Say: 'Daisy's change' her mine!' "

She began to cry—she cried and cried. I rushed out and found her mother's maid, and we locked the door and got her into a cold bath. She wouldn't let go of the letter. She took it into the tub with her and squeezed it up into a wet ball, and only let me leave it in the soap dish when she saw that it was coming to pieces like snow.

But she didn't say another word. We gave her spirits of ammonia and put ice on her forehead and hooked her back into her dress, and half an hour later, when we walked out of the room, the pearls were around her neck and the incident was over. Next day at five o'clock she married Tom Buchanan without so much as a shiver, and started off on a three months' trip to the South Seas.

I saw them in Santa Barbara when they came back, and I thought I'd never seen a girl so mad about her husband. If he left the room for a minute she'd look around uneasily, and say: "Where's Tom gone?" and wear the most abstracted expression until she saw him coming in the door. She used to sit on the sand with his head in her lap by the hour, rubbing her fingers over his eyes and looking at him with unfathomable delight. It was touching to see them together—it made you laugh in a hushed, fascinated way. That was in August. A week after I left Santa Barbara Tom ran into a wagon on the Ventura road one night, and ripped a front wheel off his car. The girl who was with him got into the papers, too, because her arm was broken—she was one of the chambermaids in the Santa Barbara Hotel.

The next April Daisy had her little girl, and they went to France for a year. I saw them one spring in Cannes, and later in Deauville, and then they came back to Chicago to settle down. Daisy was popular in Chicago, as you know. They moved with a fast crowd, all of them young and rich and wild, but she came out with an absolutely perfect reputation. Perhaps because she doesn't drink. It's a great advantage not to drink among hard-drinking people. You can hold your tongue, and, moreover, you can time any little irregularity of your own so that everybody else is so blind that they don't see or care. Perhaps Daisy never went in for amour at all—and yet there's something in that voice of hers....

Well, about six weeks ago, she heard the name Gatsby for the first time in years. It was when I asked you—do you remember?—if you knew Gatsby in West Egg. After you had gone home she came into my room and woke me up, and said: "What Gatsby?" and when I described him—I was half asleep—she said in the strangest voice that it must be the man she used to know. It wasn't until then that I connected this Gatsby with the officer in her white car.

When Jordan Baker had finished telling all this we had left the Plaza for half an hour and were driving in a Victoria through Central Park. The sun had gone down behind the tall apartments of the movie stars in the West Fifties, and the clear voices of children, already gathered like crickets on the grass, rose through the hot twilight:

"I'm the Sheik of Araby.
Your love belongs to me.
At night when you're asleep
Into your tent I'll creep——"

"It was a strange coincidence," I said.

"But it wasn't a coincidence at all."

"Why not?"

"Gatsby bought that house so that Daisy would be just across the bay."

Then it had not been merely the stars to which he had aspired on that June night. He came alive to me, delivered suddenly from the womb of his purposeless splendor.

"He wants to know," continued Jordan, "if you'll invite Daisy to your house some afternoon and then let him come over."

The modesty of the demand shook me. He had waited five years and bought a mansion where he dispensed starlight to casual moths—so that he could "come over" some afternoon to a stranger's garden.

"Did I have to know all this before he could ask such a little thing?"

"He's afraid. He's waited so long. He thought you might be offended. You see, he's a regular tough underneath it all."

Something worried me.

"Why didn't he ask you to arrange a meeting?"

"He wants her to see his house," she explained. "And your house is right next door."

"Oh!"

"I think he half expected her to wander into one of his parties, some night," went on Jordan, "but she never did. Then he began asking people casually if they knew her, and I was the first one he found. It was that night he sent for me at his dance, and you should have heard the elaborate way he worked up to it. Of course, I immediately suggested a luncheon in New York—and I thought he'd go mad:

"'I don't want to do anything out of the way!' he kept saying. 'I want to see her right next door.'

"When I said you were a particular friend of Tom's, he started to abandon the whole idea. He doesn't know very much about Tom, though he says he's read a Chicago paper for years just on the chance of catching a glimpse of Daisy's name."

It was dark now, and as we dipped under a little bridge I put my arm around Jordan's golden shoulder and drew her toward me and asked her to dinner. Suddenly I wasn't thinking of Daisy and Gatsby any more, but of this clean, hard, limited person, who dealt in universal skepticism, and who leaned back jauntily just within the circle of my arm. A phrase began to beat in my ears with a sort of heady excitement: "There are only the pursued, the pursuing, the busy and the tired."

"And Daisy ought to have something in her life," murmured Jordan to me.

"Does she want to see Gatsby?"

"She's not to know about it. Gatsby doesn't want her to know. You're just supposed to invite her to tea."

We passed a barrier of dark trees, and then the façade of Fifty-ninth Street, a block of delicate pale light, beamed down into the Park. Unlike Gatsby and Tom Buchanan, I had no girl whose disembodied face floated along the dark cornices and blinding signs, and so I drew up the girl beside me, tightening my arms. Her wan, scornful mouth smiled, and so I drew her up again closer, this time to my face.

CHAPTER V

WHEN I came home to West Egg that night I was afraid for a moment that my house was on fire. Two o'clock and the whole corner of the peninsula was blazing with light, which fell unreal on the shrubbery and made thin elongating glints upon the roadside wires. Turning a corner, I saw that it was Gatsby's house, lit from tower to cellar.

At first I thought it was another party, a wild rout that had resolved itself into "hide-and-go-seek" or "sardines-in-the-box" with all the house thrown open to the game. But there wasn't a sound. Only wind in the trees, which blew the wires and made the lights go off and on again as if the house had winked into the darkness. As my taxi groaned away I saw Gatsby walking toward me across his lawn.

"Your place looks like the World's Fair," I said.

"Does it?" He turned his eyes toward it absently. "I have been glancing into some of the rooms. Let's go to Coney Island, old sport. In my car."

"It's too late."

"Well, suppose we take a plunge in the swimming pool? I haven't made use of it all summer."

"I've got to go to bed."

"All right."

He waited, looking at me with suppressed eagerness.

"I talked with Miss Baker," I said after a moment. "I'm going to call up Daisy tomorrow and invite her over here to tea."

"Oh, that's all right," he said carelessly. "I don't want to put you to any trouble."

"What day would suit you?"

"What day would suit *you?*" he corrected me quickly. "I don't want to put you to any trouble, you see."

"How about the day after tomorrow?"

He considered for a moment. Then, with reluctance:

"I want to get the grass cut," he said.

We both looked at the grass—there was a sharp line where my ragged lawn ended and the darker, well-kept expanse of his began. I suspected that he meant my grass.

"There's another little thing," he said uncertainly, and hesitated.

"Would you rather put it off for a few days?" I asked.

"Oh, it isn't about that. At least—" He fumbled with a series of beginnings. "Why, I thought—why, look here, old sport, you don't make much money, do you?"

"Not very much."

This seemed to reassure him and he continued more confidently.

"I thought you didn't, if you'll pardon my—you see, I carry on a little business on the side, a sort of sideline, you understand. And I thought that if you don't make very much— You're selling bonds, aren't you, old sport?"

"Trying to."

"Well, this would interest you. It wouldn't take up much of your time and you might pick up a nice bit of money. It happens to be a rather confidential sort of thing."

I realize now that under different circumstances that conversation might have been one of the crises of my life. But, because the offer was obviously and tactlessly for a service to be rendered, I had no choice except to cut him off there.

"I've got my hands full," I said. "I'm much obliged but I couldn't take on any more work."

"You wouldn't have to do any business with Wolfshiem." Evidently he thought that I was shying away from the "gonnegtion" mentioned at lunch, but I assured him he was wrong. He waited a moment longer, hoping I'd begin a conversation, but I was too absorbed to be responsive, so he went unwillingly home.

The evening had made me light-headed and happy; I think I walked into a deep sleep as I entered my front door. So I don't know whether or not Gatsby went to Coney Island, or for how many hours he "glanced into rooms" while his house blazed gaudily on. I called up Daisy from the office next morning, and invited her to come to tea.

"Don't bring Tom," I warned her.

"What?"

"Don't bring Tom."

"Who is 'Tom'?" she asked innocently.

The day agreed upon was pouring rain. At eleven o'clock a man in a raincoat, dragging a lawn-mower, tapped at my front door and said that Mr. Gatsby had sent him over to cut my grass. This reminded me that I had forgotten to tell my Finn to come back, so I drove into West Egg Village to search for her among soggy whitewashed alleys and to buy some cups and lemons and flowers.

The flowers were unnecessary, for at two o'clock a greenhouse arrived from Gatsby's, with innumerable receptacles to contain it. An hour later the front door opened nervously, and Gatsby, in a white flannel suit, silver shirt, and gold-colored tie, hurried in. He was pale, and there were dark signs of sleeplessness beneath his eyes.

"Is everything all right?" he asked immediately.

"The grass looks fine, if that's what you mean."

"What grass?" he inquired blankly. "Oh, the grass in the yard." He looked out the window at it, but, judging from his expression, I don't believe he saw a thing.

"Looks very good," he remarked vaguely. "One of the papers said they thought the rain would stop about four. I think it was The Journal. Have you got everything you need in the shape of—of tea?"

I took him into the pantry, where he looked a little reproachfully at the Finn. Together we scrutinized the twelve lemon cakes from the delicatessen shop.

"Will they do?" I asked.

"Of course, of course! They're fine!" and he added hollowly, ". . . old sport."

The rain cooled about half-past three to a damp mist, through which occasional thin drops swam like dew. Gatsby looked with vacant eyes through a copy of Clay's "Economics," starting at the Finnish tread that shook the kitchen floor, and peering toward the bleared windows from time to time as if a series of invisible but alarming happenings were taking place outside. Finally he got up and informed me, in an uncertain voice, that he was going home.

"Why's that?"

"Nobody's coming to tea. It's too late!" He looked at his watch as if there was some pressing demand on his time elsewhere. "I can't wait all day."

"Don't be silly; it's just two minutes to four."

He sat down miserably, as if I had pushed him, and simultaneously there was the sound of a motor turning into my lane. We both jumped up, and, a little harrowed myself, I went out into the yard.

Under the dripping bare lilac trees a large open car was coming up the drive. It stopped. Daisy's face, tipped sideways beneath a three-cornered lavender hat, looked out at me with a bright ecstatic smile.

"Is this absolutely where you live, my dearest one?"

The exhilarating ripple of her voice was a wild tonic in the rain. I had to follow the sound of it for a moment, up and down, with my ear alone, before any words came through. A damp streak of hair lay like a dash of blue paint across her cheek, and her hand was wet with glistening drops as I took it to help her from the car.

"Are you in love with me," she said low in my ear, "or why did I have to come alone?"

"That's the secret of Castle Rackrent. Tell your chauffeur to go far away and spend an hour."

"Come back in an hour, Ferdie." Then in a grave murmur: "His name is Ferdie."

"Does the gasoline affect his nose?"

"I don't think so," she said innocently. "Why?"

We went in. To my overwhelming surprise the living-room was deserted.

"Well, that's funny!" I exclaimed.

"What's funny?"

She turned her head as there was a light dignified knocking at the front door. I went out and opened it. Gatsby, pale as death, with his hands plunged like weights in his coat pockets, was standing in a puddle of water glaring tragically into my eyes.

With his hands still in his coat pockets he stalked by me into the hall, turned sharply as if he were on a wire, and disappeared into the living-room. It wasn't a bit funny. Aware of the loud beating of my own heart I pulled the door to against the increasing rain.

For half a minute there wasn't a sound. Then from the living-room I heard a sort of choking murmur and part of a laugh, followed by Daisy's voice on a clear artificial note:

"I certainly am awfully glad to see you again."

A pause; it endured horribly. I had nothing to do in the hall, so I went into the room.

Gatsby, his hands still in his pockets, was reclining against the mantelpiece in a strained counterfeit of perfect ease, even of boredom. His head leaned back so far that it rested against the face of a defunct mantelpiece clock, and from this position his distraught eyes stared down at Daisy, who was sitting, frightened but graceful, on the edge of a stiff chair.

"We've met before," muttered Gatsby. His eyes glanced momentarily at me, and his lips parted with an abortive attempt at a laugh. Luckily the clock took this moment to tilt dangerously at the pressure of his head, whereupon he turned and caught it with trembling fingers and set it back in place.

Then he sat down, rigidly, his elbow on the arm of the sofa and his chin in his hand.

"I'm sorry about the clock," he said.

My own face had now assumed a deep tropical burn. I couldn't muster up a single commonplace out of the thousand in my head.

"It's an old clock," I told them idiotically.

I think we all believed for a moment that it had smashed in pieces on the floor.

"We haven't met for many years," said Daisy, her voice as matter-of-fact as it could ever be.

"Five years next November."

The automatic quality of Gatsby's answer set us all back at least another minute. I had them both on their feet with the desperate suggestion that they help me make tea in the kitchen when the demoniac Finn brought it in on a tray.

Amid the welcome confusion of cups and cakes a certain physical decency established itself. Gatsby got himself into a shadow and, while Daisy and I talked, looked conscientiously from one to the other of us with tense, unhappy eyes. However, as calmness wasn't an end in itself, I made an excuse at the first possible moment, and got to my feet.

"Where are you going?" demanded Gatsby in immediate alarm.

"I'll be back."

"I've got to speak to you about something before you go."

He followed me wildly into the kitchen, closed the door, and whispered: "Oh, God!" in a miserable way.

"What's the matter?"

"This is a terrible mistake," he said, shaking his head from side to side, "a terrible, terrible mistake."

"You're just embarrassed, that's all," and luckily I added: "Daisy's embarrassed too."

"She's embarrassed?" he repeated incredulously.

"Just as much as you are."

"Don't talk so loud."

"You're acting like a little boy," I broke out impatiently. "Not only that, but you're rude. Daisy's sitting in there all alone."

He raised his hand to stop my words, looked at me with unforgettable reproach, and, opening the door cautiously, went back into the other room.

I walked out the back way—just as Gatsby had when he had made his nervous circuit of the house half an hour before—and ran for a huge black knotted tree, whose massed leaves made a fabric against the rain. Once more it was pouring, and my irregular lawn, well-shaved by Gatsby's gardener, abounded in small muddy swamps and prehistoric marshes. There was nothing to look at from under the tree except Gatsby's enormous house, so I stared at it, like Kant at his church steeple, for half an hour. A brewer had built it early in the "period" craze, a decade before, and there was a story that he'd agreed to pay five years' taxes on all the neighboring cottages if the owners would have their roofs thatched with straw. Perhaps their refusal took the heart out of his plan to Found a Family—he went into an immediate decline. His children sold his house with the black wreath still on the door. Americans, while occasionally willing to be serfs, have always been obstinate about being peasantry.

After half an hour, the sun shone again, and the grocer's automobile rounded Gatsby's drive with the raw material for his servants' dinner—I felt sure he wouldn't eat a spoonful. A maid began opening the upper windows of his house, appeared momentarily in each, and, leaning from a large central bay, spat meditatively into the garden. It was time I went back. While the rain continued it had seemed like the murmur of their voices, rising and swelling a little now and then with gusts of emotion. But in the new silence I felt that silence had fallen within the house too.

I went in—after making every possible noise in the kitchen, short of pushing over the stove—but I don't believe they heard a sound. They were sitting at either end of the couch, looking at each other as if some question had been asked, or was in the air, and every vestige of embarrassment was gone.

Daisy's face was smeared with tears, and when I came in she jumped up and began wiping at it with her handkerchief before a mirror. But there was a change in Gatsby that was simply confounding. He literally glowed; without a word or a gesture of exultation a new well-being radiated from him and filled the little room.

"Oh, hello, old sport," he said, as if he hadn't seen me for years. I thought for a moment he was going to shake hands.

"It's stopped raining."

"Has it?" When he realized what I was talking about, that there were twinkle-bells of sunshine in the room, he smiled like a weather man, like an ecstatic patron of recurrent light, and repeated the news to Daisy. "What do you think of that? It's stopped raining."

"I'm glad, Jay." Her throat, full of aching, grieving beauty, told only of her unexpected joy.

"I want you and Daisy to come over to my house," he said. "I'd like to show her around."

"You're sure you want me to come?"

"Absolutely, old sport."

Daisy went upstairs to wash her face—too late I thought with humiliation of my towels—while Gatsby and I waited on the lawn.

"My house looks well, doesn't it?" he demanded. "See how the whole front of it catches the light."

I agreed that it was splendid.

"Yes." His eyes went over it, every arched door and square tower. "It took me just three years to earn the money that bought it."

"I thought you inherited your money."

"I did, old sport," he said automatically, "but I lost most of it in the big panic—the panic of the war."

I think he hardly knew what he was saying, for when I asked him what business he was in he answered: "That's my affair," before he realized that it wasn't an appropriate reply.

"Oh, I've been in several things," he corrected himself. "I was in the drug business and then I was in the oil business. But I'm not in either one now." He looked at me with more attention. "Do you mean you've been thinking over what I proposed the other night?"

Before I could answer, Daisy came out of the house and two rows of brass buttons on her dress gleamed in the sunlight.

"That huge place *there?*" she cried pointing.

"Do you like it?"

"I love it, but I don't see how you live there all alone."

"I keep it always full of interesting people, night and day. People who do interesting things. Celebrated people."

Instead of taking the short-cut along the Sound we went down to the road and entered by the big postern. With enchanting murmurs Daisy admired this aspect or that of the feudal silhouette against the sky, admired the gardens, the sparkling odor of jonquils and the frothy odor of hawthorn and plum blossoms and the pale gold odor of kiss-me-at-the-gate. It was strange to reach the marble steps and find no stir of bright dresses in and out the door, and hear no sound but bird voices in the trees.

And inside, as we wandered through Marie Antoinette music-rooms and Restoration salons, I felt that there were guests concealed behind every couch and table, under orders to be breathlessly silent until we had passed through. As Gatsby closed the door of "the Merton College Library" I could have sworn I heard the owl-eyed man break into ghostly laughter.

We went upstairs, through period bedrooms swathed in rose and lavender silk and vivid with new flowers, through dressing-rooms and poolrooms, and bathrooms with sunken baths—intruding into one chamber where a dishevelled man in pajamas was doing liver exercises on the floor. It was Mr. Klipspringer, the "boarder." I had seen him wandering hungrily about the beach that morning. Finally we came to Gatsby's own apartment, a bedroom and a bath, and an Adam study, where we sat down and drank a glass of some Chartreuse he took from a cupboard in the wall.

He hadn't once ceased looking at Daisy, and I think he revalued everything in his house according to the measure of response it drew from her well-loved eyes. Sometimes, too, he stared around at his possessions in a dazed way, as though in her actual and astounding presence none of it was any longer real. Once he nearly toppled down a flight of stairs.

His bedroom was the simplest room of all—except where the dresser was garnished with a toilet set of pure dull gold. Daisy took the brush with delight, and smoothed her hair, whereupon Gatsby sat down and shaded his eyes and began to laugh.

"It's the funniest thing, old sport," he said hilariously. "I can't— When I try to——"

He had passed visibly through two states and was entering upon a third. After his embarrassment and his unreasoning joy he was consumed with wonder at her presence. He had been full of the idea so long, dreamed it right through to the end, waited with his teeth set, so to speak, at an inconceivable pitch of intensity. Now, in the reaction, he was running down like an overwound clock.

Recovering himself in a minute he opened for us two hulking patent cabinets which held his massed suits and dressing gowns and ties, and his shirts, piled like bricks in stacks a dozen high.

"I've got a man in England who buys me clothes. He sends over a selection of things at the beginning of each season, spring and fall."

He took out a pile of shirts and began throwing them, one by one, before us, shirts of sheer linen and thick silk and fine flannel, which lost their folds as they fell and covered the table in many-colored disarray. While we admired he brought more and the soft rich heap mounted higher—shirts with stripes and scrolls and plaids in coral and apple-green and lavender and faint orange, with monograms of Indian blue. Suddenly, with a strained sound, Daisy bent her head into the shirts and began to cry stormily.

"They're such beautiful shirts," she sobbed, her voice muffled in the thick folds. "It makes me sad because I've never seen such—such beautiful shirts before."

After the house, we were to see the grounds and the swimming pool, and the hydroplane and the midsummer flowers—but outside Gatsby's window it began to rain again, so we stood in a row looking at the corrugated surface of the Sound.

"If it wasn't for the mist we could see your home across the bay," said Gatsby. "You always have a green light that burns all night at the end of your dock."

Daisy put her arm through his abruptly, but he seemed absorbed in what he had just said. Possibly it had occurred to him that the colossal significance of that light had now vanished forever. Compared to the great distance that had separated him from Daisy it had seemed very near to her, almost touching her. It had seemed as close as a star to the moon. Now it was again a green light on a dock. His count of enchanted objects had diminished by one.

I began to walk about the room, examining various indefinite objects in the half darkness. A large photograph of an elderly man in yachting costume attracted me, hung on the wall over his desk.

"Who's this?"

"That? That's Mr. Dan Cody, old sport."

The name sounded faintly familiar.

"He's dead now. He used to be my best friend years ago."

There was a small picture of Gatsby, also in yachting costume, on the bureau—Gatsby with his head thrown back defiantly—taken apparently when he was about eighteen.

"I adore it," exclaimed Daisy. "The pompadour! You never told me you had a pompadour—or a yacht."

"Look at this," said Gatsby quickly. "Here's a lot of clippings—about you."

They stood side by side examining it. I was going to ask to see the rubies when the phone rang, and Gatsby took up the receiver.

"Yes.... Well, I can't talk now.... I can't talk now, old sport.... I said a *small* town.... He must know what a small town is.... Well, he's no use to us if Detroit is his idea of a small town...."

He rang off.

"Come here *quick!*" cried Daisy at the window.

The rain was still falling, but the darkness had parted in the west, and there was a pink and golden billow of foamy clouds above the sea.

"Look at that," she whispered, and then after a moment: "I'd like to just get one of those pink clouds and put you in it and push you around."

I tried to go then, but they wouldn't hear of it; perhaps my presence made them feel more satisfactorily alone.

"I know what we'll do," said Gatsby. "We'll have Klipspringer play the piano."

He went out of the room calling "Ewing!" and returned in a few minutes accompanied by an embarrassed, slightly worn young man, with shell-rimmed glasses and scanty blond hair. He was now decently clothed in a "sport-shirt," open at the neck, sneakers, and duck trousers of a nebulous hue.

"Did we interrupt your exercises?" inquired Daisy politely.

"I was asleep," cried Mr. Klipspringer, in a spasm of embarrassment. "That is, I'd *been* asleep. Then I got up ..."

"Klipspringer plays the piano," said Gatsby, cutting him off. "Don't you, Ewing, old sport?"

"I don't play well. I don't—I hardly play at all. I'm all out of prac——"

"We'll go downstairs," interrupted Gatsby. He flipped a switch. The gray windows disappeared as the house glowed full of light.

In the music-room Gatsby turned on a solitary lamp beside the piano. He lit Daisy's cigarette from a trembling match, and sat down with her on a couch far across the room, where there was no light save what the gleaming floor bounced in from the hall.

When Klipspringer had played "The Love Nest" he turned around on the bench and searched unhappily for Gatsby in the gloom.

"I'm all out of practice, you see. I told you I couldn't play. I'm all out of prac——"

"Don't talk so much, old sport," commanded Gatsby. "Play!"

"In the morning,
In the evening,
Ain't we got fun——"

Outside the wind was loud and there was a faint flow of thunder along the Sound. All the lights were going on in West Egg now; the electric trains, men-carrying, were plunging home through the rain from New York. It was the hour of a profound human change, and excitement was generating on the air.

"One thing's sure and nothing's surer
The rich get richer and the poor get—children.
In the meantime,
In between time——"

As I went over to say good-by I saw that the expression of bewilderment had come back into Gatsby's face, as though a faint doubt had occurred to him as to the quality of his present happiness. Almost five years! There must have been moments even that afternoon when Daisy tumbled short of his dreams—not through her own fault, but because of the colossal vitality of his illusion. It had gone beyond her, beyond everything. He had thrown himself into it with a creative passion, adding to it all the time, decking it out with every bright feather that drifted his way. No amount of fire or freshness can challenge what a man will store up in his ghostly heart.

As I watched him he adjusted himself a little, visibly. His hand took hold of hers, and as she said something low in his ear he turned toward her with a rush of emotion. I think that voice held him most, with its fluctuating, feverish warmth, because it couldn't be over-dreamed—that voice was a deathless song.

They had forgotten me, but Daisy glanced up and held out her hand; Gatsby didn't know me now at all. I looked once more at them and they looked back at me, remotely, possessed by intense life. Then I went out of the room and down the marble steps into the rain, leaving them there together.

CHAPTER VI

About this time an ambitious young reporter from New York arrived one morning at Gatsby's door and asked him if he had anything to say.

"Anything to say about what?" inquired Gatsby politely.

"Why—any statement to give out."

It transpired after a confused five minutes that the man had heard Gatsby's name around his office in a connection which he either wouldn't reveal or didn't fully understand. This was his day off and with laudable initiative he had hurried out "to see."

It was a random shot, and yet the reporter's instinct was right. Gatsby's notoriety, spread about by the hundreds who had accepted his hospitality and so become authorities upon his past, had increased all summer until he fell just short of being news. Contemporary legends such as the "underground pipe-line to Canada" attached themselves to him, and there was one persistent story that he didn't live in a house at all, but in a boat that looked like a house and was moved secretly up and down the Long Island shore. Just why these inventions were a source of satisfaction to James Gatz of North Dakota isn't easy to say.

James Gatz—that was really, or at least legally, his name. He had changed it at the age of seventeen and at the specific moment that witnessed the beginning of his career—when he saw Dan Cody's yacht drop anchor over the most insidious flat on Lake Superior. It was James Gatz who had been loafing along the beach that afternoon in a torn green jersey and a pair of canvas pants, but it was already Jay Gatsby who borrowed a rowboat, pulled out to the *Tuolomee,* and informed Cody that a wind might catch him and break him up in half an hour.

I suppose he'd had the name ready for a long time, even then. His parents were shiftless and unsuccessful farm people—his imagination had never really accepted them as his parents at all. The truth was that Jay Gatsby of West Egg, Long Island, sprang from his Platonic conception of himself. He was a son of God—a phrase which, if it means anything, means just that—and he must be about His Father's business, the service of a vast, vulgar, and meretricious beauty. So he invented just the sort of Jay Gatsby that a seventeen-year-old boy would be likely to invent, and to this conception he was faithful to the end.

For over a year he had been beating his way along the south shore of Lake Superior as a clam-digger and a salmon-fisher or in any other capacity that brought him food and bed.

His brown, hardening body lived naturally through the half fierce, half lazy work of the bracing days. He knew women early, and since they spoiled him he became contemptuous of them, of young virgins because they were ignorant, of the others because they were hysterical about things which in his overwhelming self-absorption he took for granted.

But his heart was in a constant, turbulent riot. The most grotesque and fantastic conceits haunted him in his bed at night. A universe of ineffable gaudiness spun itself out in his brain while the clock ticked on the wash-stand and the moon soaked with wet light his tangled clothes upon the floor. Each night he added to the pattern of his fancies until drowsiness closed down upon some vivid scene with an oblivious embrace. For a while these reveries provided an outlet for his imagination; they were a satisfactory hint of the unreality of reality, a promise that the rock of the world was founded securely on a fairy's wing.

An instinct toward his future glory had led him, some months before, to the small Lutheran college of St. Olaf's in southern Minnesota. He stayed there two weeks, dismayed at its ferocious indifference to the drums of his destiny, to destiny itself, and despising the janitor's work with which he was to pay his way through. Then he drifted back to Lake Superior, and he was still searching for something to do on the day that Dan Cody's yacht dropped anchor in the shallows alongshore.

Cody was fifty years old then, a product of the Nevada silver fields, of the Yukon, of every rush for metal since seventy-five. The transactions in Montana copper that made him many times a millionaire found him physically robust but on the verge of soft-mindedness, and, suspecting this, an infinite number of women tried to separate him from his money. The none too savory ramifications by which Ella Kaye, the newspaper woman, played Madame de Maintenon to his weakness and sent him to sea in a yacht, were common property of the turgid journalism of 1902. He had been coasting along all too hospitable shores for five years when he turned up as James Gatz's destiny in Little Girl Bay.

To young Gatz, resting on his oars and looking up at the railed deck, that yacht represented all the beauty and glamour in the world. I suppose he smiled at Cody—he had probably discovered that people liked him when he smiled. At any rate Cody asked him a few questions (one of them elicited the brand new name) and found that he was quick and extravagantly ambitious. A few days later he took him to Duluth and bought him a blue coat, six pair of white duck trousers, and a yachting cap. And when the *Tuolomee* left for the West Indies and the Barbary Coast, Gatsby left too.

He was employed in a vague personal capacity—while he remained with Cody he was in turn steward, mate, skipper, secretary, and even jailor, for Dan Cody sober knew what lavish doings Dan Cody drunk might soon be about, and he provided for such contingencies by reposing more and more trust in Gatsby. The arrangement lasted five years, during which the boat went three times around the Continent. It might have lasted indefinitely except for the fact that Ella Kaye came on board one night in Boston and a week later Dan Cody inhospitably died.

I remember the portrait of him up in Gatsby's bedroom, a gray, florid man with a hard, empty face—the pioneer debauchee, who during one phase of American life brought back to the Eastern seaboard the savage violence of the frontier brothel and saloon. It was indirectly due to Cody that Gatsby drank so little. Sometimes in the course of gay parties women used to rub champagne into his hair; for himself he formed the habit of letting liquor alone.

And it was from Cody that he inherited money—a legacy of twenty-five thousand dollars. He didn't get it. He never understood the legal device that was used against him, but what remained of the millions went intact to Ella Kaye. He was left with his singularly appropriate education; the vague contour of Jay Gatsby had filled out to the substantiality of a man.

He told me all this very much later, but I've put it down here with the idea of exploding those first wild rumors about his antecedents, which weren't even faintly true. Moreover he told it to me at a time of confusion, when I had reached the point of believing everything and nothing about him. So I take advantage of this short halt, while Gatsby, so to speak, caught his breath, to clear this set of misconceptions away.

It was a halt, too, in my association with his affairs. For several weeks I didn't see him or hear his voice on the phone—mostly I was in New York, trotting around with Jordan and trying to ingratiate myself with her senile aunt—but finally I went over to his house one Sunday afternoon. I hadn't been there two minutes when somebody brought Tom Buchanan in for a drink. I was startled, naturally, but the really surprising thing was that it hadn't happened before.

They were a party of three on horseback—Tom and a man named Sloane and a pretty woman in a brown riding habit, who had been there previously.

"I'm delighted to see you," said Gatsby, standing on his porch. "I'm delighted that you dropped in."

As though they cared!

"Sit right down. Have a cigarette or a cigar." He walked around the room quickly, ringing bells. "I'll have something to drink for you in just a minute."

He was profoundly affected by the fact that Tom was there. But he would be uneasy anyhow until he had given them something, realizing in a vague way that that was all they came for. Mr. Sloane wanted nothing. A lemonade? No, thanks. A little champagne? Nothing at all, thanks.... I'm sorry——

"Did you have a nice ride?"

"Very good roads around here."

"I suppose the automobiles——"

"Yeah."

Moved by an irresistible impulse, Gatsby turned to Tom, who had accepted the introduction as a stranger.

"I believe we've met somewhere before, Mr. Buchanan."

"Oh, yes," said Tom, gruffly polite, but obviously not remembering. "So we did. I remember very well."

"About two weeks ago."

"That's right. You were with Nick here."

"I know your wife," continued Gatsby, almost aggressively.

"That so?"

Tom turned to me.

"You live near here, Nick?"

"Next door."

"That so?"

Mr. Sloane didn't enter into the conversation, but lounged back haughtily in his chair; the woman said nothing either—until unexpectedly, after two highballs, she became cordial.

"We'll all come over to your next party, Mr. Gatsby," she suggested. "What do you say?"

"Certainly. I'd be delighted to have you."

"Be ver' nice," said Mr. Sloane, without gratitude. "Well—think ought to be starting home."

"Please don't hurry," Gatsby urged them. He had control of himself now, and he wanted to see more of Tom. "Why don't you—why don't you stay for supper? I wouldn't be surprised if some other people dropped in from New York."

"You come to supper with *me*," said the lady enthusiastically. "Both of you."

This included me. Mr. Sloane got to his feet.

"Come along," he said—but to her only.

"I mean it," she insisted. "I'd love to have you. Lots of room."

Gatsby looked at me questioningly. He wanted to go, and he didn't see that Mr. Sloane had determined he shouldn't.

"I'm afraid I won't be able to," I said.

"Well, you come," she urged, concentrating on Gatsby.

Mr. Sloane murmured something close to her ear.

"We won't be late if we start now," she insisted aloud.

"I haven't got a horse," said Gatsby. "I used to ride in the army, but I've never bought a horse. I'll have to follow you in my car. Excuse me for just a minute."

The rest of us walked out on the porch, where Sloane and the lady began an impassioned conversation aside.

"My God, I believe the man's coming," said Tom. "Doesn't he know she doesn't want him?"

"She says she does want him."

"She has a big dinner party and he won't know a soul there." He frowned. "I wonder where in the devil he met Daisy. By God, I may be old-fashioned in my ideas, but women run around too much these days to suit me. They meet all kinds of crazy fish."

Suddenly Mr. Sloane and the lady walked down the steps and mounted their horses.

"Come on," said Mr. Sloane to Tom. "We're late. We've got to go." And then to me: "Tell him we couldn't wait, will you?"

Tom and I shook hands, the rest of us exchanged a cool nod, and they trotted quickly down the drive, disappearing under the August foliage just as Gatsby, with hat and light overcoat in hand, came out the front door.

Tom was evidently perturbed at Daisy's running around alone, for on the following Saturday night he came with her to Gatsby's party. Perhaps his presence gave the evening its peculiar quality of oppressiveness—it stands out in my memory from Gatsby's other parties that summer. There were the same people, or at least the same sort of people, the same profusion of champagne, the same many-colored, many-keyed commotion, but I felt an unpleasantness in the air, a pervading harshness that hadn't been there before. Or perhaps I had merely grown used to it, grown to accept West Egg as a world complete in itself, with its own standards and its own great figures, second to nothing because it had no consciousness of being so, and now I was looking at it again, through Daisy's eyes. It is invariably saddening to look through new eyes at things upon which you have expended your own powers of adjustment.

They arrived at twilight, and, as we strolled out among the sparkling hundreds, Daisy's voice was playing murmurous tricks in her throat.

"These things excite me *so*," she whispered. "If you want to kiss me any time during the evening, Nick, just let me know and I'll be glad to arrange it for you. Just mention my name. Or present a green card. I'm giving out green——"

"Look around," suggested Gatsby.

"I'm looking around. I'm having a marvellous——"

"You must see the faces of many people you've heard about."

Tom's arrogant eyes roamed the crowd.

"We don't go around very much," he said. "In fact, I was just thinking I don't know a soul here."

"Perhaps you know that lady." Gatsby indicated a gorgeous, scarcely human orchid of a woman who sat in state under a white-plum tree. Tom and Daisy stared, with that peculiarly unreal feeling that accompanies the recognition of a hitherto ghostly celebrity of the movies.

"She's lovely," said Daisy.

"The man bending over her is her director."

He took them ceremoniously from group to group:

"Mrs. Buchanan ... and Mr. Buchanan—" After an instant's hesitation he added: "the polo player."

"Oh no," objected Tom quickly, "not me."

But evidently the sound of it pleased Gatsby for Tom remained "the polo player" for the rest of the evening.

"I've never met so many celebrities," Daisy exclaimed. "I liked that man—what was his name?—with the sort of blue nose."

Gatsby identified him, adding that he was a small producer.

"Well, I liked him anyhow."

"I'd a little rather not be the polo player," said Tom pleasantly. "I'd rather look at all these famous people in—in oblivion."

Daisy and Gatsby danced. I remember being surprised by his graceful, conservative fox-trot—I had never seen him dance before. Then they sauntered over to my house and sat on the steps for half an hour, while at her request I remained watchfully in the garden. "In case there's a fire or a flood," she explained, "or any act of God."

Tom appeared from his oblivion as we were sitting down to supper together. "Do you mind if I eat with some people over here?" he said. "A fellow's getting off some funny stuff."

"Go ahead," answered Daisy genially, "and if you want to take down any addresses here's my little gold pencil." ... She looked around after a moment and told me the girl was "common but pretty," and I knew that except for the half hour she'd been alone with Gatsby she wasn't having a good time.

We were at a particularly tipsy table. That was my fault—Gatsby had been called to the phone, and I'd enjoyed these same people only two weeks before. But what had amused me then turned septic on the air now.

"How do you feel, Miss Baedeker?"

The girl addressed was trying, unsuccessfully, to slump against my shoulder. At this inquiry she sat up and opened her eyes.

"Wha'?"

A massive and lethargic woman, who had been urging Daisy to play golf with her at the local club tomorrow, spoke in Miss Baedeker's defense:

"Oh, she's all right now. When she's had five or six cocktails she always starts screaming like that. I tell her she ought to leave it alone."

"I do leave it alone," affirmed the accused hollowly.

"We heard you yelling, so I said to Doc Civet here: 'There's somebody that needs your help, Doc.'"

"She's much obliged, I'm sure," said another friend, without gratitude, "but you got her dress all wet when you stuck her head in the pool."

"Anything I hate is to get my head stuck in a pool," mumbled Miss Baedeker. "They almost drowned me once over in New Jersey."

"Then you ought to leave it alone," countered Doctor Civet.

"Speak for yourself!" cried Miss Baedeker violently. "Your hand shakes. I wouldn't let you operate on me!"

It was like that. Almost the last thing I remember was standing with Daisy and watching the moving-picture director and his Star. They were still under the white-plum tree and their faces were touching except for a pale, thin ray of moonlight between. It occurred to me that he had been very slowly bending toward her all evening to attain this proximity, and even while I watched I saw him stoop one ultimate degree and kiss at her cheek.

"I like her," said Daisy. "I think she's lovely."

But the rest offended her—and inarguably, because it wasn't a gesture but an emotion. She was appalled by West Egg, this unprecedented "place" that Broadway had begotten upon a Long Island fishing village—appalled by its raw vigor that chafed under the old euphemisms and by the too obtrusive fate that herded its inhabitants along a short-cut from nothing to nothing. She saw something awful in the very simplicity she failed to understand.

I sat on the front steps with them while they waited for their car. It was dark here in front; only the bright door sent ten square feet of light volleying out into the soft black morning. Sometimes a shadow moved against a dressing-room blind above, gave way to another shadow, an indefinite procession of shadows, who rouged and powdered in an invisible glass.

"Who is this Gatsby anyhow?" demanded Tom suddenly. "Some big bootlegger?"

"Where'd you hear that?" I inquired.

"I didn't hear it. I imagined it. A lot of these newly rich people are just big bootleggers, you know."

"Not Gatsby," I said shortly.

He was silent for a moment. The pebbles of the drive crunched under his feet.

"Well, he certainly must have strained himself to get this menagerie together."

A breeze stirred the gray haze of Daisy's fur collar.

"At least they are more interesting than the people we know," she said with an effort.

"You didn't look so interested."

"Well, I was."

Tom laughed and turned to me.

"Did you notice Daisy's face when that girl asked her to put her under a cold shower?"

Daisy began to sing with the music in a husky, rhythmic whisper, bringing out a meaning in each word that it had never had before and would never have again. When the melody rose her voice broke up sweetly, following it, in a way contralto voices have, and each change tipped out a little of her warm human magic upon the air.

"Lots of people come who haven't been invited," she said suddenly. "That girl hadn't been invited. They simply force their way in and he's too polite to object."

"I'd like to know who he is and what he does," insisted Tom. "And I think I'll make a point of finding out."

"I can tell you right now," she answered. "He owned some drug-stores, a lot of drug-stores. He built them up himself."

The dilatory limousine came rolling up the drive.

"Good night, Nick," said Daisy.

Her glance left me and sought the lighted top of the steps, where "Three o'Clock in the Morning," a neat, sad little waltz of that year, was drifting out the open door. After all, in the very casualness of Gatsby's party there were romantic possibilities totally absent from her world. What was it up there in the song that seemed to be calling her back inside? What would happen now in the dim, incalculable hours? Perhaps some unbelievable guest would arrive, a person infinitely rare and to be marvelled at, some authentically radiant young girl who with one fresh glance at Gatsby, one moment of magical encounter, would blot out those five years of unwavering devotion.

I stayed late that night. Gatsby asked me to wait until he was free, and I lingered in the garden until the inevitable swimming party had run up, chilled and exalted, from the black beach, until the lights were extinguished in the guest-rooms overhead. When he came down the steps at last the tanned skin was drawn unusually tight on his face, and his eyes were bright and tired.

"She didn't like it," he said immediately.

"Of course she did."

"She didn't like it," he insisted. "She didn't have a good time."

He was silent, and I guessed at his unutterable depression.

"I feel far away from her," he said. "It's hard to make her understand."

"You mean about the dance?"

"The dance?" He dismissed all the dances he had given with a snap of his fingers. "Old sport, the dance is unimportant."

He wanted nothing less of Daisy than that she should go to Tom and say: "I never loved you." After she had obliterated four years with that sentence they could decide upon the more practical measures to be taken. One of them was that, after she was free, they were to go back to Louisville and be married from her house—just as if it were five years ago.

"And she doesn't understand," he said. "She used to be able to understand. We'd sit for hours——"

He broke off and began to walk up and down a desolate path of fruit rinds and discarded favors and crushed flowers.

"I wouldn't ask too much of her," I ventured. "You can't repeat the past."

"Can't repeat the past?" he cried incredulously. "Why of course you can!"

He looked around him wildly, as if the past were lurking here in the shadow of his house, just out of reach of his hand.

"I'm going to fix everything just the way it was before," he said, nodding determinedly. "She'll see."

He talked a lot about the past, and I gathered that he wanted to recover something, some idea of himself perhaps, that had gone into loving Daisy. His life had been confused and disordered since then, but if he could once return to a certain starting place and go over it all slowly, he could find out what that thing was....

... One autumn night, five years before, they had been walking down the street when the leaves were falling, and they came to a place where there were no trees and the sidewalk was white with moonlight. They stopped here and turned toward each other. Now it was a cool night with that mysterious excitement in it which comes at the two changes of the year. The quiet lights in the houses were humming out into the darkness and there was a stir and bustle among the stars. Out of the corner of his eye Gatsby saw that the blocks of the sidewalks really formed a ladder and mounted to a secret place above the trees—he could climb to it, if he climbed alone, and once there he could suck on the pap of life, gulp down the incomparable milk of wonder.

His heart beat faster and faster as Daisy's white face came up to his own. He knew that when he kissed this girl, and forever wed his unutterable visions to her perishable breath, his mind would never romp again like the mind of God. So he waited, listening for a moment longer to the tuning-fork that had been struck upon a star. Then he kissed her. At his lips' touch she blossomed for him like a flower and the incarnation was complete.

Through all he said, even through his appalling sentimentality, I was reminded of something—an elusive rhythm, a fragment of lost words, that I had heard somewhere a long time ago. For a moment a phrase tried to take shape in my mouth and my lips parted like a dumb man's, as though there was more struggling upon them than a wisp of startled air. But they made no sound, and what I had almost remembered was uncommunicable forever.

CHAPTER VII

It was when curiosity about Gatsby was at its highest that the lights in his house failed to go on one Saturday night—and, as obscurely as it had begun, his career as Trimalchio was over. Only gradually did I become aware that the automobiles which turned expectantly into his drive stayed for just a minute and then drove sulkily away. Wondering if he were sick I went over to find out—an unfamiliar butler with a villainous face squinted at me suspiciously from the door.

"Is Mr. Gatsby sick?"

"Nope." After a pause he added "sir" in a dilatory, grudging way.

"I hadn't seen him around, and I was rather worried. Tell him Mr. Carraway came over."

"Who?" he demanded rudely.

"Carraway."

"Carraway. All right, I'll tell him."

Abruptly he slammed the door.

My Finn informed me that Gatsby had dismissed every servant in his house a week ago and replaced them with half a dozen others, who never went into West Egg Village to be bribed by the tradesmen, but ordered moderate supplies over the telephone.

The grocery boy reported that the kitchen looked like a pigsty, and the general opinion in the village was that the new people weren't servants at all.

Next day Gatsby called me on the phone.

"Going away?" I inquired.

"No, old sport."

"I hear you fired all your servants."

"I wanted somebody who wouldn't gossip. Daisy comes over quite often—in the afternoons."

So the whole caravansary had fallen in like a card house at the disapproval in her eyes.

"They're some people Wolfshiem wanted to do something for. They're all brothers and sisters. They used to run a small hotel."

"I see."

He was calling up at Daisy's request—would I come to lunch at her house tomorrow? Miss Baker would be there. Half an hour later Daisy herself telephoned and seemed relieved to find that I was coming. Something was up. And yet I couldn't believe that they would choose this occasion for a scene—especially for the rather harrowing scene that Gatsby had outlined in the garden.

The next day was broiling, almost the last, certainly the warmest, of the summer. As my train emerged from the tunnel into sunlight, only the hot whistles of the National Biscuit Company broke the simmering hush at noon. The straw seats of the car hovered on the edge of combustion; the woman next to me perspired delicately for a while into her white shirtwaist, and then, as her newspaper dampened under her fingers, lapsed despairingly into deep heat with a desolate cry. Her pocket-book slapped to the floor.

"Oh, my!" she gasped.

I picked it up with a weary bend and handed it back to her, holding it at arm's length and by the extreme tip of the corners to indicate that I had no designs upon it—but everyone nearby, including the woman, suspected me just the same.

"Hot!" said the conductor to familiar faces. "Some weather!... Hot!... Hot!... Hot!... Is it hot enough for you? Is it hot? Is it...?"

My commutation ticket came back to me with a dark stain from his hand. That anyone should care in this heat whose flushed lips he kissed, whose head made damp the pajama pocket over his heart!

... Through the hall of the Buchanans' house blew a faint wind, carrying the sound of the telephone bell out to Gatsby and me as we waited at the door.

"The master's body!" roared the butler into the mouthpiece. "I'm sorry, madame, but we can't furnish it—it's far too hot to touch this noon!"

What he really said was: "Yes... Yes... I'll see."

He set down the receiver and came toward us, glistening slightly, to take our stiff straw hats.

"Madame expects you in the salon!" he cried, needlessly indicating the direction. In this heat every extra gesture was an affront to the common store of life.

The room, shadowed well with awnings, was dark and cool. Daisy and Jordan lay upon an enormous couch, like silver idols weighing down their own white dresses against the singing breeze of the fans.

"We can't move," they said together.

Jordan's fingers, powdered white over their tan, rested for a moment in mine.

"And Mr. Thomas Buchanan, the athlete?" I inquired.

Simultaneously I heard his voice, gruff, muffled, husky, at the hall telephone.

Gatsby stood in the center of the crimson carpet and gazed around with fascinated eyes. Daisy watched him and laughed, her sweet, exciting laugh; a tiny gust of powder rose from her bosom into the air.

"The rumor is," whispered Jordan, "that that's Tom's girl on the telephone."

We were silent. The voice in the hall rose high with annoyance: "Very well, then, I won't sell you the car at all.... I'm under no obligations to you at all ... and as for your bothering me about it at lunch-time, I won't stand that at all!"

"Holding down the receiver," said Daisy cynically.

"No, he's not," I assured her. "It's a bona-fide deal. I happen to know about it."

Tom flung open the door, blocked out its space for a moment with his thick body, and hurried into the room.

"Mr. Gatsby!" He put out his broad, flat hand with well-concealed dislike. "I'm glad to see you, sir.... Nick...."

"Make us a cold drink," cried Daisy.

As he left the room again she got up and went over to Gatsby and pulled his face down, kissing him on the mouth.

"You know I love you," she murmured.

"You forget there's a lady present," said Jordan.

Daisy looked around doubtfully.

"You kiss Nick too."

"What a low, vulgar girl!"

"I don't care!" cried Daisy, and began to clog on the brick fireplace. Then she remembered the heat and sat down guiltily on the couch just as a freshly laundered nurse leading a little girl came into the room.

"Bles-sed pre-cious," she crooned, holding out her arms. "Come to your own mother that loves you."

The child, relinquished by the nurse, rushed across the room and rooted shyly into her mother's dress.

"The bles-sed pre-cious! Did mother get powder on your old yellowy hair? Stand up now, and say—How-de-do."

Gatsby and I in turn leaned down and took the small reluctant hand. Afterward he kept looking at the child with surprise. I don't think he had ever really believed in its existence before.

"I got dressed before luncheon," said the child, turning eagerly to Daisy.

"That's because your mother wanted to show you off." Her face bent into the single wrinkle of the small white neck. "You dream, you. You absolute little dream."

"Yes," admitted the child calmly. "Aunt Jordan's got on a white dress too."

"How do you like mother's friends?" Daisy turned her around so that she faced Gatsby. "Do you think they're pretty?"

"Where's Daddy?"

"She doesn't look like her father," explained Daisy. "She looks like me. She's got my hair and shape of the face."

Daisy sat back upon the couch. The nurse took a step forward and held out her hand.

"Come, Pammy."

"Good-by, sweetheart!"

With a reluctant backward glance the well-disciplined child held to her nurse's hand and was pulled out the door, just as Tom came back, preceding four gin rickeys that clicked full of ice.

Gatsby took up his drink.

"They certainly look cool," he said, with visible tension.

We drank in long, greedy swallows.

"I read somewhere that the sun's getting hotter every year," said Tom genially. "It seems that pretty soon the earth's going to fall into the sun—or wait a minute—it's just the opposite—the sun's getting colder every year.

"Come outside," he suggested to Gatsby. "I'd like you to have a look at the place."

I went with them out to the veranda. On the green Sound, stagnant in the heat, one small sail crawled slowly toward the fresher sea. Gatsby's eyes followed it momentarily; he raised his hand and pointed across the bay.

"I'm right across from you."

"So you are."

Our eyes lifted over the rose-beds and the hot lawn and the weedy refuse of the dog-days alongshore. Slowly the white wings of the boat moved against the blue cool limit of the sky. Ahead lay the scalloped ocean and the abounding blessed isles.

"There's sport for you," said Tom, nodding. "I'd like to be out there with him for about an hour."

We had luncheon in the dining-room, darkened too against the heat, and drank down nervous gayety with the cold ale.

"What'll we do with ourselves this afternoon?" cried Daisy. "And the day after that, and the next thirty years?"

"Don't be morbid," Jordan said. "Life starts all over again when it gets crisp in the fall."

"But it's so hot," insisted Daisy, on the verge of tears, "and everything's so confused. Let's all go to town!"

Her voice struggled on through the heat, beating against it, molding its senselessness into forms.

"I've heard of making a garage out of a stable," Tom was saying to Gatsby, "but I'm the first man who ever made a stable out of a garage."

"Who wants to go to town?" demanded Daisy insistently. Gatsby's eyes floated toward her. "Ah," she cried, "you look so cool."

Their eyes met, and they stared together at each other, alone in space. With an effort she glanced down at the table.

"You always look so cool," she repeated.

She had told him that she loved him, and Tom Buchanan saw. He was astounded. His mouth opened a little, and he looked at Gatsby, and then back at Daisy as if he had just recognized her as someone he knew a long time ago.

"You resemble the advertisement of the man," she went on innocently. "You know the advertisement of the man——"

"All right," broke in Tom quickly, "I'm perfectly willing to go to town. Come on—we're all going to town."

He got up, his eyes still flashing between Gatsby and his wife. No one moved.

"Come on!" His temper cracked a little. "What's the matter, anyhow? If we're going to town, let's start."

His hand, trembling with his effort at self-control, bore to his lips the last of his glass of ale. Daisy's voice got us to our feet and out on to the blazing gravel drive.

"Are we just going to go?" she objected. "Like this? Aren't we going to let anyone smoke a cigarette first?"

"Everybody smoked all through lunch."

"Oh, let's have fun," she begged him. "It's too hot to fuss."

He didn't answer.

"Have it your own way," she said. "Come on, Jordan."

They went upstairs to get ready while we three men stood there shuffling the hot pebbles with our feet. A silver curve of the moon hovered already in the western sky. Gatsby started to speak, changed his mind, but not before Tom wheeled and faced him expectantly.

"Pardon me?"

"Have you got your stables here?" asked Gatsby with an effort.

"About a quarter of a mile down the road."

"Oh."

A pause.

"I don't see the idea of going to town," broke out Tom savagely. "Women get these notions in their heads——"

"Shall we take anything to drink?" called Daisy from an upper window.

"I'll get some whiskey," answered Tom. He went inside.

Gatsby turned to me rigidly:

"I can't say anything in his house, old sport."

"She's got an indiscreet voice," I remarked. "It's full of—" I hesitated.

"Her voice is full of money," he said suddenly.

That was it. I'd never understood before. It was full of money—that was the inexhaustible charm that rose and fell in it, the jingle of it, the cymbals' song of it.... High in a white palace the king's daughter, the golden girl....

Tom came out of the house wrapping a quart bottle in a towel, followed by Daisy and Jordan wearing small tight hats of metallic cloth and carrying light capes over their arms.

"Shall we all go in my car?" suggested Gatsby. He felt the hot, green leather of the seat. "I ought to have left it in the shade."

"Is it standard shift?" demanded Tom.

"Yes."

"Well, you take my coupé and let me drive your car to town."

The suggestion was distasteful to Gatsby.

"I don't think there's much gas," he objected.

"Plenty of gas," said Tom boisterously. He looked at the gauge. "And if it runs out I can stop at a drug-store. You can buy anything at a drug-store nowadays."

A pause followed this apparently pointless remark. Daisy looked at Tom frowning, and an indefinable expression, at once definitely unfamiliar and vaguely recognizable, as if I had only heard it described in words, passed over Gatsby's face.

"Come on, Daisy," said Tom, pressing her with his hand toward Gatsby's car. "I'll take you in this circus wagon."

He opened the door, but she moved out from the circle of his arm.

"You take Nick and Jordan. We'll follow you in the coupé."

She walked close to Gatsby, touching his coat with her hand. Jordan and Tom and I got into the front seat of Gatsby's car, Tom pushed the unfamiliar gears tentatively, and we shot off into the oppressive heat, leaving them out of sight behind.

"Did you see that?" demanded Tom.

"See what?"

He looked at me keenly, realizing that Jordan and I must have known all along.

"You think I'm pretty dumb, don't you?" he suggested. "Perhaps I am, but I have a—almost a second sight, sometimes, that tells me what to do. Maybe you don't believe that, but science——"

He paused. The immediate contingency overtook him, pulled him back from the edge of the theoretical abyss.

"I've made a small investigation of this fellow," he continued. "I could have gone deeper if I'd known——"

"Do you mean you've been to a medium?" inquired Jordan humorously.

"What?" Confused, he stared at us as we laughed. "A medium?"

"About Gatsby."

"About Gatsby! No, I haven't. I said I'd been making a small investigation of his past."

"And you found he was an Oxford man," said Jordan helpfully.

"An Oxford man!" He was incredulous. "Like hell he is! He wears a pink suit."

"Nevertheless he's an Oxford man."

"Oxford, New Mexico," snorted Tom contemptuously, "or something like that."

"Listen, Tom. If you're such a snob, why did you invite him to lunch?" demanded Jordan crossly.

"Daisy invited him; she knew him before we were married —God knows where!"

We were all irritable now with the fading ale, and aware of it we drove for a while in silence. Then as Doctor T. J. Eckleburg's faded eyes came into sight down the road, I remembered Gatsby's caution about gasoline.

"We've got enough to get us to town," said Tom.

"But there's a garage right here," objected Jordan. "I don't want to get stalled in this baking heat."

Tom threw on both brakes impatiently, and we slid to an abrupt dusty stop under Wilson's sign. After a moment the proprietor emerged from the interior of his establishment and gazed hollow-eyed at the car.

"Let's have some gas!" cried Tom roughly. "What do you think we stopped for—to admire the view?"

"I'm sick," said Wilson without moving. "Been sick all day."

"What's the matter?"

"I'm all run down."

"Well, shall I help myself?" Tom demanded. "You sounded well enough on the phone."

With an effort Wilson left the shade and support of the doorway and, breathing hard, unscrewed the cap of the tank. In the sunlight his face was green.

"I didn't mean to interrupt your lunch," he said. "But I need money pretty bad, and I was wondering what you were going to do with your old car."

"How do you like this one?" inquired Tom. "I bought it last week."

"It's a nice yellow one," said Wilson, as he strained at the handle.

"Like to buy it?"

"Big chance," Wilson smiled faintly. "No, but I could make some money on the other."

"What do you want money for, all of a sudden?"

"I've been here too long. I want to get away. My wife and I want to go West."

"Your wife does!" exclaimed Tom, startled.

"She's been talking about it for ten years." He rested for a moment against the pump, shading his eyes. "And now she's going whether she wants to or not. I'm going to get her away."

The coupé flashed by us with a flurry of dust and the flash of a waving hand.

"What do I owe you?" demanded Tom harshly.

"I just got wised up to something funny the last two days," remarked Wilson. "That's why I want to get away. That's why I been bothering you about the car."

"What do I owe you?"

"Dollar twenty."

The relentless beating heat was beginning to confuse me and I had a bad moment there before I realized that so far his suspicions hadn't alighted on Tom. He had discovered that Myrtle had some sort of life apart from him in another world, and the shock had made him physically sick. I stared at him and then at Tom, who had made a parallel discovery less than an hour before—and it occurred to me that there was no difference between men, in intelligence or race, so profound as the difference between the sick and the well. Wilson was so sick that he looked guilty, unforgivably guilty—as if he had just got some poor girl with child.

"I'll let you have that car," said Tom. "I'll send it over tomorrow afternoon."

That locality was always vaguely disquieting, even in the broad glare of afternoon, and now I turned my head as though I had been warned of something behind. Over the ashheaps the giant eyes of Doctor T. J. Eckleburg kept their vigil, but I perceived, after a moment, that other eyes were regarding us with peculiar intensity from less than twenty feet away.

In one of the windows over the garage the curtains had been moved aside a little, and Myrtle Wilson was peering down at the car. So engrossed was she that she had no consciousness of being observed, and one emotion after another crept into her face like objects into a slowly developing picture. Her expression was curiously familiar—it was an expression I had often seen on women's faces, but on Myrtle Wilson's face it seemed purposeless and inexplicable until I realized that her eyes, wide with jealous terror, were fixed not on Tom, but on Jordan Baker, whom she took to be his wife.

There is no confusion like the confusion of a simple mind, and as we drove away Tom was feeling the hot whips of panic. His wife and his mistress, until an hour ago secure and inviolate, were slipping precipitately from his control. Instinct made him step on the accelerator with the double purpose of overtaking Daisy and leaving Wilson behind, and we sped along toward Astoria at fifty miles an hour, until, among the spidery girders of the elevated, we came in sight of the easygoing blue coupé.

"Those big movies around Fiftieth Street are cool," suggested Jordan. "I love New York on summer afternoons when everyone's away. There's something very sensuous about it—overripe, as if all sorts of funny fruits were going to fall into your hands."

The word "sensuous" had the effect of further disquieting Tom, but before he could invent a protest the coupé came to a stop, and Daisy signalled us to draw up alongside.

"Where are we going?" she cried.

"How about the movies?"

"It's so hot," she complained. "You go. We'll ride around and meet you after." With an effort her wit rose faintly.

"We'll meet you on some corner. I'll be the man smoking two cigarettes."

"We can't argue about it here," Tom said impatiently, as a truck gave out a cursing whistle behind us. "You follow me to the south side of Central Park, in front of the Plaza."

Several times he turned his head and looked back for their car, and if the traffic delayed them he slowed up until they came into sight. I think he was afraid they would dart down a side street and out of his life forever.

But they didn't. And we all took the less explicable step of engaging the parlor of a suite in the Plaza Hotel.

The prolonged and tumultuous argument that ended by herding us into that room eludes me, though I have a sharp physical memory that, in the course of it, my underwear kept climbing like a damp snake around my legs and intermittent beads of sweat raced cool across my back. The notion originated with Daisy's suggestion that we hire five bathrooms and take cold baths, and then assumed more tangible form as "a place to have a mint julep." Each of us said over and over that it was a "crazy idea"—we all talked at once to a baffled clerk and thought, or pretended to think, that we were being very funny …

The room was large and stifling, and, though it was already four o'clock, opening the windows admitted only a gust of hot shrubbery from the Park. Daisy went to the mirror and stood with her back to us, fixing her hair.

"It's a swell suite," whispered Jordan respectfully, and everyone laughed.

"Open another window," commanded Daisy, without turning around.

"There aren't any more."

"Well, we'd better telephone for an axe——"

"The thing to do is to forget about the heat," said Tom impatiently. "You make it ten times worse by crabbing about it."

He unrolled the bottle of whiskey from the towel and put it on the table.

"Why not let her alone, old sport?" remarked Gatsby. "You're the one that wanted to come to town."

There was a moment of silence. The telephone book slipped from its nail and splashed to the floor, whereupon Jordan whispered, "Excuse me"—but this time no one laughed.

"I'll pick it up," I offered.

"I've got it." Gatsby examined the parted string, muttered "Hum!" in an interested way, and tossed the book on a chair.

"That's a great expression of yours, isn't it?" said Tom sharply.

"What is?"

"All this 'old sport' business. Where'd you pick that up?"

"Now see here, Tom," said Daisy, turning around from the mirror, "if you're going to make personal remarks I won't stay here a minute. Call up and order some ice for the mint julep."

As Tom took up the receiver the compressed heat exploded into sound and we were listening to the portentous chords of Mendelssohn's Wedding March from the ballroom below.

"Imagine marrying anybody in this heat!" cried Jordan dismally.

"Still—I was married in the middle of June," Daisy remembered. "Louisville in June! Somebody fainted. Who was it fainted, Tom?"

"Biloxi," he answered shortly.

"A man named Biloxi. 'Blocks' Biloxi, and he made boxes—that's a fact—and he was from Biloxi, Tennessee."

"They carried him into my house," appended Jordan, "because we lived just two doors from the church. And he stayed three weeks, until Daddy told him he had to get out. The day after he left Daddy died." After a moment she added, as if she might have sounded irreverent, "There wasn't any connection."

"I used to know a Bill Biloxi from Memphis," I remarked.

"That was his cousin. I knew his whole family history before he left. He gave me an aluminum putter that I use today."

The music had died down as the ceremony began and now a long cheer floated in at the window, followed by intermittent cries of "Yea—ea—ea!" and finally by a burst of jazz as the dancing began.

"We're getting old," said Daisy. "If we were young we'd rise and dance."

"Remember Biloxi," Jordan warned her. "Where'd you know him, Tom?"

"Biloxi?" He concentrated with an effort. "I didn't know him. He was a friend of Daisy's."

"He was not," she denied. "I'd never seen him before. He came down in the private car."

"Well, he said he knew you. He said he was raised in Louisville. Asa Bird brought him around at the last minute and asked if we had room for him."

Jordan smiled.

"He was probably bumming his way home. He told me he was president of your class at Yale."

Tom and I looked at each other blankly.

"Bil*oxi*?"

"First place, we didn't have any president——"

Gatsby's foot beat a short, restless tattoo and Tom eyed him suddenly.

"By the way, Mr. Gatsby, I understand you're an Oxford man."

"Not exactly."

"Oh, yes, I understand you went to Oxford."

"Yes—I went there."

A pause. Then Tom's voice, incredulous and insulting:

"You must have gone there about the time Biloxi went to New Haven."

Another pause. A waiter knocked and came in with crushed mint and ice but the silence was unbroken by his "thank you" and the soft closing of the door. This tremendous detail was to be cleared up at last.

"I told you I went there," said Gatsby.

"I heard you, but I'd like to know when."

"It was in nineteen-nineteen, I only stayed five months. That's why I can't really call myself an Oxford man."

Tom glanced around to see if we mirrored his unbelief. But we were all looking at Gatsby.

"It was an opportunity they gave to some of the officers after the armistice," he continued. "We could go to any of the universities in England or France."

I wanted to get up and slap him on the back. I had one of those renewals of complete faith in him that I'd experienced before.

Daisy rose, smiling faintly, and went to the table.

"Open the whiskey, Tom," she ordered, "and I'll make you a mint julep. Then you won't seem so stupid to yourself.... Look at the mint!"

"Wait a minute," snapped Tom. "I want to ask Mr. Gatsby one more question."

"Go on," Gatsby said politely.

"What kind of a row are you trying to cause in my house anyhow?"

They were out in the open at last and Gatsby was content.

"He isn't causing a row." Daisy looked desperately from one to the other. "You're causing a row. Please have a little self-control."

"Self-control!" repeated Tom incredulously. "I suppose the latest thing is to sit back and let Mr. Nobody from Nowhere make love to your wife. Well, if that's the idea you can count me out.... Nowadays people begin by sneering at family life and family institutions, and next they'll throw everything overboard and have intermarriage between black and white."

Flushed with his impassioned gibberish, he saw himself standing alone on the last barrier of civilization.

"We're all white here," murmured Jordan.

"I know I'm not very popular. I don't give big parties. I suppose you've got to make your house into a pigsty in order to have any friends—in the modern world."

Angry as I was, as we all were, I was tempted to laugh whenever he opened his mouth. The transition from libertine to prig was so complete.

"I've got something to tell *you,* old sport—" began Gatsby. But Daisy guessed at his intention.

"Please don't!" she interrupted helplessly. "Please let's all go home. Why don't we all go home?"

"That's a good idea." I got up. "Come on, Tom. Nobody wants a drink."

"I want to know what Mr. Gatsby has to tell me."

"Your wife doesn't love you," said Gatsby. "She's never loved you. She loves me."

"You must be crazy!" exclaimed Tom automatically.

Gatsby sprang to his feet, vivid with excitement.

"She never loved you, do you hear?" he cried. "She only married you because I was poor and she was tired of waiting for me. It was a terrible mistake, but in her heart she never loved anyone except me!"

At this point Jordan and I tried to go, but Tom and Gatsby insisted with competitive firmness that we remain—as though neither of them had anything to conceal and it would be a privilege to partake vicariously of their emotions.

"Sit down, Daisy." Tom's voice groped unsuccessfully for the paternal note. "What's been going on? I want to hear all about it."

"I told you what's been going on," said Gatsby. "Going on for five years—and you didn't know."

Tom turned to Daisy sharply.

"You've been seeing this fellow for five years?"

"Not seeing," said Gatsby. "No, we couldn't meet. But both of us loved each other all that time, old sport, and you didn't know. I used to laugh sometimes"—but there was no laughter in his eyes—"to think that you didn't know."

"Oh—that's all." Tom tapped his thick fingers together like a clergyman and leaned back in his chair.

"You're crazy!" he exploded. "I can't speak about what happened five years ago, because I didn't know Daisy then—and I'll be damned if I see how you got within a mile of her unless you brought the groceries to the back door. But all the rest of that's a God Damned lie. Daisy loved me when she married me and she loves me now."

"No," said Gatsby, shaking his head.

"She does, though. The trouble is that sometimes she gets foolish ideas in her head and doesn't know what she's doing." He nodded sagely. "And what's more, I love Daisy too. Once in a while I go off on a spree and make a fool of myself, but I always come back, and in my heart I love her all the time."

"You're revolting," said Daisy. She turned to me, and her voice, dropping an octave lower, filled the room with thrilling scorn: "Do you know why we left Chicago? I'm surprised that they didn't treat you to the story of that little spree."

Gatsby walked over and stood beside her.

"Daisy, that's all over now," he said earnestly. "It doesn't matter any more. Just tell him the truth—that you never loved him—and it's all wiped out forever."

She looked at him blindly. "Why—how could I love him—possibly?"

"You never loved him."

She hesitated. Her eyes fell on Jordan and me with a sort of appeal, as though she realized at last what she was doing—and as though she had never, all along, intended doing anything at all. But it was done now. It was too late.

"I never loved him," she said, with perceptible reluctance.

"Not at Kapiolani?" demanded Tom suddenly.

"No."

From the ballroom beneath, muffled and suffocating chords were drifting up on hot waves of air.

"Not that day I carried you down from the Punch Bowl to keep your shoes dry?" There was a husky tenderness in his tone.... "Daisy?"

"Please don't." Her voice was cold, but the rancor was gone from it. She looked at Gatsby. "There, Jay," she said—but her hand as she tried to light a cigarette was trembling. Suddenly she threw the cigarette and the burning match on the carpet.

"Oh, you want too much!" she cried to Gatsby. "I love you now—isn't that enough? I can't help what's past." She began to sob helplessly. "I did love him once—but I loved you too."

Gatsby's eyes opened and closed.

"You loved me *too?*" he repeated.

"Even that's a lie," said Tom savagely. "She didn't know you were alive. Why—there're things between Daisy and me that you'll never know, things that neither of us can ever forget."

The words seemed to bite physically into Gatsby.

"I want to speak to Daisy alone," he insisted. "She's all excited now——"

"Even alone I can't say I never loved Tom," she admitted in a pitiful voice. "It wouldn't be true."

"Of course it wouldn't," agreed Tom.

She turned to her husband.

"As if it mattered to you," she said.

"Of course it matters. I'm going to take better care of you from now on."

"You don't understand," said Gatsby, with a touch of panic. "You're not going to take care of her any more."

"I'm not?" Tom opened his eyes wide and laughed. He could afford to control himself now. "Why's that?"

"Daisy's leaving you."

"Nonsense."

"I am, though," she said with a visible effort.

"She's not leaving me!" Tom's words suddenly leaned down over Gatsby. "Certainly not for a common swindler who'd have to steal the ring he put on her finger."

"I won't stand this!" cried Daisy. "Oh, please let's get out."

"Who are you, anyhow?" broke out Tom. "You're one of that bunch that hangs around with Meyer Wolfshiem—that much I happen to know. I've made a little investigation into your affairs—and I'll carry it further tomorrow."

"You can suit yourself about that, old sport," said Gatsby steadily.

"I found out what your 'drug-stores' were." He turned to us and spoke rapidly. "He and this Wolfshiem bought up a lot of side-street drug-stores here and in Chicago and sold grain alcohol over the counter. That's one of his little stunts. I picked him for a bootlegger the first time I saw him, and I wasn't far wrong."

"What about it?" said Gatsby politely. "I guess your friend Walter Chase wasn't too proud to come in on it."

"And you left him in the lurch, didn't you? You let him go to jail for a month over in New Jersey. God! You ought to hear Walter on the subject of *you*."

"He came to us dead broke. He was very glad to pick up some money, old sport."

"Don't you call me 'old sport'!" cried Tom. Gatsby said nothing. "Walter could have you up on the betting laws too, but Wolfshiem scared him into shutting his mouth."

That unfamiliar yet recognizable look was back again in Gatsby's face.

"That drug-store business was just small change," continued Tom slowly, "but you've got something on now that Walter's afraid to tell me about."

I glanced at Daisy, who was staring terrified between Gatsby and her husband, and at Jordan, who had begun to balance an invisible but absorbing object on the tip of her chin. Then I turned back to Gatsby—and was startled at his expression. He looked—and this is said in all contempt for the babbled slander of his garden—as if he had "killed a man." For a moment the set of his face could be described in just that fantastic way.

It passed, and he began to talk excitedly to Daisy, denying everything, defending his name against accusations that had not been made. But with every word she was drawing further and further into herself, so he gave that up, and only the dead dream fought on as the afternoon slipped away, trying to touch what was no longer tangible, struggling unhappily, undespairingly, toward that lost voice across the room.

The voice begged again to go.

"*Please*, Tom! I can't stand this any more."

Her frightened eyes told that whatever intentions, whatever courage she had had, were definitely gone.

"You two start on home, Daisy," said Tom. "In Mr. Gatsby's car."

She looked at Tom, alarmed now, but he insisted with magnanimous scorn.

"Go on. He won't annoy you. I think he realizes that his presumptuous little flirtation is over."

They were gone, without a word, snapped out, made accidental, isolated, like ghosts, even from our pity.

After a moment Tom got up and began wrapping the unopened bottle of whiskey in the towel.

"Want any of this stuff? Jordan? ... Nick?"

I didn't answer.

"Nick?" He asked again.

"What?"

"Want any?"

"No ... I just remembered that today's my birthday."

I was thirty. Before me stretched the portentous, menacing road of a new decade.

It was seven o'clock when we got into the coupé with him and started for Long Island. Tom talked incessantly, exulting and laughing, but his voice was as remote from Jordan and me as the foreign clamor on the sidewalk or the tumult of the elevated overhead. Human sympathy has its limits, and we were content to let all their tragic arguments fade with the city lights behind. Thirty—the promise of a decade of loneliness, a thinning list of single men to know, a thinning brief-case of enthusiasm, thinning hair. But there was Jordan beside me, who, unlike Daisy, was too wise ever to carry well-forgotten dreams from age to age. As we passed over the dark bridge her wan face fell lazily against my coat's shoulder and the formidable stroke of thirty died away with the reassuring pressure of her hand.

So we drove on toward death through the cooling twilight.

The young Greek, Michaelis, who ran the coffee joint beside the ashheaps was the principal witness at the inquest. He had slept through the heat until after five, when he strolled over to the garage, and found George Wilson sick in his office—really sick, pale as his own pale hair and shaking all over. Michaelis advised him to go to bed, but Wilson refused, saying that he'd miss a lot of business if he did. While his neighbor was trying to persuade him a violent racket broke out overhead.

"I've got my wife locked in up there," explained Wilson calmly. "She's going to stay there till the day after tomorrow, and then we're going to move away."

Michaelis was astonished; they had been neighbors for four years, and Wilson had never seemed faintly capable of such a statement. Generally he was one of these worn-out men: when he wasn't working, he sat on a chair in the doorway and stared at the people and the cars that passed along the road. When anyone spoke to him he invariably laughed in an agreeable, colorless way. He was his wife's man and not his own.

So naturally Michaelis tried to find out what had happened, but Wilson wouldn't say a word—instead he began to throw curious, suspicious glances at his visitor and ask him what he'd been doing at certain times on certain days. Just as the latter was getting uneasy, some workmen came past the door bound for his restaurant, and Michaelis took the opportunity to get away, intending to come back later. But he didn't. He supposed he forgot to, that's all. When he came outside again, a little after seven, he was reminded of the conversation because he heard Mrs. Wilson's voice, loud and scolding, downstairs in the garage.

"Beat me!" he heard her cry. "Throw me down and beat me, you dirty little coward!"

A moment later she rushed out into the dusk, waving her hands and shouting—before he could move from his door the business was over.

The "death car," as the newspapers called it, didn't stop; it came out of the gathering darkness, wavered tragically for a moment, and then disappeared around the next bend. Michaelis wasn't even sure of its color—he told the first policeman that it was light green. The other car, the one going toward New York, came to rest a hundred yards beyond, and its driver hurried back to where Myrtle Wilson, her life violently extinguished, knelt in the road and mingled her thick dark blood with the dust.

Michaelis and this man reached her first, but when they had torn open her shirtwaist, still damp with perspiration, they saw that her left breast was swinging loose like a flap, and there was no need to listen for the heart beneath. The mouth was wide open and ripped at the corners, as though she had choked a little in giving up the tremendous vitality she had stored so long.

We saw the three or four automobiles and the crowd when we were still some distance away.

"Wreck!" said Tom. "That's good. Wilson'll have a little business at last."

He slowed down, but still without any intention of stopping, until, as we came nearer, the hushed, intent faces of the people at the garage door made him automatically put on the brakes.

"We'll take a look," he said doubtfully, "just a look."

I became aware now of a hollow, wailing sound which issued incessantly from the garage, a sound which as we got out of the coupé and walked toward the door resolved itself into the words "Oh, my God!" uttered over and over in a gasping moan.

"There's some bad trouble here," said Tom excitedly.

He reached up on tiptoes and peered over a circle of heads into the garage, which was lit only by a yellow light in a swinging wire basket overhead. Then he made a harsh sound in his throat, and with a violent thrusting movement of his powerful arms pushed his way through.

The circle closed up again with a running murmur of expostulation; it was a minute before I could see anything at all. Then new arrivals disarranged the line, and Jordan and I were pushed suddenly inside.

Myrtle Wilson's body, wrapped in a blanket, and then in another blanket, as though she suffered from a chill in the hot night, lay on a work table by the wall, and Tom, with his back to us, was bending over it, motionless. Next to him stood a motorcycle policeman taking down names with much sweat and correction in a little book. At first I couldn't find the source of the high, groaning words that echoed clamorously through the bare garage—then I saw Wilson standing on the raised threshold of his office, swaying back and forth and holding to the doorposts with both hands. Some man was talking to him in a low voice and attempting, from time to time, to lay a hand on his shoulder, but Wilson neither heard nor saw. His eyes would drop slowly from the swinging light to the laden table by the wall, and then jerk back to the light again, and he gave out incessantly his high, horrible call:

"Oh, my Ga-od! Oh, my Ga-od! Oh, Ga-od! Oh, my Ga-od!"

Presently Tom lifted his head with a jerk and, after staring around the garage with glazed eyes, addressed a mumbled incoherent remark to the policeman.

"M-a-v—" the policeman was saying, "—o——"

"No, r—" corrected the man, "M-a-v-r-o——"

"Listen to me!" muttered Tom fiercely.

"r—" said the policeman, "o——"

"g——"

"g—" He looked up as Tom's broad hand fell sharply on his shoulder. "What you want, fella?"

"What happened?—that's what I want to know."

"Auto hit her. Ins'antly killed."

"Instantly killed," repeated Tom, staring.

"She ran out ina road. Son-of-a-bitch didn't even stopus car."

"There was two cars," said Michaelis, "one comin', one goin', see?"

"Going where?" asked the policeman keenly.

"One goin' each way. Well, she"—his hand rose toward the blankets but stopped half way and fell to his side—"she ran out there an' the one comin' from N'York knock right into her, goin' thirty or forty miles an hour."

"What's the name of this place here?" demanded the officer.

"Hasn't got any name."

A pale well-dressed negro stepped near.

"It was a yellow car," he said, "big yellow car. New."

"See the accident?" asked the policeman.

"No, but the car passed me down the road, going faster'n forty. Going fifty, sixty."

"Come here and let's have your name. Look out now. I want to get his name."

Some words of this conversation must have reached Wilson, swaying in the office door, for suddenly a new theme found voice among his gasping cries:

"You don't have to tell me what kind of car it was! I know what kind of car it was!"

Watching Tom, I saw the wad of muscle back of his shoulder tighten under his coat. He walked quickly over to Wilson and, standing in front of him, seized him firmly by the upper arms.

"You've got to pull yourself together," he said with soothing gruffness.

Wilson's eyes fell upon Tom; he started up on his tiptoes and then would have collapsed to his knees had not Tom held him upright.

"Listen," said Tom, shaking him a little. "I just got here a minute ago, from New York. I was bringing you that coupé we've been talking about. That yellow car I was driving this afternoon wasn't mine—do you hear? I haven't seen it all afternoon."

Only the negro and I were near enough to hear what he said, but the policeman caught something in the tone and looked over with truculent eyes.

"What's all that?" he demanded.

"I'm a friend of his." Tom turned his head but kept his hands firm on Wilson's body. "He says he knows the car that did it.... It was a yellow car."

Some dim impulse moved the policeman to look suspiciously at Tom.

"And what color's your car?"

"It's a blue car, a coupé."

"We've come straight from New York," I said.

Someone who had been driving a little behind us confirmed this, and the policeman turned away.

"Now, if you'll let me have that name again correct——"

Picking up Wilson like a doll, Tom carried him into the office, set him down in a chair, and came back.

"If somebody'll come here and sit with him," he snapped authoritatively. He watched while the two men standing closest glanced at each other and went unwillingly into the room. Then Tom shut the door on them and came down the single step, his eyes avoiding the table. As he passed close to me he whispered: "Let's get out."

Self-consciously, with his authoritative arms breaking the way, we pushed through the still gathering crowd, passing a hurried doctor, case in hand, who had been sent for in wild hope half an hour ago.

Tom drove slowly until we were beyond the bend—then his foot came down hard, and the coupé raced along through the night. In a little while I heard a low husky sob, and saw that the tears were overflowing down his face.

"The God Damn coward!" he whimpered. "He didn't even stop his car."

The Buchanans' house floated suddenly toward us through the dark rustling trees. Tom stopped beside the porch and looked up at the second floor, where two windows bloomed with light among the vines.

"Daisy's home," he said. As we got out of the car he glanced at me and frowned slightly.

"I ought to have dropped you in West Egg, Nick. There's nothing we can do tonight."

A change had come over him, and he spoke gravely, and with decision. As we walked across the moonlit gravel to the porch he disposed of the situation in a few brisk phrases.

"I'll telephone for a taxi to take you home, and while you're waiting you and Jordan better go in the kitchen and have them get you some supper—if you want any." He opened the door. "Come in."

"No, thanks. But I'd be glad if you'd order me the taxi. I'll wait outside."

Jordan put her hand on my arm.

"Won't you come in, Nick?"

"No, thanks."

I was feeling a little sick and I wanted to be alone. But Jordan lingered for a moment more.

"It's only half past nine," she said.

I'd be damned if I'd go in; I'd had enough of all of them for one day, and suddenly that included Jordan too. She must have seen something of this in my expression, for she turned abruptly away and ran up the porch steps into the house. I sat down for a few minutes with my head in my hands, until I heard the phone taken up inside and the butler's voice calling a taxi. Then I walked slowly down the drive away from the house, intending to wait by the gate.

I hadn't gone twenty yards when I heard my name and Gatsby stepped from between two bushes into the path. I must have felt pretty weird by that time, because I could think of nothing except the luminosity of his pink suit under the moon.

"What are you doing?" I inquired.

"Just standing here, old sport."

Somehow, that seemed a despicable occupation. For all I knew he was going to rob the house in a moment; I wouldn't have been surprised to see sinister faces, the faces of "Wolfshiem's people," behind him in the dark shrubbery.

"Did you see any trouble on the road?" he asked after a minute.

"Yes."

He hesitated.

"Was she killed?"

"Yes."

"I thought so; I told Daisy I thought so. It's better that the shock should all come at once. She stood it pretty well."

He spoke as if Daisy's reaction was the only thing that mattered.

"I got to West Egg by a side road," he went on, "and left the car in my garage. I don't think anybody saw us, but of course I can't be sure."

I disliked him so much by this time that I didn't find it necessary to tell him he was wrong.

"Who was the woman?" he inquired.

"Her name was Wilson. Her husband owns the garage. How the devil did it happen?"

"Well, I tried to swing the wheel—" He broke off, and suddenly I guessed at the truth.

"Was Daisy driving?"

"Yes," he said after a moment, "but of course I'll say I was. You see, when we left New York she was very nervous and she thought it would steady her to drive—and this woman rushed out at us just as we were passing a car coming the other way. It all happened in a minute, but it seemed to me that she wanted to speak to us, thought we were somebody she knew. Well, first Daisy turned away from the woman toward the other car, and then she lost her nerve and turned back. The second my hand reached the wheel I felt the shock—it must have killed her instantly."

"It ripped her open——"

"Don't tell me, old sport." He winced. "Anyhow—Daisy stepped on it. I tried to make her stop, but she couldn't, so I pulled on the emergency brake. Then she fell over into my lap and I drove on.

"She'll be all right tomorrow," he said presently. "I'm just going to wait here and see if he tries to bother her about that unpleasantness this afternoon. She's locked herself into her room, and if he tries any brutality she's going to turn the light out and on again."

"He won't touch her," I said. "He's not thinking about her."

"I don't trust him, old sport."

"How long are you going to wait?"

"All night, if necessary. Anyhow, till they all go to bed."

A new point of view occurred to me. Suppose Tom found out that Daisy had been driving. He might think he saw a connection in it—he might think anything. I looked at the house; there were two or three bright windows downstairs and the pink glow from Daisy's room on the second floor.

"You wait here," I said. "I'll see if there's any sign of a commotion."

I walked back along the border of the lawn, traversed the gravel softly, and tiptoed up the veranda steps. The drawing-room curtains were open, and I saw that the room was empty. Crossing the porch where we had dined that June night three months before, I came to a small rectangle of light which I guessed was the pantry window. The blind was drawn, but I found a rift at the sill.

Daisy and Tom were sitting opposite each other at the kitchen table, with a plate of cold fried chicken between them, and two bottles of ale. He was talking intently across the table at her, and in his earnestness his hand had fallen upon and covered her own. Once in a while she looked up at him and nodded in agreement.

They weren't happy, and neither of them had touched the chicken or the ale—and yet they weren't unhappy either. There was an unmistakable air of natural intimacy about the picture, and anybody would have said that they were conspiring together.

As I tiptoed from the porch I heard my taxi feeling its way along the dark road toward the house. Gatsby was waiting where I had left him in the drive.

"Is it all quiet up there?" he asked anxiously.

"Yes, it's all quiet." I hesitated. "You'd better come home and get some sleep."

He shook his head.

"I want to wait here till Daisy goes to bed. Good night, old sport."

He put his hands in his coat pockets and turned back eagerly to his scrutiny of the house, as though my presence marred the sacredness of the vigil. So I walked away and left him standing there in the moonlight—watching over nothing.

CHAPTER VIII

I COULDN'T sleep all night; a fog-horn was groaning incessantly on the Sound, and I tossed half sick between grotesque reality and savage, frightening dreams. Toward dawn I heard a taxi go up Gatsby's drive, and immediately I jumped out of bed and began to dress—I felt that I had something to tell him, something to warn him about, and morning would be too late.

Crossing his lawn, I saw that his front door was still open and he was leaning against a table in the hall, heavy with dejection or sleep.

"Nothing happened," he said wanly. "I waited, and about four o'clock she came to the window and stood there for a minute and then turned out the light."

His house had never seemed so enormous to me as it did that night when we hunted through the great rooms for cigarettes. We pushed aside curtains that were like pavilions, and felt over innumerable feet of dark wall for electric light switches—once I tumbled with a sort of splash upon the keys of a ghostly piano. There was an inexplicable amount of dust everywhere, and the rooms were musty, as though they hadn't been aired for many days. I found the humidor on an unfamiliar table, with two stale, dry cigarettes inside. Throwing open the French windows of the drawing-room, we sat smoking out into the darkness.

"You ought to go away," I said. "It's pretty certain they'll trace your car."

"Go away *now,* old sport?"

"Go to Atlantic City for a week, or up to Montreal."

He wouldn't consider it. He couldn't possibly leave Daisy until he knew what she was going to do. He was clutching at some last hope and I couldn't bear to shake him free.

It was this night that he told me the strange story of his youth with Dan Cody—told it to me because "Jay Gatsby" had broken up like glass against Tom's hard malice, and the long secret extravaganza was played out. I think that he would have acknowledged anything now, without reserve, but he wanted to talk about Daisy.

She was the first "nice" girl he had ever known. In various unrevealed capacities he had come in contact with such people, but always with indiscernible barbed wire between. He found her excitingly desirable. He went to her house, at first with other officers from Camp Taylor, then alone. It amazed him—he had never been in such a beautiful house before. But what gave it an air of breathless intensity was that Daisy lived there—it was as casual a thing to her as his tent out at camp was to him. There was a ripe mystery about it, a hint of bedrooms upstairs more beautiful and cool than other bedrooms, of gay and radiant activities taking place through its corridors, and of romances that were not musty and laid away already in lavender but fresh and breathing and redolent of this year's shining motor-cars and of dances whose flowers were scarcely withered. It excited him, too, that many men had already loved Daisy—it increased her value in his eyes. He felt their presence all about the house, pervading the air with the shades and echoes of still vibrant emotions.

But he knew that he was in Daisy's house by a colossal accident. However glorious might be his future as Jay Gatsby, he was at present a penniless young man without a past, and at any moment the invisible cloak of his uniform might slip from his shoulders. So he made the most of his time. He took what he could get, ravenously and unscrupulously—eventually he took Daisy one still October night, took her because he had no real right to touch her hand.

He might have despised himself, for he had certainly taken her under false pretenses. I don't mean that he had traded on his phantom millions, but he had deliberately given Daisy a sense of security; he let her believe that he was a person from much the same strata as herself—that he was fully able to take care of her. As a matter of fact, he had no such facilities—he had no comfortable family standing behind him, and he was liable at the whim of an impersonal government to be blown anywhere about the world.

But he didn't despise himself and it didn't turn out as he had imagined. He had intended, probably, to take what he could and go—but now he found that he had committed himself to the following of a grail. He knew that Daisy was extraordinary, but he didn't realize just how extraordinary a "nice" girl could be. She vanished into her rich house, into her rich, full life, leaving Gatsby—nothing. He felt married to her, that was all.

When they met again, two days later, it was Gatsby who was breathless, who was, somehow, betrayed. Her porch was bright with the bought luxury of star-shine; the wicker of the settee squeaked fashionably as she turned toward him and he kissed her curious and lovely mouth. She had caught a cold, and it made her voice huskier and more charming than ever, and Gatsby was overwhelmingly aware of the youth and mystery that wealth imprisons and preserves, of the freshness of many clothes, and of Daisy, gleaming like silver, safe and proud above the hot struggles of the poor.

"I can't describe to you how surprised I was to find out I loved her, old sport. I even hoped for a while that she'd throw me over, but she didn't, because she was in love with me too. She thought I knew a lot because I knew different things from her ... Well, there I was, way off my ambitions, getting deeper in love every minute, and all of a sudden I didn't care. What was the use of doing great things if I could have a better time telling her what I was going to do?"

On the last afternoon before he went abroad, he sat with Daisy in his arms for a long, silent time. It was a cold fall day, with fire in the room and her cheeks flushed. Now and then she moved and he changed his arm a little, and once he kissed her dark shining hair. The afternoon had made them tranquil for a while, as if to give them a deep memory for the long parting the next day promised. They had never been closer in their month of love, nor communicated more profoundly one with another, than when she brushed silent lips against his coat's shoulder or when he touched the end of her finger, gently, as though she were asleep.

He did extraordinarily well in the war. He was a captain before he went to the front, and following the Argonne battles he got his majority and the command of the divisional machine-guns. After the armistice he tried frantically to get home, but some complication or misunderstanding sent him to Oxford instead. He was worried now—there was a quality of nervous despair in Daisy's letters. She didn't see why he couldn't come. She was feeling the pressure of the world outside, and she wanted to see him and feel his presence beside her and be reassured that she was doing the right thing after all.

For Daisy was young and her artificial world was redolent of orchids and pleasant, cheerful snobbery and orchestras which set the rhythm of the year, summing up the sadness and suggestiveness of life in new tunes. All night the saxophones wailed the hopeless comment of the "Beale Street Blues" while a hundred pairs of golden and silver slippers shuffled the shining dust. At the gray tea hour there were always rooms that throbbed incessantly with this low, sweet fever, while fresh faces drifted here and there like rose petals blown by the sad horns around the floor.

Through this twilight universe Daisy began to move again with the season; suddenly she was again keeping half a dozen dates a day with half a dozen men, and drowsing asleep at dawn with the beads and chiffon of an evening dress tangled among dying orchids on the floor beside her bed. And all the time something within her was crying for a decision. She wanted her life shaped now, immediately—and the decision must be made by some force—of love, of money, of unquestionable practicality—that was close at hand.

That force took shape in the middle of spring with the arrival of Tom Buchanan. There was a wholesome bulkiness about his person and his position, and Daisy was flattered. Doubtless there was a certain struggle and a certain relief. The letter reached Gatsby while he was still at Oxford.

It was dawn now on Long Island and we went about opening the rest of the windows downstairs, filling the house with gray-turning, gold-turning light. The shadow of a tree fell abruptly across the dew and ghostly birds began to sing among the blue leaves. There was a slow, pleasant movement in the air, scarcely a wind, promising a cool, lovely day.

"I don't think she ever loved him." Gatsby turned around from a window and looked at me challengingly. "You must remember, old sport, she was very excited this afternoon. He told her those things in a way that frightened her—that made it look as if I was some kind of cheap sharper. And the result was she hardly knew what she was saying."

He sat down gloomily.

"Of course she might have loved him just for a minute, when they were first married—and loved me more even then, do you see?"

Suddenly he came out with a curious remark.

"In any case," he said, "it was just personal."

What could you make of that, except to suspect some intensity in his conception of the affair that couldn't be measured?

He came back from France when Tom and Daisy were still on their wedding trip, and made a miserable but irresistible journey to Louisville on the last of his army pay. He stayed there a week, walking the streets where their footsteps had clicked together through the November night and revisiting the out-of-the-way places to which they had driven in her white car. Just as Daisy's house had always seemed to him more mysterious and gay than other houses, so his idea of the city itself, even though she was gone from it, was pervaded with a melancholy beauty.

He left feeling that if he had searched harder, he might have found her—that he was leaving her behind. The day-coach—he was penniless now—was hot. He went out to the open vestibule and sat down on a folding chair, and the station slid away and the backs of unfamiliar buildings moved by. Then out into the spring fields, where a yellow trolley raced them for a minute with people in it who might once have seen the pale magic of her face along the casual street.

The track curved and now it was going away from the sun, which, as it sank lower, seemed to spread itself in benediction over the vanishing city where she had drawn her breath. He stretched out his hand desperately as if to snatch only a wisp of air, to save a fragment of the spot that she had made lovely for him. But it was all going by too fast now for his blurred eyes and he knew that he had lost that part of it, the freshest and the best, forever.

It was nine o'clock when we finished breakfast and went out on the porch. The night had made a sharp difference in the weather and there was an autumn flavor in the air. The gardener, the last one of Gatsby's former servants, came to the foot of the steps.

"I'm going to drain the pool today, Mr. Gatsby. Leaves'll start falling pretty soon, and then there's always trouble with the pipes."

"Don't do it today," Gatsby answered. He turned to me apologetically. "You know, old sport, I've never used that pool all summer?"

I looked at my watch and stood up.

"Twelve minutes to my train."

I didn't want to go to the city. I wasn't worth a decent stroke of work, but it was more than that—I didn't want to leave Gatsby. I missed that train, and then another, before I could get myself away.

"I'll call you up," I said finally.

"Do, old sport."

"I'll call you about noon."

We walked slowly down the steps.

"I suppose Daisy'll call too." He looked at me anxiously, as if he hoped I'd corroborate this.

"I suppose so."

"Well, good-by."

We shook hands and I started away. Just before I reached the hedge I remembered something and turned around.

"They're a rotten crowd," I shouted across the lawn. "You're worth the whole damn bunch put together."

I've always been glad I said that. It was the only compliment I ever gave him, because I disapproved of him from beginning to end. First he nodded politely, and then his face broke into that radiant and understanding smile, as if we'd been in ecstatic cahoots on that fact all the time. His gorgeous pink rag of a suit made a bright spot of color against the white steps, and I thought of the night when I first came to his ancestral home, three months before. The lawn and drive had been crowded with the faces of those who guessed at his corruption—and he had stood on those steps, concealing his incorruptible dream, as he waved them good-by.

I thanked him for his hospitality. We were always thanking him for that—I and the others.

"Good-by," I called. "I enjoyed breakfast, Gatsby."

Up in the city, I tried for a while to list the quotations on an interminable amount of stock, then I fell asleep in my swivel chair. Just before noon the phone woke me, and I started up with sweat breaking out on my forehead. It was Jordan Baker; she often called me up at this hour because the uncertainty of her own movements between hotels and clubs and private houses made her hard to find in any other way. Usually her voice came over the wire as something fresh and cool, as if a divot from a green golf-links had come sailing in at the office window, but this morning it seemed harsh and dry.

"I've left Daisy's house," she said. "I'm at Hempstead, and I'm going down to Southampton this afternoon."

Probably it had been tactful to leave Daisy's house, but the act annoyed me, and her next remark made me rigid.

"You weren't so nice to me last night."

"How could it have mattered then?"

Silence for a moment. Then:

"However—I want to see you."

"I want to see you, too."

"Suppose I don't go to Southampton, and come into town this afternoon?"

"No—I don't think this afternoon."

"Very well."

"It's impossible this afternoon. Various——"

We talked like that for a while, and then abruptly we weren't talking any longer. I don't know which of us hung up with a sharp click, but I know I didn't care. I couldn't have talked to her across a tea-table that day if I never talked to her again in this world.

I called Gatsby's house a few minutes later, but the line was busy. I tried four times; finally an exasperated Central told me the wire was being kept open for Long Distance from Detroit. Taking out my time-table, I drew a small circle around the three-fifty train. Then I leaned back in my chair and tried to think. It was just noon.

When I passed the ashheaps on the train that morning I had crossed deliberately to the other side of the car. I supposed there'd be a curious crowd around there all day with little boys searching for dark spots in the dust, and some garrulous man telling over and over what had happened, until it became less and less real even to him and he could tell it no longer, and Myrtle Wilson's tragic achievement was forgotten. Now I want to go back a little and tell what happened at the garage after we left there the night before.

They had difficulty in locating the sister, Catherine. She must have broken her rule against drinking that night, for when she arrived she was stupid with liquor and unable to understand that the ambulance had already gone to Flushing. When they convinced her of this, she immediately fainted, as if that was the intolerable part of the affair. Someone, kind or curious, took her in his car and drove her in the wake of her sister's body.

Until long after midnight a changing crowd lapped up against the front of the garage, while George Wilson rocked himself back and forth on the couch inside. For a while the door of the office was open, and everyone who came into the garage glanced irresistibly through it. Finally someone said it was a shame, and closed the door. Michaelis and several other men were with him; first, four or five men, later two or three men. Still later Michaelis had to ask the last stranger to wait there fifteen minutes longer, while he went back to his own place and made a pot of coffee. After that, he stayed there alone with Wilson until dawn.

About three o'clock the quality of Wilson's incoherent muttering changed—he grew quieter and began to talk about the yellow car. He announced that he had a way of finding out whom the yellow car belonged to, and then he blurted out that a couple of months ago his wife had come from the city with her face bruised and her nose swollen.

But when he heard himself say this, he flinched and began to cry "Oh, my God!" again in his groaning voice. Michaelis made a clumsy attempt to distract him.

"How long have you been married, George? Come on there, try and sit still a minute and answer my question. How long have you been married?"

"Twelve years."

"Ever had any children? Come on, George, sit still—I asked you a question. Did you ever have any children?"

The hard brown beetles kept thudding against the dull light, and whenever Michaelis heard a car go tearing along the road outside it sounded to him like the car that hadn't stopped a few hours before. He didn't like to go into the garage, because the work bench was stained where the body had been lying, so he moved uncomfortably around the office—he knew every object in it before morning—and from time to time sat down beside Wilson trying to keep him more quiet.

"Have you got a church you go to sometimes, George? Maybe even if you haven't been there for a long time? Maybe I could call up the church and get a priest to come over and he could talk to you, see?"

"Don't belong to any."

"You ought to have a church, George, for times like this. You must have gone to church once. Didn't you get married in a church? Listen, George, listen to me. Didn't you get married in a church?"

"That was a long time ago."

The effort of answering broke the rhythm of his rocking—for a moment he was silent. Then the same half knowing, half bewildered look came back into his faded eyes.

"Look in the drawer there," he said, pointing at the desk.

"Which drawer?"

"That drawer—that one."

Michaelis opened the drawer nearest his hand. There was nothing in it but a small, expensive dog-leash, made of leather and braided silver. It was apparently new.

"This?" he inquired, holding it up.

Wilson stared and nodded.

"I found it yesterday afternoon. She tried to tell me about it, but I knew it was something funny."

"You mean your wife bought it?"

"She had it wrapped in tissue paper on her bureau."

Michaelis didn't see anything odd in that, and he gave Wilson a dozen reasons why his wife might have bought the dog-leash. But conceivably Wilson had heard some of these same explanations before, from Myrtle, because he began saying "Oh, my God!" again in a whisper—his comforter left several explanations in the air.

"Then he killed her," said Wilson. His mouth dropped open suddenly.

"Who did?"

"I have a way of finding out."

"You're morbid, George," said his friend. "This has been a strain to you and you don't know what you're saying. You'd better try and sit quiet till morning."

"He murdered her."

"It was an accident, George."

Wilson shook his head. His eyes narrowed and his mouth widened slightly with the ghost of a superior "Hm!"

"I know," he said definitely. "I'm one of these trusting fellas and I don't think any harm to *no*body, but when I get to know a thing I know it. It was the man in that car. She ran out to speak to him and he wouldn't stop."

Michaelis had seen this too, but it hadn't occurred to him that there was any special significance in it. He believed that Mrs. Wilson had been running away from her husband, rather than trying to stop any particular car.

"How could she of been like that?"

"She's a deep one," said Wilson, as if that answered the question. "Ah-h-h——"

He began to rock again, and Michaelis stood twisting the leash in his hand.

"Maybe you got some friend that I could telephone for, George?"

This was a forlorn hope—he was almost sure that Wilson had no friend: there was not enough of him for his wife. He was glad a little later when he noticed a change in the room, a blue quickening by the window, and realized that dawn wasn't far off. About five o'clock it was blue enough outside to snap off the light.

Wilson's glazed eyes turned out to the ashheaps, where small gray clouds took on fantastic shapes and scurried here and there in the faint dawn wind.

"I spoke to her," he muttered, after a long silence. "I told her she might fool me but she couldn't fool God. I took her to the window"—with an effort he got up and walked to the rear window and leaned with his face pressed against it—"and I said 'God knows what you've been doing, everything you've been doing. You may fool me, but you can't fool God!'"

Standing behind him, Michaelis saw with a shock that he was looking at the eyes of Doctor T. J. Eckleburg, which had just emerged, pale and enormous, from the dissolving night.

"God sees everything," repeated Wilson.

"That's an advertisement," Michaelis assured him. Something made him turn away from the window and look back into the room. But Wilson stood there a long time, his face close to the window pane, nodding into the twilight.

By six o'clock Michaelis was worn out, and grateful for the sound of a car stopping outside. It was one of the watchers of the night before who had promised to come back, so he cooked breakfast for three, which he and the other man ate together. Wilson was quieter now, and Michaelis went home to sleep; when he awoke four hours later and hurried back to the garage, Wilson was gone.

His movements—he was on foot all the time—were afterward traced to Port Roosevelt and then to Gad's Hill, where he bought a sandwich that he didn't eat, and a cup of coffee. He must have been tired and walking slowly, for he didn't reach Gad's Hill until noon. Thus far there was no difficulty in accounting for his time—there were boys who had seen a man "acting sort of crazy," and motorists at whom he stared oddly from the side of the road. Then for three hours he disappeared from view. The police, on the strength of what he said to Michaelis, that he "had a way of finding out," supposed that he spent that time going from garage to garage thereabouts, inquiring for a yellow car. On the other hand, no garage man who had seen him ever came forward, and perhaps he had an easier, surer way of finding out what he wanted to know. By half past two he was in West Egg, where he asked someone the way to Gatsby's house. So by that time he knew Gatsby's name.

At two o'clock Gatsby put on his bathing suit and left word with the butler that if anyone phoned word was to be brought to him at the pool. He stopped at the garage for a pneumatic mattress that had amused his guests during the summer, and the chauffeur helped him pump it up. Then he gave instructions that the open car wasn't to be taken out under any circumstances—and this was strange, because the front right fender needed repair.

Gatsby shouldered the mattress and started for the pool. Once he stopped and shifted it a little, and the chauffeur asked him if he needed help, but he shook his head and in a moment disappeared among the yellowing trees.

No telephone message arrived, but the butler went without his sleep and waited for it until four o'clock—until long after there was anyone to give it to if it came. I have an idea that Gatsby himself didn't believe it would come, and perhaps he no longer cared. If that was true he must have felt that he had lost the old warm world, paid a high price for living too long with a single dream. He must have looked up at an unfamiliar sky through frightening leaves and shivered as he found what a grotesque thing a rose is and how raw the sunlight was upon the scarcely created grass. A new world, material without being real, where poor ghosts, breathing dreams like air, drifted fortuitously about ... like that ashen, fantastic figure gliding toward him through the amorphous trees.

The chauffeur—he was one of Wolfshiem's protégés—heard the shots—afterward he could only say that he hadn't thought anything much about them. I drove from the station directly to Gatsby's house and my rushing anxiously up the front steps was the first thing that alarmed anyone. But they knew then, I firmly believe. With scarcely a word said, four of us, the chauffeur, butler, gardener, and I, hurried down to the pool.

There was a faint, barely perceptible movement of the water as the fresh flow from one end urged its way toward the drain at the other. With little ripples that were hardly the shadows of waves, the laden mattress moved irregularly down the pool. A small gust of wind that scarcely corrugated the surface was enough to disturb its accidental course with its accidental burden. The touch of a cluster of leaves revolved it slowly, tracing, like the leg of a compass, a thin red circle in the water.

It was after we started with Gatsby toward the house that the gardener saw Wilson's body a little way off in the grass, and the holocaust was complete.

CHAPTER IX

AFTER two years I remember the rest of that day, and that night and the next day, only as an endless drill of police and photographers and newspaper men in and out of Gatsby's front door. A rope stretched across the main gate and a policeman by it kept out the curious, but little boys soon discovered that they could enter through my yard, and there were always a few of them clustered open-mouthed about the pool. Someone with a positive manner, perhaps a detective, used the expression "madman" as he bent over Wilson's body that afternoon, and the adventitious authority of his voice set the key for the newspaper reports next morning.

Most of those reports were a nightmare—grotesque, circumstantial, eager, and untrue. When Michaelis's testimony at the inquest brought to light Wilson's suspicions of his wife I thought the whole tale would shortly be served up in racy pasquinade—but Catherine, who might have said anything, didn't say a word. She showed a surprising amount of character about it too—looked at the coroner with determined eyes under that corrected brow of hers, and swore that her sister had never seen Gatsby, that her sister was completely happy with her husband, that her sister had been into no mischief whatever. She convinced herself of it, and cried into her handkerchief, as if the very suggestion was more than she could endure. So Wilson was reduced to a man "deranged by grief" in order that the case might remain in its simplest form. And it rested there.

But all this part of it seemed remote and unessential. I found myself on Gatsby's side, and alone. From the moment I telephoned news of the catastrophe to West Egg Village, every surmise about him, and every practical question, was referred to me. At first I was surprised and confused; then, as he lay in his house and didn't move or breathe or speak, hour upon hour, it grew upon me that I was responsible, because no one else was interested—interested, I mean, with that intense personal interest to which everyone has some vague right at the end.

I called up Daisy half an hour after we found him, called her instinctively and without hesitation. But she and Tom had gone away early that afternoon, and taken baggage with them.

"Left no address?"

"No."

"Say when they'd be back?"

"No."

"Any idea where they are? How I could reach them?"

"I don't know. Can't say."

I wanted to get somebody for him. I wanted to go into the room where he lay and reassure him: "I'll get somebody for you, Gatsby. Don't worry. Just trust me and I'll get somebody for you——"

Meyer Wolfshiem's name wasn't in the phone book. The butler gave me his office address on Broadway, and I called Information, but by the time I had the number it was long after five, and no one answered the phone.

"Will you ring again?"

"I've rung them three times."

"It's very important."

"Sorry. I'm afraid no one's there."

I went back to the drawing-room and thought for an instant that they were chance visitors, all these official people who suddenly filled it. But, as they drew back the sheet and looked at Gatsby with unmoved eyes, his protest continued in my brain:

"Look here, old sport, you've got to get somebody for me. You've got to try hard. I can't go through this alone."

Someone started to ask me questions, but I broke away and going upstairs looked hastily through the unlocked parts of his desk—he'd never told me definitely that his parents were dead. But there was nothing—only the picture of Dan Cody, a token of forgotten violence, staring down from the wall.

Next morning I sent the butler to New York with a letter to Wolfshiem, which asked for information and urged him to come out on the next train. That request seemed superfluous when I wrote it. I was sure he'd start when he saw the newspapers, just as I was sure there'd be a wire from Daisy before noon—but neither a wire nor Mr. Wolfshiem arrived; no one arrived except more police and photographers and newspaper men. When the butler brought back Wolfshiem's answer I began to have a feeling of defiance, of scornful solidarity between Gatsby and me against them all.

Dear Mr. Carraway. This has been one of the most terrible shocks of my life to me I hardly can believe it that it is true at all. Such a mad act as that man did should make us all think. I cannot come down now as I am tied up in some very important business and cannot get mixed up in this thing now. If there is anything I can do a little later let me know in a letter by Edgar. I hardly know where I am when I hear about a thing like this and am completely knocked down and out.

Yours truly

MEYER WOLFSHIEM

and then hasty addenda beneath:

Let me know about the funeral etc do not know his family at all.

When the phone rang that afternoon and Long Distance said Chicago was calling I thought this would be Daisy at last. But the connection came through as a man's voice, very thin and far away.

"This is Slagle speaking ..."

"Yes?" The name was unfamiliar.

"Hell of a note, isn't it? Get my wire?"

"There haven't been any wires."

"Young Parke's in trouble," he said rapidly. "They picked him up when he handed the bonds over the counter. They got a circular from New York giving 'em the numbers just five minutes before. What d'you know about that, hey? You never can tell in these hick towns——"

"Hello!" I interrupted breathlessly. "Look here—this isn't Mr. Gatsby. Mr. Gatsby's dead."

There was a long silence on the other end of the wire, followed by an exclamation ... then a quick squawk as the connection was broken.

I think it was on the third day that a telegram signed Henry C. Gatz arrived from a town in Minnesota. It said only that the sender was leaving immediately and to postpone the funeral until he came.

It was Gatsby's father, a solemn old man, very helpless and dismayed, bundled up in a long cheap ulster against the warm September day. His eyes leaked continuously with excitement, and when I took the bag and umbrella from his hands he began to pull so incessantly at his sparse gray beard that I had difficulty in getting off his coat. He was on the point of collapse, so I took him into the music-room and made him sit down while I sent for something to eat. But he wouldn't eat, and the glass of milk spilled from his trembling hand.

"I saw it in the Chicago newspaper," he said. "It was all in the Chicago newspaper. I started right away."

"I didn't know how to reach you."

His eyes, seeing nothing, moved ceaselessly about the room.

"It was a madman," he said. "He must have been mad."

"Wouldn't you like some coffee?" I urged him.

"I don't want anything. I'm all right now, Mr.——"

"Carraway."

"Well, I'm all right now. Where have they got Jimmy?"

I took him into the drawing-room, where his son lay, and left him there. Some little boys had come up on the steps and were looking into the hall; when I told them who had arrived, they went reluctantly away.

After a little while Mr. Gatz opened the door and came out, his mouth ajar, his face flushed slightly, his eyes leaking isolated and unpunctual tears. He had reached an age where death no longer has the quality of ghastly surprise, and when he looked around him now for the first time and saw the height and splendor of the hall and the great rooms opening out from it into other rooms, his grief began to be mixed with an awed pride. I helped him to a bedroom upstairs; while he took off his coat and vest I told him that all arrangements had been deferred until he came.

"I didn't know what you'd want, Mr. Gatsby——"

"Gatz is my name."

"—Mr. Gatz. I thought you might want to take the body West."

He shook his head.

"Jimmy always liked it better down East. He rose up to his position in the East. Were you a friend of my boy's, Mr.——?"

"We were close friends."

"He had a big future before him, you know. He was only a young man, but he had a lot of brain power here."

He touched his head impressively, and I nodded.

"If he'd of lived, he'd of been a great man. A man like James J. Hill. He'd of helped build up the country."

"That's true," I said, uncomfortably.

He fumbled at the embroidered coverlet, trying to take it from the bed, and lay down stiffly—was instantly asleep.

That night an obviously frightened person called up, and demanded to know who I was before he would give his name.

"This is Mr. Carraway," I said.

"Oh!" He sounded relieved. "This is Klipspringer."

I was relieved too, for that seemed to promise another friend at Gatsby's grave. I didn't want it to be in the papers and draw a sightseeing crowd, so I'd been calling up a few people myself. They were hard to find.

"The funeral's tomorrow," I said. "Three o'clock, here at the house. I wish you'd tell anybody who'd be interested."

"Oh, I will," he broke out hastily. "Of course I'm not likely to see anybody, but if I do."

His tone made me suspicious.

"Of course you'll be there yourself."

"Well, I'll certainly try. What I called up about is——"

"Wait a minute," I interrupted. "How about saying you'll come?"

"Well, the fact is—the truth of the matter is that I'm staying with some people up here in Greenwich, and they rather expect me to be with them tomorrow. In fact, there's a sort of picnic or something. Of course I'll do my very best to get away."

I ejaculated an unrestrained "Huh!" and he must have heard me, for he went on nervously:

"What I called up about was a pair of shoes I left there. I wonder if it'd be too much trouble to have the butler send them on. You see, they're tennis shoes, and I'm sort of helpless without them. My address is care of B. F.——"

I didn't hear the rest of the name, because I hung up the receiver.

After that I felt a certain shame for Gatsby—one gentleman to whom I telephoned implied that he had got what he deserved. However, that was my fault, for he was one of those who used to sneer most bitterly at Gatsby on the courage of Gatsby's liquor, and I should have known better than to call him.

The morning of the funeral I went up to New York to see Meyer Wolfshiem; I couldn't seem to reach him any other way. The door that I pushed open, on the advice of an elevator boy, was marked "The Swastika Holding Company," and at first there didn't seem to be anyone inside. But when I'd shouted "hello" several times in vain, an argument broke out behind a partition, and presently a lovely Jewess appeared at an interior door and scrutinized me with black hostile eyes.

"Nobody's in," she said. "Mr. Wolfshiem's gone to Chicago."

The first part of this was obviously untrue, for someone had begun to whistle "The Rosary," tunelessly, inside.

"Please say that Mr. Carraway wants to see him."

"I can't get him back from Chicago, can I?"

At this moment a voice, unmistakably Wolfshiem's, called "Stella!" from the other side of the door.

"Leave your name on the desk," she said quickly. "I'll give it to him when he gets back."

"But I know he's there."

She took a step toward me and began to slide her hands indignantly up and down her hips.

"You young men think you can force your way in here any time," she scolded. "We're getting sickantired of it. When I say he's in Chicago, he's in Chi*ca*go."

I mentioned Gatsby.

"Oh-h!" She looked at me all over again. "Will you just— What was your name?"

She vanished. In a moment Meyer Wolfshiem stood solemnly in the doorway, holding out both hands. He drew me into his office, remarking in a reverent voice that it was a sad time for all of us, and offered me a cigar.

"My memory goes back to when first I met him," he said. "A young major just out of the army and covered over with medals he got in the war. He was so hard up he had to keep on wearing his uniform because he couldn't buy some regular clothes. First time I saw him was when he come into

Winebrenner's poolroom at Forty-third Street and asked for a job. He hadn't eat anything for a couple of days. 'Come on have some lunch with me,' I sid. He ate more than four dollars' worth of food in half an hour."

"Did you start him in business?" I inquired.

"Start him! I made him."

"Oh."

"I raised him up out of nothing, right out of the gutter. I saw right away he was a fine-appearing, gentlemanly young man, and when he told me he was an Oggsford I knew I could use him good. I got him to join up in the American Legion and he used to stand high there. Right off he did some work for a client of mine up to Albany. We were so thick like that in everything"—he held up two bulbous fingers—"always together."

I wondered if this partnership had included the World's Series transaction in 1919.

"Now he's dead," I said after a moment. "You were his closest friend, so I know you'll want to come to his funeral this afternoon."

"I'd like to come."

"Well, come then."

The hair in his nostrils quivered slightly, and as he shook his head his eyes filled with tears.

"I can't do it—I can't get mixed up in it," he said.

"There's nothing to get mixed up in. It's all over now."

"When a man gets killed I never like to get mixed up in it in any way. I keep out. When I was a young man it was different—if a friend of mine died, no matter how, I stuck with them to the end. You may think that's sentimental, but I mean it—to the bitter end."

I saw that for some reason of his own he was determined not to come, so I stood up.

"Are you a college man?" he inquired suddenly.

For a moment I thought he was going to suggest a "gonnegtion," but he only nodded and shook my hand.

"Let us learn to show our friendship for a man when he is alive and not after he is dead," he suggested. "After that my own rule is to let everything alone."

When I left his office the sky had turned dark and I got back to West Egg in a drizzle. After changing my clothes I went next door and found Mr. Gatz walking up and down excitedly in the hall. His pride in his son and in his son's possessions was continually increasing and now he had something to show me.

"Jimmy sent me this picture." He took out his wallet with trembling fingers. "Look there."

It was a photograph of the house, cracked in the corners and dirty with many hands. He pointed out every detail to me eagerly. "Look there!" and then sought admiration from my eyes. He had shown it so often that I think it was more real to him now than the house itself.

"Jimmy sent it to me. I think it's a very pretty picture. It shows up well."

"Very well. Had you seen him lately?"

"He come out to see me two years ago and bought me the house I live in now. Of course we was broke up when he run off from home, but I see now there was a reason for it. He knew he had a big future in front of him. And ever since he made a success he was very generous with me."

He seemed reluctant to put away the picture, held it for another minute, lingeringly, before my eyes. Then he returned the wallet and pulled from his pocket a ragged old copy of a book called "Hopalong Cassidy."

"Look here, this is a book he had when he was a boy. It just shows you."

He opened it at the back cover and turned it around for me to see. On the last fly-leaf was printed the word SCHEDULE, and the date September 12, 1906. And underneath:

Rise from bed	6.00	A.M.
Dumbbell exercise and wall-scaling	6.15–6.30	"
Study electricity, etc.	7.15–8.15	"
Work	8.30–4.30	P.M.
Baseball and sports	4.30–5.00	"
Practice elocution, poise and how to attain it	5.00–6.00	"
Study needed inventions	7.00–9.00	"

GENERAL RESOLVES

No wasting time at Shafters or [a name, indecipherable]
No more smokeing or chewing.
Bath every other day
Read one improving book or magazine per week
Save $5.00 [crossed out] $3.00 per week
Be better to parents

"I come across this book by accident," said the old man. "It just shows you, don't it?"

"It just shows you."

"Jimmy was bound to get ahead. He always had some resolves like this or something. Do you notice what he's got about improving his mind? He was always great for that. He told me I et like a hog once, and I beat him for it."

He was reluctant to close the book, reading each item aloud and then looking eagerly at me. I think he rather expected me to copy down the list for my own use.

A little before three the Lutheran minister arrived from Flushing, and I began to look involuntarily out the windows for other cars. So did Gatsby's father. And as the time passed and the servants came in and stood waiting in the hall, his eyes began to blink anxiously, and he spoke of the rain in a worried, uncertain way. The minister glanced several times at his watch, so I took him aside and asked him to wait for half an hour. But it wasn't any use. Nobody came.

About five o'clock our procession of three cars reached the cemetery and stopped in a thick drizzle beside the gate—first a motor-hearse, horribly black and wet, then Mr. Gatz and the minister and I in the limousine, and a little later four or five servants and the postman from West Egg, in Gatsby's station wagon, all wet to the skin. As we started through the gate into the cemetery I heard a car stop and then the sound of someone splashing after us over the soggy ground. I looked around. It was the man with owl-eyed glasses whom I had found marvelling over Gatsby's books in the library one night three months before.

I'd never seen him since then. I don't know how he knew about the funeral, or even his name. The rain poured down his thick glasses, and he took them off and wiped them to see the protecting canvas unrolled from Gatsby's grave.

I tried to think about Gatsby then for a moment, but he was already too far away, and I could only remember, without resentment, that Daisy hadn't sent a message or a flower. Dimly I heard someone murmur "Blessed are the dead that the rain falls on," and then the owl-eyed man said "Amen to that," in a brave voice.

We straggled down quickly through the rain to the cars. Owl Eyes spoke to me by the gate.

"I couldn't get to the house," he remarked.

"Neither could anybody else."

"Go on!" He started. "Why, my God! they used to go there by the hundreds."

He took off his glasses and wiped them again, outside and in.

"The poor son-of-a-bitch," he said.

One of my most vivid memories is of coming back West from prep school and later from college at Christmas time. Those who went farther than Chicago would gather in the old dim Union Station at six o'clock of a December evening, with a few Chicago friends, already caught up into their own holiday gayeties, to bid them a hasty good-by. I remember the fur coats of the girls returning from Miss This-or-That's and the chatter of frozen breath and the hands waving overhead as we caught sight of old acquaintances, and the matchings of invitations: "Are you going to the Ordways'? the Herseys'? the Schultzes'?" and the long green tickets clasped tight in our gloved hands. And last the murky yellow cars of the Chicago, Milwaukee & St. Paul railroad looking cheerful as Christmas itself on the tracks beside the gate.

When we pulled out into the winter night and the real snow, our snow, began to stretch out beside us and twinkle against the windows, and the dim lights of small Wisconsin stations moved by, a sharp wild brace came suddenly into the air. We drew in deep breaths of it as we walked back from dinner through the cold vestibules, unutterably aware of our identity with this country for one strange hour, before we melted indistinguishably into it again.

That's my Middle West—not the wheat or the prairies or the lost Swede towns, but the thrilling returning trains of my youth, and the street lamps and sleigh bells in the frosty dark and the shadows of holly wreaths thrown by lighted windows on the snow. I am part of that, a little solemn with the feel of those long winters, a little complacent from growing up in the Carraway house in a city where dwellings are still called through decades by a family's name. I see now that this has been a story of the West, after all—Tom and Gatsby, Daisy and Jordan and I, were all Westerners, and perhaps we possessed some deficiency in common which made us subtly unadaptable to Eastern life.

Even when the East excited me most, even when I was most keenly aware of its superiority to the bored, sprawling, swollen towns beyond the Ohio, with their interminable inquisitions which spared only the children and the very old—even then it had always for me a quality of distortion. West Egg, especially, still figures in my more fantastic dreams. I see it as a night scene by El Greco: a hundred houses, at once conventional and grotesque, crouching under a sullen, overhanging sky and a lustreless moon. In the foreground four solemn men in dress suits are walking along the sidewalk with a stretcher on which lies a drunken woman in a white evening dress. Her hand, which dangles over the side, sparkles cold with jewels. Gravely the men turn in at a house—the wrong house. But no one knows the woman's name, and no one cares.

After Gatsby's death the East was haunted for me like that, distorted beyond my eyes' power of correction. So when the blue smoke of brittle leaves was in the air and the wind blew the wet laundry stiff on the line I decided to come back home.

There was one thing to be done before I left, an awkward, unpleasant thing that perhaps had better have been let alone.

But I wanted to leave things in order and not just trust that obliging and indifferent sea to sweep my refuse away. I saw Jordan Baker and talked over and around what had happened to us together, and what had happened afterward to me, and she lay perfectly still, listening, in a big chair.

She was dressed to play golf, and I remember thinking she looked like a good illustration, her chin raised a little jauntily, her hair the color of an autumn leaf, her face the same brown tint as the fingerless glove on her knee. When I had finished she told me without comment that she was engaged to another man. I doubted that, though there were several she could have married at a nod of her head, but I pretended to be surprised. For just a minute I wondered if I wasn't making a mistake, then I thought it all over again quickly and got up to say good-by.

"Nevertheless you did throw me over," said Jordan suddenly. "You threw me over on the telephone. I don't give a damn about you now, but it was a new experience for me, and I felt a little dizzy for a while."

We shook hands.

"Oh, and do you remember"—she added—"a conversation we had once about driving a car?"

"Why—not exactly."

"You said a bad driver was only safe until she met another bad driver? Well, I met another bad driver, didn't I? I mean it was careless of me to make such a wrong guess. I thought you were rather an honest, straightforward person. I thought it was your secret pride."

"I'm thirty," I said. "I'm five years too old to lie to myself and call it honor."

She didn't answer. Angry, and half in love with her, and tremendously sorry, I turned away.

One afternoon late in October I saw Tom Buchanan. He was walking ahead of me along Fifth Avenue in his alert, aggressive way, his hands out a little from his body as if to fight off interference, his head moving sharply here and there, adapting itself to his restless eyes. Just as I slowed up to avoid overtaking him he stopped and began frowning into the windows of a jewelry store. Suddenly be saw me and walked back, holding out his hand.

"What's the matter, Nick? Do you object to shaking hands with me?"

"Yes. You know what I think of you."

"You're crazy, Nick," he said quickly. "Crazy as hell. I don't know what's the matter with you."

"Tom," I inquired, "what did you say to Wilson that afternoon?"

He stared at me without a word, and I knew I had guessed right about those missing hours. I started to turn away, but he took a step after me and grabbed my arm.

"I told him the truth," he said. "He came to the door while we were getting ready to leave, and when I sent down word that we weren't in he tried to force his way upstairs. He was crazy enough to kill me if I hadn't told him who owned the car. His hand was on a revolver in his pocket every minute he was in the house—" He broke off defiantly. "What if I did tell him? That fellow had it coming to him. He threw dust into your eyes just like he did in Daisy's, but he was a tough one. He ran over Myrtle like you'd run over a dog and never even stopped his car."

There was nothing I could say, except the one unutterable fact that it wasn't true.

"And if you think I didn't have my share of suffering—look here, when I went to give up that flat and saw that damn box of dog biscuits sitting there on the sideboard, I sat down and cried like a baby. By God it was awful——"

I couldn't forgive him or like him, but I saw that what he had done was, to him, entirely justified. It was all very careless and confused. They were careless people, Tom and Daisy—they smashed up things and creatures and then retreated back into their money or their vast carelessness, or whatever it was that kept them together, and let other people clean up the mess they had made....

I shook hands with him; it seemed silly not to, for I felt suddenly as though I were talking to a child. Then he went into the jewelry store to buy a pearl necklace—or perhaps only a pair of cuff buttons—rid of my provincial squeamishness forever.

Gatsby's house was still empty when I left—the grass on his lawn had grown as long as mine. One of the taxi drivers in the village never took a fare past the entrance gate without stopping for a minute and pointing inside; perhaps it was he who drove Daisy and Gatsby over to East Egg the night of the accident, and perhaps he had made a story about it all his own. I didn't want to hear it and I avoided him when I got off the train.

I spent my Saturday nights in New York because those gleaming, dazzling parties of his were with me so vividly that I could still hear the music and the laughter, faint and incessant, from his garden, and the cars going up and down his drive. One night I did hear a material car there, and saw its lights stop at his front steps. But I didn't investigate. Probably it was some final guest who had been away at the ends of the earth and didn't know that the party was over.

On the last night, with my trunk packed and my car sold to the grocer, I went over and looked at that huge incoherent failure of a house once more. On the white steps an obscene word, scrawled by some boy with a piece of brick, stood out clearly in the moonlight, and I erased it, drawing my shoe raspingly along the stone. Then I wandered down to the beach and sprawled out on the sand.

Most of the big shore places were closed now and there were hardly any lights except the shadowy, moving glow of a ferryboat across the Sound. And as the moon rose higher the inessential houses began to melt away until gradually I became aware of the old island here that flowered once for Dutch sailors' eyes—a fresh, green breast of the new world. Its vanished trees, the trees that had made way for Gatsby's house, had once pandered in whispers to the last and greatest of all human dreams; for a transitory enchanted moment man must have held his breath in the presence of this continent, compelled into an aesthetic contemplation he neither understood nor desired, face to face for the last time in history with something commensurate to his capacity for wonder.

And as I sat there brooding on the old, unknown world, I thought of Gatsby's wonder when he first picked out the green light at the end of Daisy's dock. He had come a long way to this blue lawn, and his dream must have seemed so close that he could hardly fail to grasp it. He did not know that it was already behind him, somewhere back in that vast obscurity beyond the city, where the dark fields of the republic rolled on under the night.

Gatsby believed in the green light, the orgastic future that year by year recedes before us. It eluded us then, but that's no matter—tomorrow we will run faster, stretch out our arms farther.... And one fine morning——

So we beat on, boats against the current, borne back ceaselessly into the past.

HISTORY OF THE TEXT

Composition and publication

In June 1922, F. Scott Fitzgerald began work on a novel, then untitled, that he would publish three years later as *The Great Gatsby*. He was living at White Bear Lake, a resort town near St. Paul, Minnesota. He had recently sent revised proof to Scribner's for *Tales of the Jazz Age*, his second collection of short stories. He began now to think about his next novel. On June 20, he wrote to Maxwell Perkins, his editor at Scribner's, that the new novel would have a "catholic element" and would be set in "the middle west and New York of 1885."[1] Fitzgerald worked on the manuscript for this novel intermittently during 1922 and 1923 but was dissatisfied with what he was producing. At this point he was writing in an omniscient voice; Nick Carraway had not yet emerged as the narrator.

In the early spring of 1924, Fitzgerald took a new approach. He allowed Nick to tell the story and placed the action in

[1] *Dear Scott/Dear Max: The Fitzgerald–Perkins Correspondence*, ed. John Kuehl and Jackson R. Bryer (New York: Charles Scribner's Sons, 1971): 61.

a fictionalized version of Great Neck, New York, where he was then living. He composed three chapters in March and April; later in April he and his wife and daughter sailed to France for an extended stay. While living on the French Riviera during the summer and early fall of 1924, Fitzgerald continued to work on the narrative, composing in longhand and working with typists, often through several drafts, to produce a setting copy for the publisher. On October 27, he sent a full typescript of the novel to Perkins via transatlantic mail.

Perkins had the novel typeset, in monotype, at the Scribner Press. Two sets of galley proofs, a working set and a final set, were pulled and sent to Fitzgerald in late December. In their correspondence, which survives, Perkins offered praise to Fitzgerald but also made suggestions about bringing Jay Gatsby's character into better focus. Perkins' advice prompted Fitzgerald to make heavy revisions to the text. In the galleys he moved much material about, changed the order of chapters, cut lengthy passages of exposition, and composed new description and dialogue. In this revision, he made Nick a more likeable character than he had been in the initial text, provided information about Jay Gatsby's early life, and added suggestions about the sources of his money. Fitzgerald also chose a title: *The Great Gatsby*.

The author mailed a set of galleys bearing his final revisions to Scribner's in February 1925. (He kept the working galleys for himself; they survive among his papers at Princeton.) He was now living in Italy; there was not enough time for the publisher to send another round of proofs to him there. Perkins took over at this point, supervising the galley revisions and seeing the novel through the press. Fitzgerald made matters more difficult by continuing to send in revisions, by letter and cable, until almost the day of publication. Perkins and his colleagues at Scribner's did a commendable job; the novel was published on schedule, on April 10, 1925. Some 20,870 copies were printed by the initial run of the presses. For each copy, the sheets were folded and gathered into fourteen unsigned gatherings of eight leaves each. These were case-bound in dark green linen, with blind-stamping on the front cover and gold-stamping on the spine. The endpapers were of white wove stock. The top and bottom edges of the text block were trimmed, the fore edge untrimmed. The price for one copy was $2.00.[2]

Dust jacket

During a visit to the Scribner's offices in April 1924, shortly before he departed for Europe, Fitzgerald saw a painting, a gouache on paper, by the artist Francis Cugat. This painting, which depicts a woman's eyes floating over an amusement-park scene at night, caught Fitzgerald's attention. He asked that the image be reserved for the dust jacket of the novel he had in progress. "For Christs sake don't give anyone that jacket you're saving for me," he reminded Perkins in a letter sent from France in late August. "I've written it into the book" (*Dear Scott/Dear Max*, 76). Fitzgerald probably took the inspiration for Doctor T. J. Eckleburg's eyes on page 28 of the Centennial edition from Cugat's painting. The front panel of the Scribner's jacket is reproduced in the section of plates for this edition.

[2] For a full analysis of the text of the first edition, the reader should consult the prefatory and back matter for *The Great Gatsby: A Variorum Edition*, ed. James L. W. West III (Cambridge and New York: Cambridge University Press, 2019). Physical details of the first printing are taken from Matthew J. Bruccoli, *F. Scott Fitzgerald: A Descriptive Bibliography*, rev. ed. (Pittsburgh: University of Pittsburgh Press, 1987): 64.

Title

Fitzgerald was not altogether satisfied with *The Great Gatsby* as a title. During composition he had considered several other titles: "Among the Ash Heaps and Millionaires," "Gold-Hatted Gatsby," "Trimalchio," "Trimalchio in West Egg," "The High-Bouncing Lover," "On the Road to West Egg," and "Gatsby." On March 19, three weeks before publication, he sent this cable to Perkins: "CRAZY ABOUT TITLE UNDER THE RED WHITE AND BLUE STOP WHART WOULD DELAY BE." Perkins answered the next day: "Advertised and sold for April tenth publication. Change suggested would mean some weeks delay, very great psychological damage. Think irony is far more effective under less leading title. Everyone likes present title. Urge we keep it." Fitzgerald conceded in a March 22 cable: "YOURE RIGHT."[3] The novel was published as *The Great Gatsby*.

Emoluments and reputation

Writing was Fitzgerald's calling, his vocation, but it was also his profession. He wrote for money, and he made a great deal of it from *The Great Gatsby*. Sales of the book version were disappointing (ca. 22,000 copies) but still yielded some $7,000 in royalties. Syndicate, stage, and movie rights brought in a great deal more—approximately $26,000. Altogether, Fitzgerald's earnings for *The Great Gatsby* during 1925–6 translate into more than $450,000 in buying power today. After its initial run at the bookshops, *The Great Gatsby* became a backlist title,

[3] A facsimile of the March 19 cable, with the typo "WHART" for "WHAT," is reproduced in *Correspondence of F. Scott Fitzgerald*, ed. Matthew J. Bruccoli, Margaret M. Duggan, and Susan Walker (New York: Random House, 1980): 153.

selling only a few copies each year. The last royalty statement Fitzgerald received during his lifetime (dated August 1, 1940) reported the sale of only seven copies during the preceding twelve months. Fitzgerald died on December 21, 1940. In the years that followed, his reputation underwent a revival. *The Great Gatsby* in particular won a following among teachers, students, and readers. Over time, the novel has come to be regarded as a foundational text in American literature. It has been interpreted by generations of critics, taught in high-school and college classrooms, and read by millions of readers.

Later printings and editions

The textual history of *The Great Gatsby* is complicated. Six alterations in the electrotype plates were introduced for a second printing, executed in August 1925. Four of these changes were requested by Fitzgerald; the other two were corrections of typographical errors. The six alterations for the second printing are listed below by page and line number in the Centennial text. The first reading is from the first printing; the second reading (which follows the bracket) is from the second printing.

53.23 chatter [echolalia
101.20 northern [southern
139.21 it's [its
140.2 away [away.
172.19 sick in tired [sickantired
177.11 Union Street station [Union Station

A seventh alteration in the text appears first in a set of duplicate plates that were cast and shipped to Chatto & Windus in London for its "edition" of *The Great Gatsby*, published in February 1926. The change is the correction of "self-absorbtion" to "self-absorption" at 101.6 of the Centennial text.

Fitzgerald penciled more than thirty revisions, all of them stylistic, onto the pages of his personal copy of *The Great Gatsby*. This copy survives among his papers at Princeton. The changes do not, however, appear to have resulted from a thorough revision of the text for a new typesetting. They seem rather to have been made from time to time, according to no pattern, as Fitzgerald reread portions of the text. These changes have been incorporated into several subsequent editions of the novel, including the Centennial text.[4]

The second edition of *The Great Gatsby* (i.e., the second typesetting) was published in 1941, the year after Fitzgerald's death, in a volume with *The Last Tycoon*, the novel he had in progress when he died, and with five of his best short stories. This edition was edited by Edmund Wilson, a friend from Fitzgerald's years at Princeton who had become a prominent literary critic.[5] The appearance of this 1941 edition did much to resurrect Fitzgerald's reputation and to make *The Great Gatsby* available to a new generation of readers. Wilson, however, took liberties with the text. Among the changes: the epigraph was omitted; the dedication to Fitzgerald's wife, Zelda Sayre, was dropped; several lines of text were left out; the word "orgastic" on the last page was altered to "orgiastic." Most editions of the novel published during the following fifty years took the Wilson text as their starting point and reproduced these errors.

[4] Changes marked in Fitzgerald's copy were first introduced into the text by the critic Malcolm Cowley for a sub-edition of *The Great Gatsby* included in *Modern Standard Authors: Three Novels of F. Scott Fitzgerald*, published by Charles Scribner's Sons in 1953. For lists of Fitzgerald's alterations, and of additional changes made by Cowley, see the Cambridge Variorum edition, pp. xxxvii–xxxviii, 227–8.

[5] *The Last Tycoon, An Unfinished Novel … Together with The Great Gatsby and Selected Stories*, ed. Edmund Wilson (New York: Charles Scribner's Sons, 1941).

Copyright on *The Great Gatsby* expired on January 1, 2021. The novel is now in the public domain. As of this writing, more than forty new editions have appeared. These include inexpensive paperbacks, gift editions, and student editions. Many of the errors that entered the text during its long history of publication are still afloat in these new editions. Five of the new editions, for example, leave out the epigraph, and seventeen omit the dedication to Zelda. Several of the new editions add their own sophistications and "improvements."[6]

The Centennial edition

In 2019, Cambridge University Press published a variorum edition of *The Great Gatsby* as the eighteenth and final volume of the Cambridge Edition of the Works of F. Scott Fitzgerald. The variorum text is based on the surviving manuscripts and proofs and the first two printings. It includes the alterations in Fitzgerald's copy of the novel but does not incorporate the changes introduced by Wilson in the 1941 edition. The variorum traces the history of the text from its inception in 1922 through initial publication and numerous subsequent typesettings until 2018. The variorum includes an extensive apparatus listing alterations and errors in major editions subsequent to the first. New editions of *The Great Gatsby* will continue to appear in the years to come; the Cambridge variorum, however, is the text of record. The Centennial edition presents the variorum text.

[6] For a review of the post-2021 editions, see James L. W. West III, "Proliferating in the Public Domain: New Editions of *The Great Gatsby*," *F. Scott Fitzgerald Review* 19 (2021): 222–38. A longer version of this review appears in West, *Business Is Good: F. Scott Fitzgerald, Professional Author* (University Park, PA: Penn State Press, 2023): 148–65.

SELECTED EDITIONS OF THE NOVEL

Primary editions

The Great Gatsby. New York: Charles Scribner's Sons, 1925. The first edition.*

The Last Tycoon, An Unfinished Novel … Together with The Great Gatsby and Selected Stories. Edited by Edmund Wilson. New York: Charles Scribner's Sons, 1941.

The Great Gatsby. Edited by Matthew J. Bruccoli. Cambridge and New York: Cambridge University Press, 1991.

The Great Gatsby: A Variorum Edition. Edited by James L. W. West III. Cambridge and New York: Cambridge University Press, 2019.

* Copies of the original first edition, first printing, of *The Great Gatsby* have for many years been among the most desirable and scarce of the modern firsts offered on the rare book market. In August 2023, for example, the twelve copies without jacket listed for sale by dealers ranged in price from $3,000 to $12,500, depending on condition. Only two copies in dust jacket were listed: one (in a repaired jacket) for $55,000 and the other (in a near-fine jacket) for $85,000.

Other editions

Full-color digital reproductions of both the manuscript and the revised galley proofs of *The Great Gatsby* are available on the Special Collections website, Princeton University Library.

The Great Gatsby: A Facsimile of the Manuscript. Edited by Matthew J. Bruccoli. Washington, DC: Microcard Editions Books, 1973.

The Great Gatsby: The Revised and Rewritten Galleys. Edited by Matthew J. Bruccoli. New York and London: Garland Publishing, Inc., 1990. Facsimile of the revised galley proofs.

The Great Gatsby. New York: Collectors Reprints/First Edition Library, 1991. Photo-facsimile of the first-impression text. Green cloth, enclosed in a facsimile of the first-edition dust jacket.

Trimalchio: An Early Version of The Great Gatsby. Edited by James L. W. West III. Cambridge and New York: Cambridge University Press, 2000. The text of the unrevised galley proofs, with editorial emendations.

The Great Gatsby. Cambremer, France: Éditions des Saints Pères, 2017. Facsimile of the manuscript.

The Great Gatsby: An Edition of the Manuscript. Edited by James L. W. West III and Don C. Skemer. Cambridge and New York: Cambridge University Press, 2018. The unemended manuscript text.

ANNOTATIONS AND IDENTIFICATIONS

Many of the references in *The Great Gatsby*—to persons, places, popular songs, works of literature, public figures, entertainers, and social customs—are unfamiliar to current readers. These references are identified and annotated below. The annotations are keyed to the Centennial text by page and line number.

9.10 sent a substitute] The Enrollment Act of 1863 made it possible for men from the Northern states to hire a substitute in order to avoid conscription into the Union Army.

9.14 I graduated from New Haven] "New Haven," for Nick, is a casual way of referring to Yale University in New Haven, Connecticut.

10.4 eighty a month] In 1922, the year in which the novel is set, $80 would have had the approximate value of $1,300 today (ca. 2023).

11.15–16 the less fashionable of the two] East Egg and West Egg are meant to suggest Manhasset Neck (old money) and Great Neck (new money) on Long Island. In the manuscript of the novel, Jordan gives Tom a description of West Egg (with a

Fitzgerald misspelling): "Most expensive town on Long Island. Full of moving picture people, playrites, singers and cartoonists and kept women. You'd love it." (See Frontispiece.) From October 1922 until April 1924, Fitzgerald rented a house on Great Neck and lived there with his wife and young daughter.

13.22 the same senior society] Every spring, the six senior societies at Yale each elected fifteen rising seniors to membership. Being chosen by a society was a significant honor. Members of the societies maintained friendships with each other into their adult lives.

16.21 Miss Baker] During Nick's college years, young men and women of the high bourgeoisie addressed each other as "Mr." and "Miss" until they became better acquainted. Nick still observes these customs in the novel. In Chapter II, however, Myrtle insists "after the first drink" that she and Nick use first names.

18.32 'The Rise of the Colored Empires'] Tom is trying to remember the title of *The Rising Tide of Color against White World-Supremacy*, a book published in 1920 by Lothrop Stoddard (1883–1950), an American historian and white supremacist. Stoddard believed that a racial world war would break out if Africans and Asians were allowed to migrate to western countries.

21.19–20 Cunard or White Star Line] The two major British transatlantic passenger lines of the period. The Cunard liners included the *Mauretania*, the *Aquitania*, and the *Berengaria*; the White Star liners, which could be identified by their black-topped funnels, included the *Olympic*, the *Britannic*, and the *Titanic*.

23.21 the Saturday Evening Post] This popular middle-class magazine was Fitzgerald's major outlet for short fiction during the peak earning years of his career.

24.7 *Jor*dan Baker] Here Fitzgerald has brought together the names of two automobile companies, both of which manufactured sporty vehicles for women drivers. The Jordan Motor Car Company was known for its stylish runabouts; the Baker Motor Vehicle Company specialized in electric two-seaters.

24.10 rotogravure pictures] The "rotogravure," an illustrated supplement found in most Sunday newspapers, featured photographs of celebrities, society people, stage and movie stars, and sports figures (such as Jordan). Rotogravure images were printed from intaglio cylinders mounted on rotary presses.

24.10–11 Asheville and Hot Springs and Palm Beach] These luxury resorts, located in North Carolina, Arkansas, and Florida, were known for their golf courses, which would have been familiar to Jordan.

31.10 Town Tattle] A fictional magazine. Fitzgerald's readers would have thought of *Town Topics*, a gossip sheet that specialized in scandalous stories about the wealthy and famous. (See the plate section for a color image.)

31.22 John D. Rockefeller] Rockefeller (1839–1937) founded the Standard Oil Company in 1870. He was the wealthiest man in America during the 1920s and was widely known for his philanthropy.

33.16–17 "Simon Called Peter"] The British author Robert Keable (1887–1927) published this semi-scandalous novel in the US in 1921. The protagonist, an army chaplain, loses his ideals during the First World War. (See the plate section for a color image.)

36.18 Montauk Point] This area, at the easternmost tip of Long Island, is known for its lighthouse, erected in 1796, and for its wildlife and natural scenery.

36.26–27 a cousin of Kaiser Wilhelm's] Wilhelm II (1859–1941), known as "Kaiser Bill" in the popular press, was the ruler of the German Empire and the Kingdom of Prussia from 1888 to 1918. His military alliance with Austria-Hungary led to the involvement of Germany in the First World War. (See the plate section for an image.)

42.4 Pennsylvania Station] Penn Station, then the largest train terminal in New York City, was bounded by 31st and 33rd Streets and Seventh and Eighth Avenues. The architect Charles Follen McKim (1847–1909) designed Penn Station to resemble the Baths of Caracalla in Rome. The building no longer stands; it was demolished in 1963.

42.4 the morning Tribune] This New York newspaper, conservative in politics, was founded by Horace Greely in 1841. In 1924, the *Tribune* merged with the *New York Herald* to form the *New York Herald–Tribune*. Gatsby reads a much more racy sheet—the *Journal*. See the gloss at **86.22.**

43.7 aquaplanes] Before the advent of water-skiing, aquaplaning was a popular water sport. Participants rode on flat boards called "aquaplanes," towed by a motorboat. (See the plate section for an image.)

45.11–12 moving her hands like Frisco] The woman is mimicking the dancing style of Joe Frisco (1889–1958), a 1920s comedian famous for inventing a soft-shoe shuffle called the "Frisco Dance."

45.15–16 Gilda Gray's understudy from the Follies] Gilda Gray (1901–59), a popular dancer and cabaret singer of the period, has been credited with inventing the Shimmy. ("I'm shaking my shimmy, that's what I'm doing.")

50.2 "Stoddard Lectures"] John L. Stoddard (1850–1931), a popular speaker, used the stereopticon, an early image-projection device, during his lectures. The lectures were issued in a series of bound volumes beginning in 1897. They were aimed at middlebrow audiences and would have been among the volumes that a book supplier might have placed on the shelves of Gatsby's library. Lothrop Stoddard, mentioned in the annotation for 18.32, was the son of John L. Stoddard.

50.4 a regular Belasco] The Broadway dramatist and producer David Belasco (1853–1931) was known for creating lifelike illusions on stage. He is remembered for his productions of *Lord Chumley* (1888) and *The Girl of the Golden West* (1905).

50.6 didn't cut the pages] During the 1920s, some books were still issued with untrimmed edges. One would read these books with a paper knife or letter-opener ready at hand, separating the leaves as one progressed. Owl Eyes is suggesting that Gatsby's books have been purchased and shelved but are unread.

51.21 hydroplane] A hydroplane (not an aquaplane, glossed earlier at 43.7) is an aircraft that can take off and land on water.

60.8 the Yale Club] The Yale Club, at the corner of Vanderbilt and East 44th Street, is a private establishment for graduates and faculty of Yale University. It is centrally located, near Grand Central Station and (then as now) close to fashionable shops and restaurants.

60.14 the old Murray Hill Hotel] This traditional hotel, with late Victorian architecture and decor, had one entrance on Park Avenue and another on 40th Street.

63.6–7 nephew to Von Hindenburg] During the First World War, Paul von Hindenburg (1847–1934) was field marshal of the German armed forces. He served as president of the Weimar Republic after the war.

66.12 balancing himself on the dashboard] In cars of this period, the "dashboard" was a narrow platform beneath each door. It was later called a "running-board."

68.21 Argonne Forest] This campaign in northeastern France was the most important of the engagements participated in by American troops in the First World War. Fighting in the Argonne Forest commenced in late September 1918 and ended in November. The success of the US forces against the Germans helped to bring about the armistice that ended the war on November 11.

68.21–25 so far forward ... Lewis guns] Gatsby's exploits bring to mind the story of the "Lost Battalion," a unit of the 77th Division that fought in the Meuse-Argonne Forest Offensive. The battalion advanced beyond its flank support but held its ground. Of the 554 men in the battalion, only 194 survived. The Lewis gun was a one-man air-cooled machine gun with a circular cartridge drum.

68.28 Montenegro] During the First World War, Montenegro, a small sovereign state on the Adriatic, was among the Allied Powers. After the Treaty of Versailles, it was absorbed by Yugoslavia.

69.15 Trinity Quad] Trinity College, Oxford, is one of the largest of the colleges of the university. The photograph would have been taken in its main quadrangle.

69.22 the Grand Canal] This major waterway, known as the *Canalazzo*, winds like an inverted letter S through the city of Venice. Palaces belonging to wealthy Venetian families lined the Grand Canal.

72.11 "Highballs?"] This whiskey drink, mixed with ginger ale or soda water, is served in a tall glass over ice. The date is 1922; Prohibition was in force but was largely ignored in metropolitan establishments.

72.20 The old Metropole] Gatsby speaks this line. Wolfshiem's recollections, which begin on the next line, are based on the murder of the gangster Herman Rosenthal on July 16, 1912, at the Metropole Hotel, 147 West 43rd Street.

75.17 the man who fixed the World's Series] Arnold Rothstein (1882–1928), the original for Wolfshiem, was a gambler and racketeer. He was said to have fixed the 1919 World's Series in the infamous "Black Sox" scandal.

76.16 the Plaza Hotel] The Plaza, luxurious and fashionable, is located at Fifth Avenue and 59th Street, across from Central Park. (See the plate section for an image.)

77.31 after the armistice] This agreement specified that fighting should stop on November 11, 1918, at 11:00 a.m. This was the eleventh hour of the eleventh day of the eleventh month (Matthew 20:1–16).

80.5 a Victoria] Nick and Jordan are riding in a horse-drawn carriage called a "Victoria." This vehicle had a calash top and a perch for the driver in front.

80.10 I'm the Sheik of Araby.] These lyrics are from the 1921 hit song "The Sheik of Araby." Readers might also have been reminded of *The Sheik*, a 1921 silent movie that starred Rudolph Valentino (1895–1926), the first "Latin lover" screen idol. (See the plate section for a color image of the sheet music.)

86.22 The Journal] The *New York Evening Journal*, which sold for 1 cent, was a Hearst newspaper known for its sensationalist reporting and its daily comic-strip page. Nick reads the *Tribune*, a more conservative newspaper (**42.4**).

86.32 Clay's "Economics"] Gatsby holds a copy of *Economics: An Introduction for the General Reader*, first published in the US in 1918. The author, British economist and lecturer Henry Clay (1883–1954), was primarily concerned with redistributing wealth to the lower levels of society—surely an ironic touch here.

87.28 Castle Rackrent] The regional novel *Castle Rackrent* (1800), by the Anglo-Irish novelist Maria Edgeworth (1767–1849), recounts the misadventures of three generations of Irish landowners named Rackrent.

90.19–20 like Kant at his church steeple] Immanuel Kant (1724–1804), the German philosopher best known for *The Critique of Pure Reason* (1781), was said to gaze at a church steeple visible from the windows of his writing room while contemplating metaphysical matters.

93.9 "the Merton College Library"] The library at Merton College, Oxford, is considered to be among the most beautiful at the university. The library at Cottage Club (Fitzgerald's club at Princeton) is modeled on the Merton library. (See the plate section for a color image.)

93.18 an Adam study] "Adam style" furniture, ornate and neoclassical, was developed by the Scottish brothers James and Robert Adam.

95.25 The pompadour!] Hair in a pompadour was swept upward from the sides and forehead. The construction was held in place with hair gel or oil. The style was popular with young men in the 1910s—but not with young men in Daisy's social class.

97.4 "The Love Nest"] This popular song was first heard in *Mary*, a hit Broadway show in 1920. A sample: "Just a love nest, / Cozy with charm, / Like a dove nest, / Down on a farm ... Better than a palace with a gilded dome, / Is a love nest / You can call home." The lyrics that follow seven lines on are from "Ain't We Got Fun" (1921). In the third from last line, Klipspringer sings the variant "children" for "poorer."

100.3–4 underground pipe-line] A popular myth during the years of Prohibition was that liquor was being run through an underground pipe-line from Canada into the United States. Illegal alcohol did indeed enter the country from Canada; the lengthy border was difficult to police.

101.19 St. Olaf's] This small institution in Northfield, Minnesota (properly St. Olaf College) was founded by Norwegian Lutherans in 1874.

102.2 Madame de Maintenon] Françoise d'Aubigné, Marquise de Maintenon (1635–1719), became the second wife of Louis XIV (1638–1715) in 1683. Pious and narrow-minded, she influenced the king during his final years.

110.27 "Three o'Clock in the Morning"] This song by Julián Robledo was popular during the early 1920s. Paul Whiteman's orchestra recorded an instrumental version on the Victor label in 1922.

115.3 Trimalchio] Fitzgerald is referring to "Trimalchio's Feast," a chapter in the *Satyricon*, by the Roman author Petronius (ca. AD 27–66). Trimalchio is a freed slave who has grown wealthy. He gives ostentatious parties, with food, drink, and gifts for the guests. Many of them do not know his name and speak slightingly of him when he is absent from the room. The narrator of "Trimalchio's Feast" is Encolpius, an observer and recorder who resembles Nick. "Trimalchio" and "Trimalchio in West Egg" were among the titles that Fitzgerald considered before settling on *The Great Gatsby*. The penultimate version of the novel, taken from the unrevised galley proofs, was published under the title *Trimalchio* by Cambridge University Press in 2000.

117.3–4 National Biscuit Company] Nick refers here to the whistle from a large Nabisco plant in Long Island City.

120.9 preceding four gin rickeys] This cooling drink is made from gin, fruit syrup, lime juice, and selzer. A gin rickey is served in a lowball glass over ice, often with a wedge of lime.

123.16–17 You can buy anything at a drug-store nowadays.] Some Prohibition-era drug-stores engaged in bootlegging. Tom means to imply that Gatsby is no more than a bootlegger.

125.4 Tom threw on both brakes] Most automobiles during the 1920s were equipped with both hand brakes and pedal-operated brakes. Later in the novel, just after Daisy has run down Myrtle, Gatsby pulls on the hand brakes to stop his yellow car.

129.32 Biloxi, Tennessee] This city is located in Harrison County, Mississippi, on the Gulf Coast. Daisy, who is upset, places Biloxi in Tennessee.

134.17–21 Kapiolani ... the Punch Bowl] Kapiolani is a park in Hawaii; the Punch Bowl is an extinct volcano crater on Honolulu. Both are popular spots for hikers and sightseers.

153.19 "Beale Street Blues"] This blues tune by the songwriter and pianist W. C. Handy (1873–1958) was first issued as sheet music in 1917.

158.12 an exasperated Central] During the early 1920s, telephones had no dialing mechanisms. One spoke to a "Central" operator and gave the number; the operator then placed the call using a switchboard. Long-distance calls, which usually passed through several interchanges, had to be cleared in advance.

F. Scott and Zelda Fitzgerald, ca. 1922. Princeton University Library.

James Rennie and Florence Eldridge as Gatsby and Daisy, onstage in the 1926 Broadway adaptation of the novel by the playwright Owen Davis. New York Public Library for the Performing Arts.

Photograph of bearer

Description of bearer

Height 5 feet 8 1/2 inches
Hair blond
Eyes green
Distinguishing marks or features

Place of birth St. Paul, Minn.
Date of birth Sept. 24, 1896
Occupation author

F. Scott Fitzgerald
Signature of bearer

Fitzgerald family passport.
Princeton University Library.

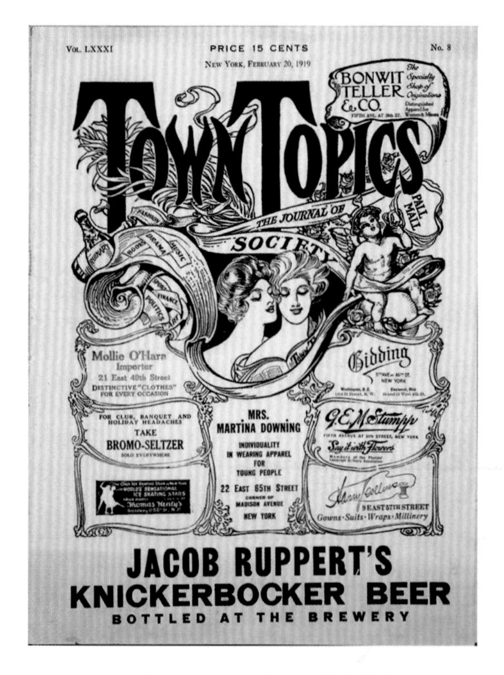

Town Topics, a New York gossip and scandal sheet (*Town Tattle* in Chapter II).

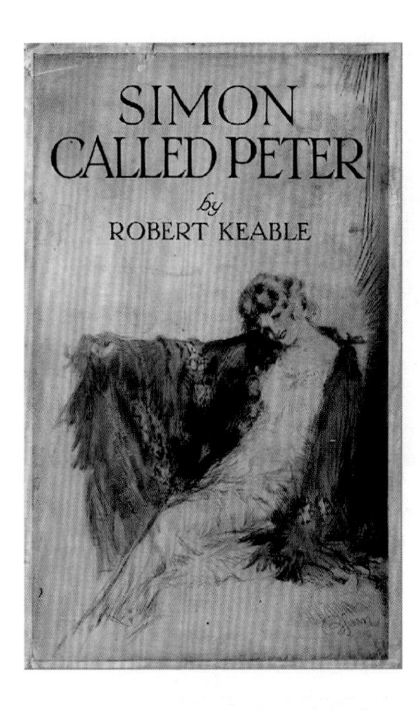

Dust jacket, Robert Keable, *Simon Called Peter* (1921). A risqué novel that Nick finds in Tom and Myrtle's love nest.

Aquaplaning, from Chapter III: "… while his two motor-boats slit the waters of the Sound, drawing aquaplanes over cataracts of foam."

Contemporary photograph of the library at University Cottage Club, Fitzgerald's club at Princeton. This library is patterned after the library at Merton College, Oxford. The library in Gatsby's mansion (Owl Eyes examines the books there) is also an imitation of the Merton College Library.

Sheet music for "Come Along," sung by the Follies star Gilda Gray (1922). One of the guests at Gatsby's first party, in Chapter III of the novel, is rumored to be her understudy.

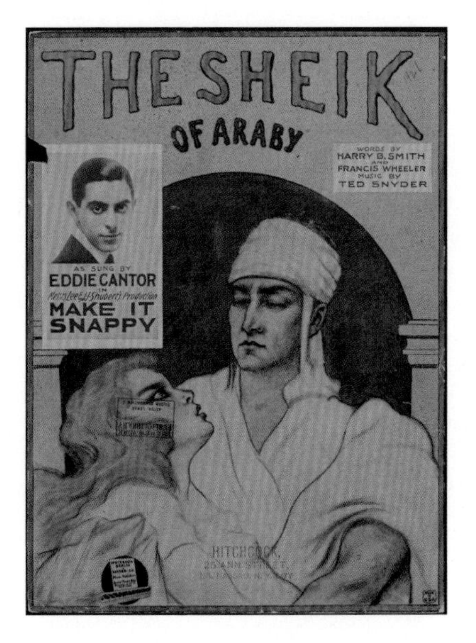

Poster for *The Sheik*, a 1921 movie starring the "Latin lover" Rudolph Valentino. In Chapter IV of Fitzgerald's novel, children playing in Central Park sing lyrics from "The Sheik of Araby," a popular song of that year. Romantic young men during the 1920s were sometimes called "sheiks."

The Plaza Hotel, ca. 1925. At Fifth Avenue and 59th Street, across from the southeast corner of Central Park. This is the scene of the confrontation between Tom and Gatsby.

Wilhelm II (1859–1941) ruled Germany and Prussia during the First World War. Jay Gatsby is rumored to be "a cousin of Kaiser Wilhelm's."

Photo courtesy of Getty Images.

Paul von Hindenburg (1847–1934). Prussian-German field marshal and statesman von Hindenburg, in military uniform, 1918. Gatsby is also said to be a "nephew to Von Hindenburg."

Photo courtesy of the Estate of Emil Bieber / Klaus.

The Seelbach Hotel, Louisville, Kentucky, where Tom and Daisy have their wedding in June 1919.

James J. Hill, a railroad executive and financier from St. Paul, Minnesota, Fitzgerald's home town. In Chapter IX, Gatsby's father thinks that his son might have become "a great man … like James J. Hill."

Photo courtesy of Heritage Images / Getty Images.

Clarence E. Mulford, *Hopalong Cassidy* (1910). The book in which Jimmy Gatz sets down his "Schedule" (Chapter IX).

Poster for the 1926 silent movie of *The Great Gatsby*, starring Warner Baxter as Gatsby, Lois Wilson as Daisy, Neil Hamilton as Nick, and Georgia Hale as Myrtle.

El Greco, *View of Toledo*, ca. 1600. Nick's dreams in Chapter IX are haunted by "a night scene by El Greco." Metropolitan Museum of Art, New York City.

(14)

~~around so possessively at every object that I thought~~ ~~asked if she lived here whereupon Myrtle told~~ ~~me haughtily that she lived with a girl friend. This~~ [inquiry] ~~seemed to insult everyone present, even Tom, and I~~ ~~was told haughtily that this "belonged to Tom and~~ ~~Myrtle Catherine shouldn't~~ But when ~~I asked her she shook her head in a~~ shocked way ~~and told me she lived with a girl friend~~ [just off Riverside Drive].

Mrs. Wilson had changed her ~~clothes~~ [costume] some time before and was now attired in an ~~elaborate~~ ~~aftern~~ elaborate afternoon dress of cream colored chiffon which gave out a continual russel as she ~~moved from room to~~ [swept about the] room. With ~~the change~~ [The influence of the dress] her personality had changed also. The intense vitality, ~~that so amazing~~ [that had seemed] in the garage ~~that it seemed like~~ [like] a scarcely restrained lust, was converted into ~~an absurd haughtiness~~ [vehement hauteur]. Her laughter, her gestures her ~~sentences~~ [assertions] became more [transparently] affected ~~with~~ [moment] ~~every~~ [by] moment and as she expanded the rooms grew ~~seemed to grow~~ smaller ~~and smaller~~ around her. ~~until I wondered how she could breathe at all~~ until she seemed to be turning round and ~~round~~ on a pivot through the smoky air.

"My dear," she told her sister in a high mincing shout, "I ~~told~~ [let] him [know] to his face that [he] dint any right to charge ~~ten dollars~~ fifty dollars" — ~~for some incalculable reason~~ she was having summer covers made for the ~~chairs~~ [furniture], " — ~~Some~~ [Most] of

Chapter III, leaf 14, from the manuscript of *The Great Gatsby*. From the scene in Tom and Myrtle's atelier on West 158th Street, Chapter II of the published book. Princeton University Library.

(5)

casualness of Gatsby's party there were romantic possibilities totally absent from her world. What was it up there in the song that seemed to be calling her back inside? What would happen now in the dim uncalculable hours? Perhaps some unbelievable guest would arrive, a person infinitely rare and to be marvelled at, some authentically radiant young girl who with one fresh glance at Gatsby, one moment of magical encounter, would blot out those five years of unwavering devotion.

Leave one space here.

I stayed late that night, Gatsby asked me to wait until he was free and I lingered in the garden until the inevitable swimming party had run up, chilled and exalted, from the black beech, until the lights were extinguished in the guestrooms overhead. When he came down the steps at last the tanned skin was drawn unusually tight on his face, and his eyes were bright and tired.

"She didn't like it", he said immediately.

"Of course she did".

"She didn't like it", he insisted, "She didn't have a good time".

He was silent ~~for a moment~~ and I guessed at his unutterable depression.

"I feel far away from her", he said, "It's hard to make her understand".

"You mean about the dance?"

"The dance?" He dismissed all the dances he had given with a snap of his fingers, "Old sport, the dance is unimportant".

He wanted nothing less of Daisy than that she should go to Tom and say: "I never loved you". After she had obliterated four years with that sentence they could decide upon the more practical measures to be taken. One of them was that after she was free they were to go back to Louisville and be married from her house — just as if it were five years ago.

"And she doesn't understand", he said dispairingly, "She used to be able to understand. We'd sit for hours ----"

He broke off and began to walk up and down a desolate path of fruit rinds and paper fans and crushed flowers.

"I wouldn't ask too much of her", I ventured, "You can't repeat the past".

"Can't repeat the past?" he cried incredulously, "Why of course you can!"

He looked around him wildly, as if the past were lurking here in the shadow of his house, just out of reach of his hand.

"I'm going to fix everything just the way it was before", he said, nodding determinedly, "She'll see".

He talked a lot about the past and I gathered that he wanted to recover something, some idea of

New material, typescript and holograph, for Chapter VI, inserted by Fitzgerald into the galley proofs when he revised the novel for publication. Princeton University Library.

His hand, trembling with his effort of self-control, reached down and bore to his lips the last of his glass of ale. Carrying the situation on her voice Daisy got us to our feet and out on to the blazing gravel drive.

"Are we just going to go?" she objected, "Like this? Aren't we going to let anyone smoke a cigarette first?"

"Everybody smoked all through lunch," said Tom truculently.

"Well, personally Jordan and I are going to powder our nose."

They went in. We three men stood there shuffling the hot pebbles with our feet. A silver curve of the moon hovered already in the western sky.

"Have you got your stables here?" asked Gatsby.

"About quarter of a mile down the road."

"Oh."

A pause.

"I don't see the idea of going to town," broke out Tom savagely, "Women get these ideas in their head—"

"Shall we take anything to drink?" called Daisy from an upper window.

"I'll get some whiskey," answered Tom. He went inside.

Gatsby turned to me, his eyes glittering with happiness.

"She loves you," I agreed, "That voice is full of wonder."

"It's full of money."

Chapter VI, leaf 11, manuscript of *The Great Gatsby*. A fair copy of this portion of the text. "It's full of money." Princeton University Library.

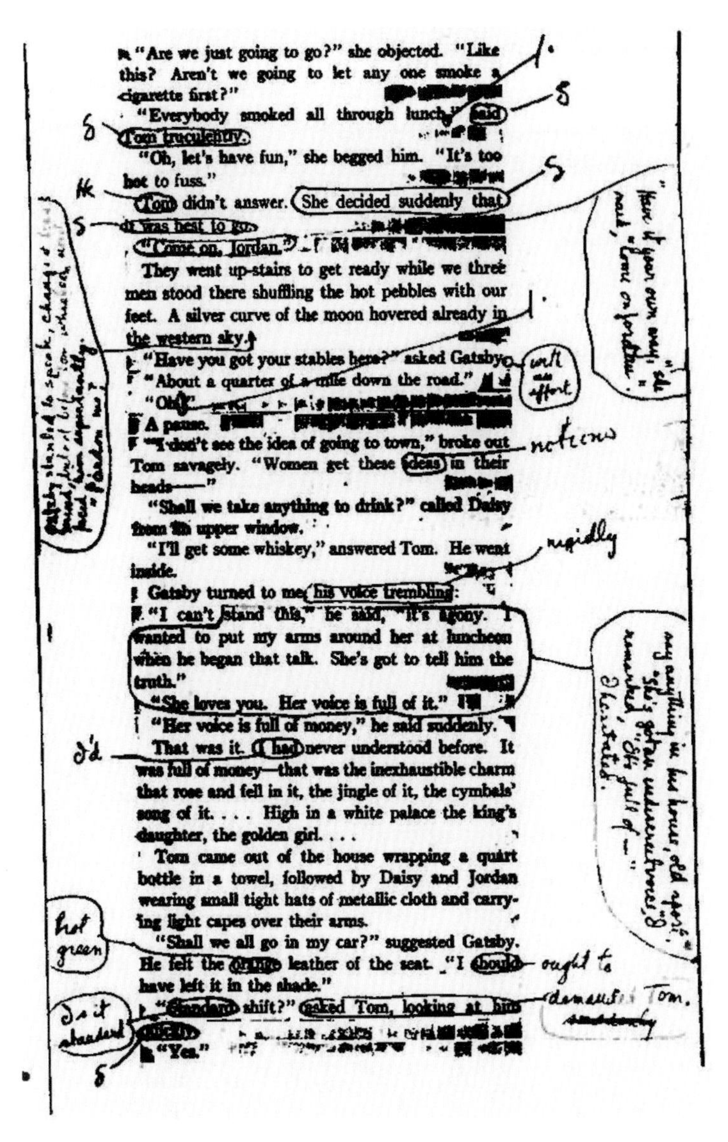

"Are we just going to go?" she objected. "Like this? Aren't we going to let any one smoke a cigarette first?"

"Everybody smoked all through lunch," said Tom truculently.

"Oh, let's have fun," she begged him. "It's too hot to fuss."

Tom didn't answer. She decided suddenly that it was best to go.

"Come on, Jordan."

They went up-stairs to get ready while we three men stood there shuffling the hot pebbles with our feet. A silver curve of the moon hovered already in the western sky.

"Have you got your stables here?" asked Gatsby.

"About a quarter of a mile down the road."

"Oh."

A pause.

"I don't see the idea of going to town," broke out Tom savagely. "Women get these ideas in their heads——"

"Shall we take anything to drink?" called Daisy from an upper window.

"I'll get some whiskey," answered Tom. He went inside.

Gatsby turned to me, his voice trembling:

"I can't stand this," he said, "it's agony. I wanted to put my arms around her at luncheon when he began that talk. She's got to tell him the truth."

"She loves you. Her voice is full of it."

"Her voice is full of money," he said suddenly.

That was it. I had never understood before. It was full of money—that was the inexhaustible charm that rose and fell in it, the jingle of it, the cymbals' song of it. . . . High in a white palace the king's daughter, the golden girl. . . .

Tom came out of the house wrapping a quart bottle in a towel, followed by Daisy and Jordan wearing small tight hats of metallic cloth and carrying light capes over their arms.

"Shall we all go in my car?" suggested Gatsby. He felt the orange leather of the seat. "I should have left it in the shade."

"Standard shift?" asked Tom, looking at him quickly.

"Yes."

From galley 37, proofs of *The Great Gatsby*. "Her voice is full of money ..." from Chapter VII. Princeton University Library.

~~Laugh in a flabbergasted way.~~

~~"It's the funniest thing," he said hilariously, shaking his head from side to side. "I can't to think — when I think —"~~

~~Recovering his dignity with an effort he flung open~~ two hulking patent cabinets which held his massed suits and dressing gowns and ties, and his shirts piled like bricks in stacks a dozen ~~[illegible]~~ high.

"I've got a man in England who buys me things," he said, "He sends a bunch of things over at the beginning of ~~every~~ each season, spring and fall."

He took out a pile of shirts and began throwing them one by one on the table, ~~linen shirts, flannel~~ shirts of sheer linen and thick silk and fine flannel that lost their folds as they fell and covered the table in many colored disarray. ~~[illegible]~~ While we admired ~~[illegible]~~ he brought out more and the soft rich heap mounted higher — shirts with stripes and scrolls and plaids in ~~pink~~ coral and ~~[illegible]~~ apple green and lavender and faint orange with ~~monograms~~ with ~~[illegible]~~ monograms of Indian blue. Suddenly with a strained sound Daisy bent her head into the shirts and began to cry ~~violently~~ stormily.

"They're such beautiful shirts," she sobbed, her voice muffled in the ~~said in a~~

Chapter V, leaf 13, manuscript of *The Great Gatsby*. Fitzgerald revises the description of Jay Gatsby's shirts. Princeton University Library.

Record for 1926

Stories	Your Way and Mine	$1750.00	Com 10%	1575	00
	The Dance	2000.00	"	1800	00
	Total			3375	00
English Rights	Love in the Night ([illegible]	91.75	Com 15%	78	00
	One of Our Oldest Friends	97.00	"	83	45
	A Penny Spent	76.38	"	61	92
	The Adolescent Marriage	76.23	"	64	80
	Total			288	17
Syndicate ed.	Adjuster, Pusher in the Face, Oldest Friends	239.19	Com 10% + 7.60	222	68
Article	How to Waste Material	100.00	"	90	00
Books (inc. English)	This Side of Paradise			44	00
	Flappers and Philosophers			35	80
	The Beautiful and Damned			33	10
	Tales of the Jazz Age			21	20
	The Great Gatsby			508	25
	All the Sad Young Men			1181	25
	Total			1833	20
Foreign	Danish and Swedish Rights to Gatsby			213	00
Moving Pictures	The Great Gatsby	16,666.00	Com 10% (twice)	13500	00
Play (The Great Gatsby)	New York Run (Deduct last years advance)	3907.76	Com 6%	2616	98
	Chicago "	2971.07	"	2673	97
	Road Run " (Detroit, Brklyn, Balt, St. Louis, Chi, Denver, Phila)	751.38	"	673	26
				5964	21
Total				$26,686	05
	Love in the Night (English)			97	75

Page 60 from Fitzgerald's business ledger, showing income from stories, novels, and other writings, and from the stage and movie adaptations of *The Great Gatsby*. Bruccoli Collection, University of South Carolina.

Front of the dust jacket for the Scribner's 1925 first edition of *The Great Gatsby*, preserved in Fitzgerald's scrapbook for the novel. Princeton University Library.

170.22–23 James J. Hill] Hill's base of operations was in St. Paul, Minnesota, Fitzgerald's home city. Hill (1838–1916) was a self-made man, a wealthy financier and railroad executive. His mansion still stands on Summit Avenue in St. Paul. (See the plate section for an image.)

172.1 Swastika] In 1920, five years before the publication of *The Great Gatsby*, the newly established Nazi Party in Germany adopted the swastika as one of its emblems. The swastika was used on flags, badges, posters, and armbands. Fitzgerald, who was living in France when he wrote the final chapters of the novel, likely knew of this association and was using "The Swastika Holding Company" here in an ironic way.

172.8 "The Rosary"] This tune, popular in the 1920s, was quite sentimental: "The hours I spent with thee, dear heart, / Are as a string of pearls to me; / I count them over, every one apart, / My rosary, my rosary!"

174.32 "Hopalong Cassidy"] The hero of this cowboy book was the creation of Clarence E. Mulford (1883–1956), who published a series of boys' stories and novels about "Hoppy" beginning in 1904. (See the plate section for a color image.)

176.25 "Blessed are the dead ... "] These words are from the poem "Rain" (1916), by the British poet Edward Thomas (b. 1878), who perished on the Western Front on April 9, 1917, at the Battle of Arras.

178.19 El Greco] The Greek painter and sculptor Doménikos Theotokópoulos (1541–1614) was known as "El Greco." He is known for his elongated figures and surreal subject matter. (See the Introduction to this edition, pp. xxxvi–xl, and the plate section for a color image.)

THREE CRUXES

There are several textual cruxes in *The Great Gatsby*—readings that might require correction, emendation, or preservation depending on the editorial approach employed. The textual policy of the Centennial edition is conservative; very few emendations have been made in the text. The arguments below for and against emendation, in three particular cases, will be of interest to the reader.[1]

1. "dazzled by the alabaster light …"

Early in chapter I of the novel, Nick describes his first view of Daisy Buchanan and Jordan Baker. The two women are reclining on an enormous couch:

> They were both in white, and their dresses were rippling and fluttering as if they had just been blown back in after a short flight around the house. I must have stood for a few moments listening to the whip and snap of the curtains and the groan of

[1] For discussion of various cruxes in the novel, see James L. W. West III, "Decisions, Decisions: Editing *The Great Gatsby*," in *Business Is Good: F. Scott Fitzgerald, Professional Author* (University Park: Penn State Press, 2023): 128–47.

> a picture on the wall. Then there was a boom as Tom Buchanan shut the rear windows and the caught wind died out about the room, and the curtains and the rugs and the two young women ballooned slowly to the floor.
>
> (Centennial text, 14)

Eight words might be missing from this passage—one of the most memorable in the novel. On leaf 12 in chapter I of the surviving manuscript, the words "on the threshold, dazzled by the alabaster light," take up a complete line, the fourth line on that leaf. Fitzgerald, who could not type, used a stenographic service to produce the setting-copy typescript that he mailed to Perkins. The typist worked from the author's handwritten draft. The missing words might have resulted from "eyeskip." The stenographer would have typed "moments," the last word in line 3 of the manuscript, then skipped over the next line and typed "listening," the first word in the fifth line. The reading "on the threshold, dazzled by the alabaster light," would have been omitted. No obvious error would have resulted: the typescript (which is no longer extant) would have read "for a few moments listening to the whip and snap … " Unless Fitzgerald remembered the original wording as he was reviewing the typescript, he would not have noticed the absence of the eight words. The altered sentence, without "on the threshold, dazzled by the alabaster light," appears in the galley proofs, which do survive. The altered sentence is present in the first edition.

The typist, of course, might have typed the sentence as it appears in the manuscript, without leaving out line 4. Fitzgerald, in revising, might have cut the eight words. If that is what happened, then the sentence in the first edition reads as he meant for it to read. No emendation has been made for the Centennial text. The possibility of eyeskip is speculative. The rhythm of the sentence would be altered by restoring the eight words, and the meaning would be changed a bit. Nick, our narrator, would be "dazzled" by the entire scene—the impressive house and grounds, the furniture and décor, the two reclining women, the evidence of money and privilege and ease. The sentence with the eight words restored reads as follows: "I must have stood for a few moments on the threshold, dazzled by the alabaster light, listening to the whip and snap of the curtains and the groan of a picture on the wall."

2. Mendelssohn or Wagner?

On page 129 of the Centennial edition, one encounters what appears to be a factual error. Tom, Daisy, Nick, Jordan, and Gatsby have checked into the room at the Plaza Hotel. The heat is oppressive; the men open the windows of the room to admit "a gust of hot shrubbery from the Park." Tom picks up the room telephone and orders ice for mint juleps. This sentence follows: "As Tom took up the receiver the compressed heat exploded into sound and we were listening to the portentous chords of Mendelssohn's Wedding March from the ballroom below." The music, from a society wedding taking place downstairs at the Plaza, brings to mind Tom and Daisy's wedding three years earlier. Tom, Daisy, and Jordan (a bridesmaid in that wedding) begin to reminisce. They tell stories about a freeloader named "Blocks" Biloxi, who somehow was invited to the ceremony and fainted at the event. He was taken to Jordan's house to recover and stayed there for three weeks. Gatsby is impatient with this small talk. He wants Daisy to tell her husband that she does not love him and never has, and that she is leaving him. Gatsby wants to erase Daisy's wedding to Tom, then marry her himself in her house in Louisville, where he courted her.

He and she will "repeat the past." This time it will come out as he desires.

On page 130, we read: "The music had died down as the ceremony *began* and now a long cheer floated in at the window, followed by intermittent cries of 'Yea—ea—ea!' and finally by a burst of jazz as the dancing began" (my emphasis). The problem here is that Fitzgerald has given the wrong work of music earlier in the passage. The proper musical work, if the wedding is *beginning*, would be a processional, most likely the "Bridal Chorus" from Wagner's *Lohengrin* (which most people think of as "Here Comes the Bride"). The "Wedding March" from Mendelssohn's incidental music for *A Midsummer Night's Dream* is the *recessional* heard at many weddings. It is played after the vows have been completed, as the bride and groom leave the church. The difficulty is with the pacing of the scene. Not enough time is provided in the first edition for processional, vows, recessional, cheers, and jazz. Replacing Mendelssohn with Wagner does not fix things. No emendation has been made in the Centennial text, but the problem can be solved by emending "began," the word that was italicized above, to "ended." By changing this word, the processional and the vows have already taken place. The ceremony is coming to an end, and Mendelssohn's "Wedding March," floating through the window, is the proper music. The guests can cheer, and the dancing can begin.

3. Mavromichaelis or Michaelis?

The third crux involves the name of the "young Greek" who runs a diner near George Wilson's garage in the Valley of Ashes. In the manuscript, his name is "Mavromichaelis." Somewhere between manuscript and galley proof, probably in typescript, Fitzgerald changed the character's name to

"Michaelis." At 165.12 of the first edition, however, we find an occurrence of "Mavromichaelis" that survived into the published text. Fitzgerald changed the name to "Michaelis" at that spot in his personal copy; everyone will agree that this emendation, in Fitzgerald's hand, should be introduced into the text. But two pages later on in the first edition (page 141 of the Centennial text), the change in name causes confusion. Myrtle has been struck by Gatsby's yellow car and lies dead on a table in the garage. Curious passers-by have crowded into the space. Wilson screams "Oh, my Ga-od!" Tom, Nick, and Jordan, on their way back to East Egg in Tom's car, have pulled off the road and have entered the garage. A policeman on the scene is asking questions of Michaelis. He is trying to write down Michaelis' name, but the name he is attempting to spell is "Mavromichaelis," not "Michaelis." Here is how the passage reads in the first edition:

> "M-a-v—" the policeman was saying, "—o——"
> "No, r—" corrected the man, "M-a-v-r-o——"
> "Listen to me!" muttered Tom fiercely.
> "r—" said the policeman, "o——"
> "g——"
> "g—" He looked up as Tom's broad hand fell sharply on his shoulder. "What you want, fella?"
> "What happened?—that's what I want to know."
>
> (First edition, 167)

No alteration has been made in the Centennial text. Repair work would involve rather much emendation, but the adjustment could be made. The passage could be altered so that the policeman is trying to spell "Michaelis":

> "M-i-k—" the policeman was saying, "—a——"
> "No, c—" corrected the man, "M-i-c-h-a——"
> "Listen to me!" muttered Tom fiercely.

"c—" said the policeman, "h——"

"a——"

"a—" He looked up as Tom's broad hand fell sharply on his shoulder. "What you want, fella?"

"What happened?—that's what I want to know."

ALTERNATIVE PASSAGES FROM THE MANUSCRIPT AND GALLEY PROOFS

In composing *The Great Gatsby*, Fitzgerald discarded a great deal of material. Some of these passages reveal the growth and development of his characters and themes. The five passages below, from the manuscript and the galley proofs, tell us much about Fitzgerald's efforts to depict Jay Gatsby, who was unfocused and shadowy in earlier versions of the text, and about the composition of the ending of the novel.

1. Gatsby's song

Gatsby has come to visit Nick at his cottage. He is trying to explain to Nick his fascination with Daisy—with her image, with what she has come to represent to him. In this passage from the manuscript, Fitzgerald is presenting Gatsby's inner thoughts and memories, a narrative problem that he handles skillfully in the published book but awkwardly here. In this early version of the text, Gatsby is conventionally sentimental. He admits to Nick that he is "empty"—something we sense in the published book, though it is never stated there.

> We sat for a few minutes in silence. Then he asked me if he could tell me about something that was on his mind, something that

had happened to him when he first knew Daisy several years ago.

"Will it bore you?" He looked up quickly. "For God's sake tell me if it'll bore you."

"It won't bore me."

They had been walking together down the street one autumn night when the leaves were falling, and they came to a place where there were no trees and the sidewalk was white with moonlight. They stopped here and turned toward each other. Now it was a cool night with that mysterious excitement in it which comes at the two changes of the year, and Gatsby became aware that everything was alive. The quiet lights in the houses were humming out into the darkness and there was a stir and bustle among the stars. He took a step toward her, perceiving out of the corner of his eye that the blocks of the sidewalk formed a ladder and mounted to a roof garden above the trees where one could suck on the pap of life, gulp down the incomparable milk of wonder.

His heart beat faster and faster as Daisy's white face came up to his own. He knew that when he kissed this girl, and forever wed his unutterable visions to her perishable breath, his mind would never romp again like the mind of God. So he waited, listening for a moment longer to the humming and the song. Then he kissed her. At his lips' touch she blossomed for him like a flower, and the incarnation was complete.

... He didn't really say any of this. What he said was that she had been an "ideal" of his, and that he'd never have such ideals about things or girls anymore.

"We all grow old," I told him. "It seems to me you've come pretty close to getting all your desires."

"I haven't got anything," he said simply. "I thought for awhile I had a lot of things, my house—" He looked up at it for an instant—"and things like that. But the truth is I'm empty and I guess people feel it. That must be why they keep on making up things about me, so I won't be so empty. Why,—Daisy's all I've got left from a world that was so wonderful that when I think of it I feel sick all over." He looked around with wild regret. "Let me sing you a song—I want to sing you a song!"

He began to sing a song in a low unmusical baritone. The tune seemed to be a vague compendium of all the tunes of twenty years ago. It went about like this:

> "*We hear the tinkle of the gay guitars*
> *We see the shining Southern moon;*
> *Where the fire-flies flit*
> *And the June bugs sit*
> *Drones the cricket's single tune.*
> *We hear the lapping of the wavelets*
> *Where the lonesome nightbirds sing*
> *And the soft warm breeze*
> *Tells the tall palm trees*
> *The Dreamy Song of Spring.*"

"I made it up when I was fourteen," he said eagerly, "and the sound of it makes me perfectly happy. But I don't sing it often now because I'm afraid I'll use it up."

Through all he said, even through the doggerel of the song, I was reminded of something—an elusive time, a fragment of lost words that I had heard somewhere a long time ago. For a moment a phrase tried to take shape in my mouth and my lips parted like a dumb man's, as though there was more struggling upon them than a wisp of startled air. But they made no sound and what it was that I had almost remembered was incommunicable forever.

(*The Great Gatsby: An Edition of the Manuscript*, 91–3)

2. "Her voice is full of money …"

Fitzgerald often produced his best verbal effects in revision. A good example occurs in *The Great Gatsby*. Nick, our narrator, is standing in the driveway outside the Buchanan house; Gatsby and Tom are with him. Daisy and Jordan are inside the house, preparing for an automobile trip into New York City. Nick and Gatsby are talking. Three versions of this passage survive—in the manuscript, the galley proofs, and the first edition (see the plate section for images). Here is the exchange as it appears in Fitzgerald's handwritten manuscript:

> "Shall we take anything to drink?" called Daisy from an upper window.
> "I'll get some whiskey," answered Tom. He went inside.
> Gatsby turned to me, his eyes glittering with happiness.
> "She loves you," I agreed. "That voice is full of wonder."
> "It's full of money."
>
> (*The Great Gatsby: An Edition of the Manuscript*, 97)

At this point in the narrative it is not clear why Gatsby should be happy, nor is it obvious that Daisy loves him. Nick's comment that Daisy's voice is "full of wonder" seems vague; Gatsby's response, that her voice is "full of money," is unprepared for—blunt and flat. Gatsby seems resentful of Daisy's self-assurance and of the ease and gentility suggested by her voice.

Here is the passage after Fitzgerald has revised it. This intermediate version is preserved in the proofs of the novel, published by Cambridge in 2000 as *Trimalchio*. This is the text that Fitzgerald submitted to Maxwell Perkins in October 1924:

> "Shall we take anything to drink?" called Daisy from an upper window.
> "I'll get some whiskey," answered Tom. He went inside.
> Gatsby turned to me, his voice trembling.
> "I can't stand this," he said, "it's agony. I wanted to put my arms around her at luncheon when he began that talk. She's got to tell him the truth."
> "She loves you. Her voice is full of it."
> "Her voice is full of money," he said suddenly.
>
> (*Trimalchio*, 96)

Gatsby has been uneasy throughout luncheon, waiting for Daisy to confront Tom and tell him that she is leaving him. Daisy has not done so. Gatsby is upset, and Nick is attempting to console him. He assures Gatsby that Daisy's voice is full of love, but Gatsby seems unconvinced. "Her voice is full of money," he says. Gatsby blurts out the comment as if the insight has only just occurred to him. He seems here to sense that, in the end, Daisy will stay with Tom—but we are not yet ready for this insight.

Fitzgerald revised the passage further in galley proofs. He produced the passage below, the final version that appears on page 144 of the first edition and in the Cambridge Centennial text:

> "Shall we take anything to drink?" called Daisy from an upper window.
> "I'll get some whiskey," answered Tom. He went inside.
> Gatsby turned to me rigidly:
> "I can't say anything in his house, old sport."
> "She's got an indiscreet voice," I remarked. "It's full of—" I hesitated.
> "Her voice is full of money," he said suddenly.
>
> (Centennial edition, 122)

Gatsby is now tense: he wants to behave properly but is angry. He uses the expression "old sport," as he often does when he wants to appear casual and confident. Nick, struggling to describe Daisy's voice, uses the word "indiscreet," but that is not quite correct. "It's full of—" Nick begins, but Gatsby breaks in. "Her voice is full of money," he says in a level tone. This time the statement carries authority, as if Gatsby has had this thought many times before. To us the remark is a surprise, something we have only sensed but that Gatsby has known all along.

3. The masquerade party

The second party at Gatsby's estate was originally a masquerade. Nick attends as a farmer in overalls, Daisy as a Provençal peasant. Celebrated people from the stage and screen are in attendance. Gatsby assumes that Daisy will be impressed; he does not yet understand the attitude of the very rich toward newspaper fame and celebrity. This becomes clear to him in an exchange with Daisy which occurs toward the end of the passage as it appears in the galley proofs. Gatsby is talking to Daisy about her hairstyle. He is certain that she would like to have her "look" imitated. He learns quickly that she wants nothing of the sort.

> Whether Tom, seeking new fields of amusement, brought Daisy, or Daisy suggested it to Tom I don't know—they were at Gatsby's house the following Saturday night. The party was a little more elaborate than any of the others; there were two orchestras for example—jazz in the gardens and intermittent "classical stuff" from the veranda above. It was a harvest dance with the immemorial decorations—sheaves of wheat, crossed rakes, and corncobs in geometrical designs—straw knee deep on the floor and a negro dressed as a field hand serving cider, which nobody wanted, at a straw covered bar. The real bar was outside, under a windmill whose blades, studded with colored lights, revolved slowly through the summer air.
>
> Only about a third of the guests were in costume, and this included the orchestra who were dressed as "village constables." As most of the others were village constables also the effect was given that the members of the orchestra got up at intervals and danced with the ladies present—an illusion which added to the pleasant confusion of the scene. For those who came without country costumes straw hats and sunbonnets were provided at the door.
>
> I dislike fancy dress enormously but as the nearest neighbor I cooperated to the extent of a pair of overalls and a grey goatee. The goatee kept getting in my mouth all evening until finally I tore it off ferociously, and much of my chin came with it. I've got a sort of deep dimple in my chin that's always bothered me shaving—it caught in that.

Tom came in a dinner coat, but Daisy, buttoned into a tight Provençal peasant costume, was lovelier than I had ever seen her lovely. Her eyes were bright too and her voice was playing gay murmurous tricks in her throat.

"It's wonderful," she whispered. "These things excite me *so*. If you want to kiss me any time during the evening, Nick, just let me know and I'll be glad to arrange it for you. Just mention my name. Or present a green—or present a green card. I'm giving out green——"

"I thought you'd like it," said Gatsby, his eyes glittering with happiness. "Just look around."

"I know. It's wonderful——"

"I mean the people," he interrupted. "You must see many faces of people you've heard of."

Tom's eyes roved here and there among the guests.

"We don't go round very much," he said. "In fact, I was just thinking that I don't know a soul here."

Gatsby stared at him, first incredulously and then with tolerance.

"I mean their pictures," he explained more formally. "For instance there's——"

In a low voice he began a roster of the more prominent names.

"But it will be a privilege to introduce you," he said. And as we moved off he added, reassuringly: "They're all as natural and unaffected as they can be."

He took us politely from group to group until Tom and Daisy had met everyone of consequence in the garden. Finally we approached the moving picture celebrity whom I had seen there before. She was surrounded by at least a dozen men who from a distance seemed to be making violent love to her. Coming closer, however, we discovered that the men were some less important members of the moving picture profession, and that their attitude was one of marked respect. They swayed toward her, not with passion, but lest they miss one of the jokes to which she was addicted, and which they applauded with hilarious laughter. Through this reverent entourage Gatsby made way.

"Mrs. Buchanan—" he introduced her, "and Mr. Buchanan—" after an instant's hesitation he added, "the polo player."

"Oh, no," said Tom quickly. "Not me."

However the sound of it evidently pleased Gatsby, and Tom remained "the polo player" throughout the rest of the tour.

"I've never met so many grand celebrities before," said Daisy. "I like that man, what was his name, with the sort of blue nose——"

"Augustus Waize," said Gatsby. "Oh, he's just a small producer. He only does one play a year."

"I liked him anyhow. And it must be fascinating to know them all."

"They like to come here," he admitted, "and I enjoy having them."

"I'd a little rather not be the polo player," said Tom pleasantly. "I'd rather look at all these famous people in—in oblivion."

He meant incognito but in any case Gatsby was surprised. He felt that in placing Tom, in attesting him as a spectacular figure among these other spectacular figures, he had done him a service.

Daisy and Gatsby danced; it was the first time I had ever seen him dance. Formally, with neither awkwardness nor grace, he moved at a conservative foxtrot around the platform. They were both very solemn about it, as if it were a sort of rite—perhaps they were thinking of some other summer night when they had danced together back in the old, sad, poignant days of the war. Once she looked up at him in such a way that I glanced sharply around to see if Tom were watching. But he'd found amusement elsewhere—he was bringing some girl a cocktail from the bar.

When the music stopped Daisy and Gatsby strolled over to me.

"Where's Tom?" she inquired. Then she saw: "Oh—well, don't let's disturb him. She's pretty, isn't she. Common but——"

She stopped herself suddenly but Gatsby was occupied in looking around the garden.

"There's several other people I want you to meet," he said, "but one of them hasn't arrived yet."

"We'll wait till they all get here," she suggested. "We'll leave Nick here in case there's a fire or a flood or anything and wander around. You'll tell us, Nick, in case there's a fire or a flood—or any act of God? We insured the house last week and I remember——"

The tumultuous clamor, like a prolongation of the nervous sounds of New York, soothed me, and I felt at home. But I tried to imagine how the party would appear to Daisy, how it had appeared to me on that June night two months before. It seemed less bizarre now—it seemed a world complete in itself, with its own standards and its own great figures, bounded, to its own satisfaction, by its own wall. It was second to nothing because it had no consciousness of being so. But Daisy might well regard it as the preposterous and rather sinister fringe of the universe.

"Listen, Nick——" She was back beside me. "Would you mind if we went over and sat on the steps of your bungalow or whatever it is?"

"You and Tom?"

"No, Jay and me."

She never saw any humor except her own—not always that.

"It's so noisy here," she explained, "and I have this ear drum, you see. I thought if we sat on your steps I'd get all—— What's that girl yelling about?"

"She's tight and she has hysterics."

"Oh! ... Well, we want to sit on your steps." She hesitated. "If Tom starts paging me around the garden you'll come and tell us won't you. I wouldn't want him to think I was bad."

She winked solemnly and I began to laugh as she went back toward the house.

An hour later Tom asked me casually if I'd seen Daisy; I sent him inside. Crossing the two lawns I found them sitting on the steps in the bright moonlight.

"Nick," she called.

"Yes."

"We're having a row."

"What about?"

"Oh, about things," she replied vaguely. "About the future—the future of the black race. My theory is we've got to beat them down."

"You don't know what you want," said Gatsby suddenly.

She didn't answer. Without haste we strolled back over the dark lawn to the area of hilarity, and Daisy and I danced. Gatsby made a complete circuit of the garden, speaking to people here and there, and then stood alone for a while in his habitual place on the steps.

"Do you think I'm making a mistake?" asked Daisy, leaning back and looking up into my face.

"I don't understand."

"Well, I'm going to leave Tom."

I was illogically startled.

"Do you mean immediately?"

"No. When I'm ready. When it can be arranged." Her eyes were sincere, her voice was full and sad.

"Have you told Tom?"

"No, not yet. I'm not going to do anything for a month or two. Then I'll decide."

"I thought you'd decided."

"Yes, but—then I'll decide the details and all that." She laughed. "You know if you've never gone through a thing like this it's not so easy. In fact—I want to just go, and not tell Tom anything.

"Do you think I'm making a mistake?"

"I don't know Gatsby well," I said cautiously. "I like him, but I'm not competent to give advice."

"He's wonderful," she said confidently.

As we sat down at a table I found that I was illogically depressed at what she had told me. These break-ups, however justified, however wise, always have a tragic irony of their own.

Supper was being served. Gatsby joined us at the table and, discovering us, Tom came across the garden.

"Mind if I sit with some people over here?" he inquired. "It's that man with the blue nose. He's been getting off some funny stuff."

"Go right ahead," said Daisy genially. "If you want to take down any more addresses here's my gold pencil."

Tom laughed and hurried away.

Gatsby, who had been talking to the moving picture celebrity, remarked suddenly that she had been very complimentary about Daisy. His voice was proud and pleased.

"And, here's a chance to become famous—-she wants to know where you got your hair cut."

"You tell her I think she's lovely too," said Daisy pleasantly.

Gatsby took out a pencil and a notebook.

"Where do you get your hair cut? I promised her I'd ask you."

"It's a secret," whispered Daisy. "It's a man I discovered myself and I wouldn't tell anybody for the world."

"You don't understand," he said impressively. "She'll probably have hers done the same way and you'll be the originator of a new vogue all over the country."

"No thanks," said Daisy lightly. The disappointment in his face bothered her, and she added: "Do you think I want that person to go around with her hair cut exactly like mine? It'd spoil it for me."

Without a word Gatsby replaced the notebook in his pocket.

"We're together here in your garden, Jay—your beautiful garden," broke out Daisy suddenly. "It doesn't seem possible, does it? I can't believe it's possible. Will you have somebody look up in the encyclopedia and see if it's really true. Look it up under G."

For a moment I thought this was casual chatter—then I realized that she was trying to drown out from us, from herself, a particularly obscene conversation that four women were carrying on at a table just behind.

"I thought if we ever met it'd be when we were old—and decrepit——" She broke off and glanced around in a frightened way. "What is it?" she whispered. "Why is that woman acting like that? Is she drunk?"

"I think you're probably nervous," said Gatsby. "She's just having a good time." He hesitated. "I don't know what's the matter tonight; very few people seem to be enjoying themselves."

Her wandering eyes caught his and perceived his disappointment.

"Why, they are, Jay," she cried quickly. "Everybody's having a wonderful time. Have I said something that you—here——!"

With her little gold pencil she wrote an address on the tablecloth. "There's where I get my hair cut. Is that what she wanted to know?"

But there was no such intimacy between them as would allow them to criticize each other's friends. Gatsby took out his pencil and slowly obliterated her markings with his own.

(*Trimalchio*, 80–6)

4. The confrontation

In the manuscript, Fitzgerald set the confrontation between Tom and Gatsby at two locations in New York City that would have been familiar to his readers—the Polo Grounds, a baseball stadium in upper Manhattan near the Harlem River, and at a café in Central Park, which begins at 90th Street and extends to 110th. Neither location proved suitable for this pivotal scene: both were public spaces where the two men could not speak openly. In this early version, Tom presents some evidence of Gatsby's criminal activities, but Gatsby is not convincingly defeated. For the published book, Fitzgerald moved the confrontation to a private room at the Plaza Hotel, at Fifth Avenue and 90th Street. The argument in this later version (on pp. 128–37 of the Centennial text) is longer and less restrained than it is in the manuscript. Tom has additional evidence of Gatsby's malefactions; Gatsby is defeated; his affair with Daisy is over.

There is no confusion like the confusion of a simple mind, and Tom was feeling the cold touch of panic—both his wife and his mistress, until an hour ago secure and inviolate, were slipping unexpectedly out of his control. His first instinct made him step hard on the accelerator with the double purpose of overtaking

Daisy and leaving Wilson behind. We covered the open road between Flushing and Jackson Heights at fifty miles an hour and at Astoria came in sight of the easygoing blue coupé.

He slowed down behind them, never taking his eyes from Gatsby and Daisy whose heads were visible through the rear oval of glass. Suddenly the coupé stopped and Daisy's hand emerged from the window waving us by.

"You go first," she called as we came abreast.

"What's the idea?"

There was undoubtedly an idea—or at least an unmistakable intensity about Daisy and Gatsby. They looked flagrantly alone.

"We'd rather follow you."

At the shrill, cursing whistle of a truck Tom pulled in by the curb ahead and walked back to the coupé.

"We ought to have stayed in East Egg," said Jordan. "This looks like a row to me."

After several minutes Tom returned frowning.

"We're going to the baseball game," he informed us briefly. "Daisy says the movies are too hot."

In spite of all the things he had concealed, Tom was not a secretive man and he felt alone in this unfamiliar silence. He looked at us several times as if he wanted us to talk, to comment—seeking not so much an idea as an arrangement of words that he could hang onto until his existence could right itself in action.

We crossed the bridge and split the city heat northward toward the Polo Grounds. At every corner Tom turned his head and sought eagerly for the other car; if the traffic delayed them he slowed up himself and waited until they came into sight. It was all so sudden to him that I think he expected them to dart down a side street any minute and out of his life forever.

At the Polo Grounds we got out and waited—after a blank moment the coupé appeared with insolent leisure around a corner.

"Is this the Polo Grounds?" inquired Daisy absently.

She showed no inclination to move, glanced uncertainly at Gatsby who regarded the wheel with an interested stare.

"Get out," ordered Tom. "We're going to the game."

"It looks so hot," she complained. "You go."

"Who?"

"Whoever wants to," she said evasively. "We'll ride around and meet you after."

"What's the point," demanded Tom, seeing it more clearly every minute. "Why can't we all stick together."

No answer. A wild roar went up inside the ball park....

"It's so hot I can hardly breathe," said Daisy unhappily, "much less decide."

Suddenly she and Tom were in a short fierce argument as to which one had proposed the trip to New York. Jordan retired to the shadow of the grandstand where she stood eating an ice cream cone and talking to a little boy. If she would give him fifty cents, the little boy explained, he could get in and see the game.

"Let's get out," she whispered as I joined her.

But we didn't. They were with us suddenly and we all went to the game.

I enjoyed that afternoon. It was so hot that my underwear climbed like a damp snake around my legs, so hot that when I took off my coat beads of sweat raced cold across my back—but the smell of peanuts and hot butter and cigarettes mingled agreeably in the air and someone was thrown violently from the bleachers for being drunk or sober or wrong, and a pitcher with an exquisitely eccentric delivery warmed up near us on the grass. The Chicago Cubs were the visiting team and Tom applauded with perfunctory patriotism whenever they hit safely or pulled off a good play. But when he urged Daisy to do likewise she answered that she and Gatsby were for New York—after that he took no interest in the game.

Somebody won and we swept out with the crowd into the late afternoon. We had a drink in a little café set amid the hot sparse shrubbery of Central Park—and suddenly Tom was quarreling violently with Gatsby over her emotions.

"Be quiet, Tom," said Daisy a little frightened. "There're people here. That Mrs. Rolf from Hempstead is here—"

Tom kept looking at Gatsby.

"What kind of a row are you trying to cause in my house anyhow?"

"He isn't causing any row," whispered Daisy tensely. "You're causing a row. Please have a little self control."

"Self control!" repeated Tom incredulously. "Self con*trol!*"

"That's it," said Daisy brightly. "What's more, if we're going to the Dashboards' tonight we ought to be starting home."

"What Dashboards?"

"I don't know. They're your friends. You ought to—"

"You mean the Dashiels. Austin Dashiel."

"Well, whoever they are. You made the engagement and if you want to keep it we'd better be—"

For a moment I thought she was going to get him away but unfortunately Gatsby, who hadn't said a word, looked up at Daisy suddenly with adoring eyes.

"Self control," repeated Tom sardonically. "I suppose the latest thing is to sit back and let Mr. Nobody from Nowhere make love to your wife. Well, I may not be so bright but if that's what things are coming to you can count me out. You begin by sneering at family life and family institutions and the next thing you'll throw everything overboard and have intermarriage between black and white!"

Flushed with his own impassioned gibberish he stood there on the last barrier of civilization alone.

"We're all white here," murmured Jordan.

"And that's about all," insisted Tom fiercely. He turned back to Gatsby. "Who the devil are you anyway?"

Gatsby looked at Daisy as if seeking permission to reply.

"You're one of that bunch that hangs around Meyer Wolfshiem," went on Tom. "That much I happen to know."

Daisy got up from the table.

"Come on. Let's go home."

"All right," agreed Tom, "but I want your friend here to realize that his little flirtation is over."

Gatsby looked at Daisy.

"He says it's a little flirtation."

She sat down again helplessly.

"Is it?" asked Gatsby.

She wanted passionately to evade the question but saw with dismay that it was too late.

"No," she admitted in a low voice.

At this point Jordan and I tried to go. Human sympathy has its limits and we were bored with their self-absorption, repelled by their conflicting desires. They thought we were leaving out of delicacy and insisted effusively, generously, that we stay, as though it were a privilege to partake vicariously of their emotions.

The people at the next table left the restaurant, sweeping inquisitively near as they went out the door. Daisy drew a relieved breath and Gatsby addressed his first remark to Tom.

"I don't think your wife loves you very much," he said. "Do you, Daisy?"

"No." Her answer was almost inaudible. The music had faded suddenly out of her voice.

"You're presumptuous," said Tom savagely. "Of course she loves me."

"On the contrary, I think she'd like to get a divorce from you." He reddened with embarrassment at the abrupt sound of the word. "Wouldn't you, Daisy?"

"Yes."

Suddenly Daisy and Jordan burst into nervous laughter.

"It sounds so silly when you say it," she explained, now on the verge of tears. "I've often heard people t-talk about it but when you actually come to—to—"

"Oh, it's a great little joke, all right," said Tom, choking. "It's a great little joke, isn't it Nick?"

"What's that?" I asked abstractedly.

"Weren't you listening?"

They looked at me with injured eyes.

"I just remembered this is my birthday."

I was thirty. Beside that realization their importunities were dim and far away. Before me stretched the portentous, menacing road of a new decade.

"I don't pretend to be a saint," said Tom so often that he convinced himself a saint wasn't worth being, "but I'm not ashamed to love my wife. Sometimes I go off on a spree and make an ass of myself but in my heart I love her all the time."

"You're revolting," she said.

But now that Tom knew this was no obscure slap at him from heaven, but only a romantic and comprehensible desire, his vitality asserted itself—he began talking with complete confidence, with a sort of husky tenderness about their honeymoon.

"She never loved you," interrupted Gatsby uncomfortably. "She only married you because you were rich and she was tired. Isn't that true, Daisy?"

"... Yes."

But her reluctance was so perceptible, and a shadow of doubt crossed Gatsby's face.

"She's always loved me," said Tom with rising confidence. He loved her now—it was in his voice. Daisy lit a trembling cigarette and glanced at her husband, feeling the massive solidity of his presence there.

Watching her face but unwilling to believe what he saw, Gatsby reached over the table and laid an imploring hand on her arm.

"Tell him you never loved him," he said urgently. "Just tell him the simple truth, that you never loved him."

She hesitated. Suddenly a light went on overhead, and another, and a long row that bordered the corner of the roof. I realized that the café was filling up swiftly with people coming for dinner, and that the head waiter was standing inquiring beside our table. It was the last one still bare.

"Your party is dining here?"

Tom and I looked at our watches. It was half past seven.

"By God!" he exclaimed. "I'll have to call up Austin Dashiel."

"I'll call," offered Daisy in wild relief.

For a moment Tom tasted the situation, looking with a contemptuous smile into Gatsby's tragic eyes.

"No, I'll telephone. You go along with your beau here in his circus wagon. He'll bring you right home. I think he understands now that you're my wife."

(*The Great Gatsby: An Edition of the Manuscript*, 104–9)

5. "the green glimmer ..."

Perhaps the most famous passage in *The Great Gatsby* appears on the final two pages of the novel in a luminous evocation by Fitzgerald of American innocence, aspiration, and hope. Some of the lines in this passage came to him early in the composition of the novel, as he was finishing the first chapter. Below is the ending of that chapter in the manuscript. Nick has returned from his evening with the Buchanans; he is sitting on an "abandoned grass roller" on the lawn in front of his cottage. He sees his neighbor, "Mr. Gatsby himself," contemplating the "local heavens," but before he can call out, Gatsby vanishes. These two paragraphs follow:

> The sense of being in an unfamiliar place deepened on me and as the moon rose higher the inessential houses seemed to melt away until I was aware of the old island here that flowered once for Dutch sailors' eyes—a fresh green breast of the new world. Its vanished trees, the very trees that had made way for Gatsby's house, had once pandered in whispers to the last and greatest of all human dreams—for a transitory and enchanted moment man must have held his breath in the presence of this continent, compelled into an aesthetic contemplation he neither understood nor desired, face to face for the last time in history with something commensurate to his capacity for wonder.
>
> And as I sat there brooding on the old unknown world I too held my breath and waited, until I could feel the motion of America as it turned through the hours—my own blue lawn and the tall incandescent city on the water and beyond that the dark fields of the republic rolling on under the night.
>
> (*The Great Gatsby: An Edition of the Manuscript*, 17–18)

This passage appears too early in the narrative for the reader. Fitzgerald seems to have realized this: he saved the two paragraphs, revised and expanded them, and transferred them to the end of the novel. Here are the final five paragraphs as they read in the manuscript:

> On the last night, with my trunk packed and my car sold to the grocer, I went over and looked at that huge incoherent failure of a house once more. On the white steps an obscene word, scrawled by some boy with a piece of brick, stood out clearly in the moonlight and I erased it, drawing my shoe raspingly along the stone. Then I wandered down to the beach and sprawled out in the sand.
>
> Most of the big shore places were closed now and there were hardly any lights except the shadowy glow of a ferryboat across the Sound. And as the moon rose higher the inessential houses themselves began to melt away until suddenly I became aware of the old island here that flowered once for Dutch sailors' eyes—a fresh, green breast of the new world. Its vanished trees, the trees that had made way for Gatsby's house, had once pandered in whispers to the last and greatest of all human dreams; for a transitory and enchanted moment man must have held his breath in the presence of this continent, compelled into an aesthetic contemplation he neither understood nor desired, face to face for the last time in history with something commensurate to his capacity for wonder.
>
> And as I sat there, brooding on the old unknown world, I thought of Gatsby when he picked out the green light at the end of Daisy's dock. He had come a long way to this blue lawn, but now his dream must have seemed so close that he could hardly fail to grasp it. He did not know that it was all behind him, back in that vast obscurity on the other side of the city, where the dark fields of the republic rolled on under the night.
>
> He believed in the green glimmer, in the orgastic future that year by year recedes before us. It eluded us then but never mind—tomorrow we will run faster, stretch out our arms farther. And one fine morning—
>
> So we beat on, a boat against the current, borne back ceaselessly into the past.
>
> (*The Great Gatsby: An Edition of the Manuscript*, 156–7)

Fitzgerald revised these paragraphs slightly in subsequent versions of the text. The "green glimmer" became the "green light"; "never mind" was altered to "that's no matter"; "a boat against the current" became "boats against the current." In its essentials, however, the text remains the same, giving us the familiar ending that appears in the first edition and in the Centennial text.

ACKNOWLEDGMENTS

We are grateful to Eleanor Blake Hazard, Eleanor Lanahan, and Chris Byrne, the Trustees of the F. Scott Fitzgerald Estate, for advice, permissions, and support. At Princeton University Library, we thank the Manuscripts Division, Department of Rare Books and Special Collections, for access to the F. Scott Fitzgerald Papers and to the Archives of Charles Scribner's Sons. For many courtesies we are grateful to Don C. Skemer, Curator of Manuscripts, Emeritus, and to his staff. For their expertise and assistance, we thank our fellow Fitzgerald scholars Jackson Bryer, Kirk Curnutt, Anne Margaret Daniel, and Bryant Mangum. Thanks also to Mary Lee Carns (who *is* related to Kaiser Wilhelm) for help with the illustrations.

S. C.

J. L. W. W. III